Murder
by the
Book

by
Rayne Romo

Green Ivy Publishing
1 Lincoln Centre
18W140 Butterfield Road
Suite 1500
Oakbrook Terrace IL 60181-4843
www.greenivybooks.com

Murder by the Book/Rayne Romo
ISBN: 978-1-946775-81-8
Ebook: 978-1-946775-82-5

I

Joe Olsen was a cop. His grandfather was an MP in the service, and his dad, Daniel Olsen, was in the service. Born in 1953, Joe was an only child. His parents didn't have time for him, let alone any other siblings. Joe was on his own, basically left by himself most of the time. Needless to say, Joe moved around a lot in his youth, finding it hard to keep friends. He didn't have a hard time making friends, just keeping them. As soon as he got comfortable with a town, and the people, they would move on. That's the way it was in a military family. Joe had to grow up fast, and be the man of the house. He thought he had to be there for his mom, a strong and confident woman, who loved moving in the higher circles with the other military wives. It was pretty unusual for a woman to be so independent in that day and age, although not unusual for a military wife. Joe learned early on that his mom could take care of herself.

The young family soon moved to Hawaii, where Joe entered high school. There, he met a beautiful young girl named Ailani. Joe called her Ali, and they soon became inseparable. Ali was also an only child, and a military brat. They fell in love, and got married just after graduating in 1971. Ali was a beautiful girl, dark- skinned, with long, black hair. In stark contrast to Joe's light skin, and blonde hair, they made a striking couple. After marrying, the young couple moved to Los Angeles. There, Joe went to college for two years studying criminal justice. Joe knew from a very young age that he wanted to be a cop, so he entered the police academy when he turned twenty-one. Joe's parents were not happy when he didn't join the military, but were proud of him nonetheless. They didn't live to see him earn the top spot in the academy, as they died in a car accident soon after Joe and Ali were married.

Joe graduated top of his class at the academy and was hired at the Los Angeles police department shortly after graduating. Ali was there to support her husband, and enjoyed setting a hot meal on the table for Joe when he came home from his shift. Life was pretty good for the young couple. They had their ups and downs like any other marriage, but all in all, things were good. Money was short in the beginning, so Joe started moonlighting at the club downtown. He enjoyed working security at the gentlemen's club. Rubbing elbows with the movers and shakers of LA. He figured it wouldn't hurt to know people when he made his way to the top. Joe had ambitions of eventually working in homicide, and becoming chief one day. So, he kept his nose to the grindstone and started making his mark in the Los Angeles police department.

Before long, Ali and Joe bought a home, and their first child was born, a beautiful little girl they named Sara. Sara was a perfect blend of both parents, with huge brown eyes, like her mother, and a tuft of blonde hair, like her daddy. She was the apple of her daddy's eye, quickly becoming a daddy's girl. Joe would come home after a long day at work, but no matter how tired he was, he always took time to read Sara a nursery rhyme or two out of her favorite book. Her daddy bought it for her when she was born. Ali loved being a mom, and a cop's wife.

Two years later, little Ann was born. Ann was so different from Sara. With dark hair and dark eyes, she looked just like her mom. Sara was thrilled to have a little sister, and didn't mind sharing her parents' affection. Even though Sara was only two, she loved Ann and was always holding her and cuddling with her.

When Sara turned eight, and Ann was six, Joe finally got into the homicide division, where he always wanted to be. Ecstatic, he took the whole family out for a celebratory dinner. The two girls got to dress up in their prettiest dresses. Sara was growing to be a stunning young girl with her long, blonde hair, and big brown eyes. Ann was equally pretty, with her dark hair and eyes. It was a fun and memorable evening for everyone, including Ali. She was happy for Joe getting his dream job, but knew in her heart that their days of spending a lot of time together were probably coming to an end. The life of a homicide detective was brutal, always on call, pretty much twenty-four-seven.

By the time the evening ended, the two little girls were tired. Although Sara and Ann fell asleep on the way home from the restaurant, they still insisted on at least three nursery rhymes to be read to them. Joe tucked them in and grabbed the book, starting where he always did. "Hey diddle diddle, the cat and the fiddle, the cow jumped over the moon."

He smiled, as his two little beauties fell asleep before he could finish the rhyme. As he kissed Sara on the cheek, he whispered. "I'll always love you, daddy's big girl." Joe carried Ann to her bed and leaned down to kiss her cheek. "Daddy loves you Ann, you're a special girl, always remember that." He tiptoed out of the room and made his way down the hall to his and Ali's bedroom.

The very next year, Sara and Ann started to feel the tension between their parents. The girls didn't understand what was going on, but they could tell something was wrong. They were seeing less and less of their dad. Sara and Ann would try and wait up for him to read to them. They usually ended up falling asleep, or Mom had to tell them that they needed to go to bed. The girls both were in school now, and Sara would sometimes read to Ann out of their book. Sara, being the oldest, was always trying to be the big girl. "It's okay Annie, I'll read to you. Daddy will be here tomorrow."

But Daddy wasn't there the next day, or the day after that. Sara would often hear her mommy crying herself to sleep at night. When Joe was home, they were fighting and arguing about someone. Sara thought she heard a name, but couldn't make it out. She would hear her dad leave the house after most of these arguments, and she and Ann would watch from the window as he drove away.

Ann would always ask Sara. "Where is Daddy going, Sara? He forgot to read to us again." She would whimper, and her lower lip would start to quiver.

Sara, always the strong one, even at nine years old, would try to comfort her sister. "I don't know where he's going, Ann. Probably to work again. Come on, I'll read to you." Sara would put her arm around Ann and put her to bed, reading softly to her until she fell asleep.

Ali wasn't sure if the rumors she was hearing about her husband and his partner Liz were true. The other detectives' wives were trying to give her advice and telling Ali to let it go. "It happens a lot Ali. He will grow tired of her and you'll always be there for him to come home to. She's his partner, they spend every day, all day together. They're bound to grow close." Were they sleeping together? Joe denied it, of course. They just ended up fighting about it and he would take off. It seemed as though Joe didn't care about his family anymore, not even spending time with Sara and Ann. She just did not know what to do. Should she confront Liz, or take the other wives advice and back off? Ali wiped the tears off her face, and tried to fall asleep, sobbing lightly so the girls would not hear her.

Joe opened the hotel room door, letting Liz in the dimly lit room. The two lovers did not spend much time talking. Their time was too short together this way. He knew it was wrong, but Liz was his partner. She understood what being a detective was all about. There was no complaining about the long hours spent on the job, getting calls in the middle of the night, and all the other things the job entailed.

Liz Rommel loved her husband, Kurt, but Joe was so different. Kurt was a cop too, working in the drug enforcement division. He would spend weeks undercover, each time coming home a little bit different. It was hard to see Kurt changing that way. They were definitely growing apart. She didn't know if Kurt knew, or even cared, that Liz and Joe were together. Liz just couldn't help herself. She was falling in love with Joe. She knew in her heart that Joe loved Ali, but there was always that hope that he would love her too. Right now, she would take what she could get.

Kurt Rommel walked into his house. He was beyond tired after spending two weeks undercover, and finally breaking one of the biggest drug rings in Los Angeles. Sometimes, he had to go deep undercover to get these drugs off the street, even using drugs himself to stay believable as a drug lord. It was hard sometimes to shed the persona when he was done with a case, getting harder and harder actually. Kurt was often called into his captain's office and reprimanded for his tactics on the job. He figured it shouldn't matter as long as he was getting the job done.

As Kurt walked into the bedroom, he wondered where his wife was, although he figured she was at work. He threw his keys on the dresser and noticed her badge lying on the top of some crumpled up notes. Picking it up, Kurt frowned. "Why would she leave for work without her badge?"

He shrugged, setting it back down on the dresser. Kurt mixed himself a drink, then headed for the shower. The more he thought about it, the more curious he became, so he went back and picked up Liz's badge, reading some of the notes underneath it. There was a lot from her partner,

Joe, but that wasn't unusual. They did work together after all. Frowning, he went through her dresser drawer, and saw Joe's handwriting show up on notes he found there, too. Sitting on the edge of the bed, Kurt stared at the notes. Some were work related, but some seemed pretty personal.

As Kurt read on, the notes started getting more and more personal. "Where should we meet tonight? Can you get away tonight?" One note from Liz to Joe even said, "I love you." Kurt was seeing red by this time. He threw the badge and notes across the room.

It only took another year for things to come to a head in the Olsen household, as well as the Rommels. Ali finally gave Joe an ultimatum, threatening to leave him if he didn't break it off with Liz, and Kurt Rommel was going off the deep end. Liz didn't care, she just wanted Joe. That's all that mattered to her.

It was becoming more than Ali could handle. Ali begged her husband. "Joe, I love you, and I forgive you, but you need to come back to your family. We need you."

Joe nodded. "I know, Ali. I love you too." He hung his head. "I'll break it off with Liz tonight, I promise."

That's just what he did. Liz didn't take it well. It was increasingly hard to work together, and she couldn't do her job. Liz was fired from the force, and her marriage to Kurt broke up soon after.

Kurt Rommel blamed Joe for everything wrong in his life, from his spiral downward at work, to his broken marriage. He was heavy into drugs now, and it was showing in his work. The higher ups were noticing Kurt driving new cars, and buying boats, so it looked as though he was on the take. Problem was, they couldn't prove it. They fired Kurt, and he went to the other side. The bad side. By the end of that year, Kurt was in bad shape. Liz was who knows where, and Joe and Ali were back on track, happier than ever.

Kurt Rommel sat outside Joe Olsen's house, snorting cocaine and drinking heavily. "Damn you, Olsen! You ruined my life. Now I am going to ruin yours. You don't deserve what you have. You stole my wife, and my job, and you will pay." He sneered, and guzzled the bottle of whiskey sitting beside him.

Sara awoke to the smell of smoke in the air. Scared, she groped around through the thick smoke, choking and coughing, trying to find her little sister. Sara tried to remember what the nice firemen taught them at the assembly at school on fire safety. One of the things they said was to stay low to the ground, because smoke rises. Sara got on her hands and knees and crawled to Ann's bed. She found her little sister curled into a ball in the middle of the bed.

"It's okay, Annie. It's Sara. Come on, we need to get out of here."

Sara grabbed her hand, squeezing it to calm Ann down. By this time, they could barely breathe. The smoke was so dense. Sara took Ann by the hand, and started crawling to the window. As the two girls crawled slowly toward where Sara hoped the window was, two strong arms wrapped around them and picked them up.

"Sara, it's Dad. I've got you, honey. I'm going to take you to the window. Then I want you to run to the neighbors, and don't look back, okay? I will get your mom, and meet you there. Here's your book. I promise I'll read it to you when we get over there. I need you to be daddy's big girl now, okay? You can do it, Sara. Ann, stick right by your sister's side and you'll be alright."

"Okay, Daddy. I'll be big, I promise." Sara whimpered.

Ann started to cry, as Joe dropped them on the other side of the open window. Joe took a deep breath of fresh air as he turned and headed back into the burning house. The girls ran as fast as they could to the nearest neighbor, doing as their dad said and not looking back.

Sara watched from the neighbor's window as the firefighters arrived, lights blinking and sirens blaring. Ann was in the corner holding her hands over her ears, trying to block out the noise. Sara couldn't look away. As the flames licked the night sky, the windows blew outward. "Mommy, Daddy, where are you? Why can't I see you?" She clutched her book tightly to her chest, crying herself into a restless sleep. She held Ann's hand tightly, trying to calm her down. They would never see their mom and dad again.

As the firefighters rolled up their equipment and started getting ready to leave, the fire inspector approached the chief. "What do you think about this one, Chief?"

The fireman turned. "I smelled gasoline when we entered the house. We couldn't get to the victims. There was just too much smoke and flames. Two victims inside. You tell me what you think when you check out the house. It's okay to enter now. Good luck."

"Okay, I'll head in and let you know what I find out."

They both turned as two bodies in black body bags were being brought out of the house. The bodies were to be taken to the coroner's office for positive identification and cause of death. The two men had to look away.

Looking over the house, the arson squad discovered a trail of gasoline leading from the front door into the living area and down the hallway. "This was definitely arson. These people didn't stand a chance of getting out of here. It's a miracle the girls did." When his phone rang, he answered on the first ring. "Yes, Doc Miller, what can I do for you---? So it's confirmed then. It was Joe and Ailani Olsen? Cause of death was smoke inhalation. Got it. Well, it was arson, so they were murdered, unless it was murder-suicide. I'll call you later."

When Sara woke up the next day, there was a blanket covering her and Ann. She squinted, wrinkling her nose at the smell of smoke. After sniffing her clothes, Sara coughed. She was trying to figure out where she was at. Remembering last night, Sara jumped up. "Mommy, Daddy!" Ann woke up and instantly started crying. "Come on, Ann. Let's go find Dad and Mom."

They ran to the other room. "Mommy, Daddy, are you here?" The girls almost collided with the Avery's, the kind people who lived next door. They had worried looks on their faces, and standing next to them was the local priest from the Olsen's church.

"Where's my mom and dad? Are they here?" Sara looked from one to the other.

The priest spoke first. "Sara, Ann, please sit down. I have something to tell you. Girls, you remember the fire last night?" Sara nodded. "Well, I'm so sorry, girls, but your parents...they didn't make it out of the house. I'm afraid they're gone."

Sara just stared at the Priest. Ann fell to the floor, crying and rocking back and forth.

Just a few days after that, Kurt Rommel was found with a self-inflicted gunshot to the head. He had written a suicide note, confessing to the arson that caused the deaths of the Olsens. Doc Miller confirmed the suicide. "Guess Kurt couldn't live with the fact that he left two little girls without parents."

Joe and Ailani Olsen were buried three days later, with the full police force in attendance. Sara and Ann stood in the front, holding hands. Sara's head was held high. Ann was clinging to her sister, sobbing uncontrollably. After the funeral, Sara overheard people talking around her.

"What is going to happen to the girls? Did they have any family?"

"The only family they found was a great-aunt, right here in Los Angeles. She's agreed,--somewhat reluctantly, I'm afraid,---to take the girls in."

Sara was never so scared in her life.

2

*S*ara and Ann had been living in Los Angeles with their great-aunt Elda for four years now. It was awful. The old woman didn't want them there, and she didn't mind telling the two girls that every day. Ann was becoming more rebellious by the minute, and Sara was just trying to hold it together long enough to get the hell out of there. "The aunt,"as the girls called her, made them do all the cleaning in the old house, and paid them a meager amount to buy their clothes and such.

"This is just like living in a prison!" Ann whined. "We even have to do chores to earn enough money for our clothes!"

Sara had to chuckle. "Ann, there's nothing wrong with earning your keep. Besides, that's the least of the horrors of this place!" Sara cringed as she looked around the old house. Ann was right, it felt like a prison here. Sara thought it was more like a dungeon, cold and empty of any personal things. She shivered again, as they left the house and headed off to school. Sara was just going into her freshman year, and she was excited.

Ann, on the other hand, was in Junior High, and hated every minute of it. "If Mom and Dad were here, I wouldn't be at that awful school. I bet I'd be in a fancy boarding school or something."

Sara let her think that, not wanting to burst her bubble. Ann had blocked out most of that terrifying night when they lost their parents. Sara, on the other hand, could never forget it. The only thing they had left of their parents was Sara's book. There were no pictures, and no other mementos of them, just the book. Sara cherished it and still read from it every night.

Sara got a part-time job as a waitress at the local diner to help pay for some of the things she and Ann needed. It got her out of that dungeon anyway. She felt guilty, leaving Ann alone there with 'the aunt,' but she didn't have much of a choice.

Cheerleading tryouts were next week, so she needed the money to buy her uniform should she make the squad. Sara had a crush on the quarterback of the football team, Jake Long. "He's so hot, and nice too." She told her friend Lacey one day. "If I get on the cheerleading squad, maybe he'll notice me."

Jake was two years older than Sara. He was captain of the football team, and got straight A's besides. Tall, and with hair the color of caramel, Jake was well-liked and chased by all the girls. Lacey reminded Sara of that fact. "I don't see Jake noticing you, Sara. You're just a freshman, and he could have anybody he wanted. I wouldn't get my hopes up if I were you."

It's too late for that. Sara thought as she headed for her next class.

The next week went by quickly, while Sara practiced for her tryouts. While doing cartwheels in the house one day, she and Ann were laughing and giggling when Ann tried a cartwheel. They hadn't felt like laughing in such a long time, it sure felt good.

The 'aunt' walked in just as Ann fell for the tenth time, rolling on the floor, and giggling. "You girls stop this nonsense and get your chores done. Sara, what's going on here?"

Sara straightened her spine. "I'm trying out for the cheerleading squad tomorrow, so I'm just practicing my cartwheels."

Their aunt scoffed at that. "You're not good enough for cheerleading. Besides, you don't have time for that nonsense. I'm not going to give my consent for that."

"But, Aunt Elda, you can't do that! I've been practicing hard, and I will use my own money for everything I need!"

"*Hmph.* Well, I'll see. Go get the dishes done, and I'll think about it." She shuffled down the hall, heading for her bedroom.

For once, it was Ann who grabbed Sara and headed for the kitchen. "Come on, Sara. Let's go do dishes."

Sara wanted to make a smart remark to her aunt, but kept her mouth shut. She didn't want to hurt her chances for getting Aunt Elda to sign the consent form so she could try out for cheerleading.

The next day at tryouts, Sara was so nervous, she thought she might throw up. Hearing her aunt's voice in her ear. *You're not good enough for cheerleading.* Sara was having second thoughts. "I don't know, Lacey. I almost wish Aunt Elda hadn't signed the consent form. It would have saved me from the humiliation of not making the team."

"Don't be silly, Sara, we'll do great! Just wait and see!"

It didn't help the butterflies in Sara's stomach. When their names got called, the two girls took a deep breath, and high-fived each other as they ran out on the floor.

Jake Long got home from a long day at school and football practice. Throwing his car keys on the table, he yelled. "Hey, Mom, I'm starving! What's to eat?"

Jake's mom tried to sound stern. "Good grief, Jake! Between the two of you, and Tom too, when he's home, we can't keep any food in the house!"

Jake kissed his mom on the cheek. "Growing boys, Mom. That's what you get for raising three of us. Besides, we know how much you love to cook for us."

"You're right, son, I do love it! Where is your brother? I thought Sam would be home by now."

Jake had two brothers, one older, and one younger. Tom, the oldest, was in Las Vegas, already climbing his way up the ladder in the police force. He was single, saying it was better that way. No family tying him down, keeping him from getting what he wanted, being the Chief of Police. Sam was just a freshman, and he was enjoying life as only a handsome young man could do.

"Sam is the wild one." Their dad always said. "If I get that boy raised, I'll be happy."Jake's dad, Vern Long, was a cop in Los Angeles. He loved being a cop, and was so proud of Tom, for following in his footsteps. "I'm proud of all three of you boys. Just be good men, and always respect people, and they will show you respect." Vern has been a cop in Los Angeles for twenty-five years. He passed up a few promotions, knowing that if he didn't, he wouldn't be there for his wife and three boys like he wanted to. He was a good man, and he expected his boys to be good men too. Vern always said he didn't care what the boys wanted to do with their lives, just as long as they did their best. No matter what they chose for a profession.

Jake already knew that he wanted to be a police officer, just like his dad, and his brother Tom. He couldn't speak for Sam, but Jake figured he felt the same way as the other two boys. Jake's mom, Bonnie, stayed home, and worked hard at raising the three boys. Vern and Bonnie Long never missed a game that the boys participated in. Whether it was basketball, football, track, or anything else they joined. Jake and his brothers were very competitive, and had always brought each other to the top of their game. They had a houseful of trophies to prove it, which were displayed proudly all over the house. Along with the many scholastic awards, of course. Jake's dad always joked that it was a good thing they quit at three children, as they didn't have enough room in the house for any more awards.

The first football game of the year was that weekend, and, of course, the Longs were there in full force. Tom even showed up from Las Vegas to cheer his brother on. Everyone cheered loudly when Jake's name was called for the starting lineup. A cheerleader on the sidelines was cheering extra hard. Sara jumped high and cheered Jake's name, along with the other starters, but she had eyes for only one player out there. The game was a hard-fought battle between two rivals, and Arcadia came out on top. The whole team played well, but Jake had a great game, with four touchdown passes. He also ran one in himself for a touchdown. Jake and the other football players were flying high after their first win of the season.

High-fiving each other, Jake and his teammates ran off the field. After breaking out of the huddle, Jake glanced toward the cheering section, looking for his parents and brother, Tom. His eyes were immediately drawn to a beautiful blonde standing on the sidelines. Jake elbowed his friend Toby, next to him. "Who is the cute new cheerleader? Do you know her?"

Toby looked over to where the cheerleaders stood. "Nope, don't know her, but I think she's a freshman."

"*Hmm.* She's in Sam's class. I'll have to ask him about her." Jake took one last look before he got engulfed in a mob of fans and players.

Sara felt eyes on her, so she glanced over at the football team. "Oh my gosh! I think Jake just looked at me!"

She smiled shyly, and when Jake Long winked at her, she nearly fainted. Sara went to bed that night happier than she had felt in a long time.

Jake was still flying high from the game when he got home that night. He couldn't get that pretty cheerleader off his mind. He went to his brother Sam's room to see if he was still awake. Sam was sprawled out on his bed, books and notebooks spread everywhere. "Whatcha doin' bro?"

"What's it look like I'm doing, Jake? Having a party? *Sheesh*, I'm trying to finish my homework. Why do we have to learn history anyway! It's all over and done with." Sam threw his history book on the bed, exasperated.

Jake had to chuckle. His brother never did like schoolwork. "I don't know how you manage to get *A*'s and *B*'s, Sam. All you ever do is complain about school. I just came in to ask you a question, but the way it looks, maybe I should wait."

"No, no way, I need a break from this crap anyway. What's up?"

"Well, I noticed a gorgeous blonde cheerleader tonight after the game. Toby thought she was a freshman. Do you know her?"

Sam snorted. "Good grief, Jake! Another blonde? You certainly have a type. Well, if it's who I think it is, she may be out of your league, Jake. I'm not sure of her whole story. She lives out at that old haunted-looking house with her sister. Old lady Elda is her aunt, or something like that. I wouldn't go near that place, or that woman. Rumor has it she's got bodies buried around there."

Jake shook his head and frowned. "Well, I'm not afraid of ghosts, or that old lady, not if there's a beautiful girl involved. What's her name, Sam? Come on, spill!"

"Sara Olsen. I think she works at the S & W. Good luck with this one, Jake."

"I don't need luck, bro, just my good looks and charm." Jake ducked, as the pillow Sam threw at him just missed his head.

Jake didn't have a chance to talk to Sara until two weeks later, when he spotted her in the hallway of AHS. He made a beeline to where she was standing with some other cheerleaders. Jake swaggered over to the girls. "Well, hello ladies."

The girls all giggled, and got red in the face, not used to the captain of the football team talking to them. All but one lowered their heads.

Sara looked Jake straight in the eye and smiled. "Hi, Jake. You had another great game the other night."

"Why, thank you. What might your name be, pretty lady?"

"Sara Olsen. I'm in your brother Sam's class."

"Well, Sara, don't hold him against me, okay? I'm nothing like my brother."

Sara smiled again. "Okay, I won't." The bell rang. Sara frowned, not wanting this moment to end. "Well, I'd better get to class."

"Sara, maybe I'll see you after the next football game?"

"Oh, I'll be there, cheering you on." Sara quipped as she turned to leave. "See ya around, Jake."

Jake watched as Sara walked down the hall. "Wow! She's not only gorgeous, she's nice too! Irresistible combo."

Sara floated through the rest of the week, waiting for the next football game that weekend. "Oh my gosh, Lacey!" Jake said he'd catch me after the game! Do you think he will talk to me?"

"One thing I know about Jake, if he said he'd catch you after the game, he will. Homecoming is only two weeks away. Maybe he'll ask you to go with him!"

Sara could barely wait until after the game to talk to Jake. She cheered loudly, but AHS ended up losing a close one. Jake had an interception, and the other team ran it back for a touchdown to win the game. Everyone was bummed. Sara figured she wouldn't be seeing Jake after losing the game. She was just walking off the field when she heard him calling her name.

"Sara, wait up!"

She turned, and saw Jake running toward her. He still had on his football jersey. Sara thought she had never seen anyone as handsome as Jake in her life.

When Sara turned and smiled, Jake almost tripped over his own feet. *Whoa! Settle down! She's just another girl with a beautiful smile, Jake.* But in his heart, Jake knew he was wrong. This one was different, and he was in deep trouble.

"Sorry about the game, Jake."

"Thanks." Jake said, as he stopped in front of Sara. "Can't win 'em all, I guess. What are you doing right now? Do you want to go grab a burger or something?"

Sara frowned, and looked around. "I'd love to, but my little sister Ann is here with me...somewhere. Sorry, Jake. Another time?"

"It's okay if you want to bring Ann along. I'd like to meet her too." Jake just didn't want to go another night without spending some time with Sara, even if it meant her little sister tagging along.

"Well...Let me find her, and I'll see what she says. We have to be home by eight to do our chores though."

Jake crossed his chest with his fingers. "I promise to have you home in plenty of time. What do you say?"

Sara hesitated, wondering briefly what Aunt Elda would say when they didn't come home right after the game. Well, Sara wasn't going to pass up a chance to go out with Jake. "Sure, hang on. I'll find Ann."

Jake was happy that Sara agreed to go out with him. "I'm just going to grab my gear, and let my parents know what's going on. I'll meet you back here in twenty minutes, okay?"

"Okay." Sara had to stop herself from jumping up and clicking her heels as she ran to find Ann.

The burgers were delicious, the company was even better. Jake was so kind to Ann, giving her coins to play the video games while she and Jake talked.

"So, I know you're a football star, what else do you like to do?"

"I'm no star, but I do enjoy football. I play basketball too, and run track. I have two annoying brothers. You know Sam, Tom is the oldest. But enough about me, tell me about yourself."

Sara wondered just how much to tell Jake about her past. She opted for as close to truth as she could without delving into her parent's deaths too closely. "Well, my parents died when I was ten. We moved in with our great-aunt Elda. It's okay most of the time, but it's harder on Ann. She's so young. I'll be fifteen next month, and she's only twelve. As long as we stay out of Elda's way, and do our chores, she leaves us alone for the most part." Realizing she may have said too much, Sara changed the subject. "So you're a junior. What are your plans after graduation?"

"My dad is a policeman here in Los Angeles, and my older brother, Tom, is a cop in Las Vegas. My grandfather was a cop too. I want to follow in their footsteps."

Sara sat up straight in her chair. "A cop? Are you sure you want to do that? It's a brutal job for sure." Sara thought his next answer could be the deal breaker for them having any kind of a relationship.

"Things could change in the next few years, I suppose. But yeah, for now, that's what I want to do." Jake was a bit taken aback by Sara's tone of voice, when she wanted to go home all of a sudden.

"Ann, come on. We need to get home and do our chores. Thanks for the burger, Jake. This was fun."

"*Whoa*, wait a minute! You're not getting off that easy, I'll give you a ride home. Hang on, I'll take care of the bill."

Even with his revelation about his career choice, Sara didn't want this night to end. "Okay. Thanks, Jake."

When Jake pulled up to the old house, he let out a low whistle. "Wow! Sam wasn't kidding when he said this place looked like a haunted house. Have you seen any ghosts, Sara?"

Sara flinched a little, startled by the question. "Of course not. There are no ghosts here, just us and one cranky old woman."

Jake had to laugh at that reply. "Sara, I'd like to ask you something."

"Hang on. Ann, will you head in and start the dishes please?"

"I guess so." Ann said, dragging herself out of the car and trudging up to the spooky old house.

Sara laughed. "I suppose she thinks I won't come in and help her with dishes."

"Well, as much as I would like to have you stay here and talk to me all night, you better not leave all the dishes for her to do alone." Jake cleared his throat. "Sara, homecoming is coming up soon. Would you go with me to the dance?"

Sara almost lost it. She was so excited. "I'll have to check with my aunt, but I would like that, Jake."

He resisted the urge to do a fist pump. "Okay, let me know for sure at school tomorrow."

Sara opened the door and leaned back in. "Okay, Jake. I'll ask tonight and let you know."

"Hang on, I'll walk you to the door."

"No, that's okay, I can make it. Good night, Jake."

"Night, Sara. See you tomorrow."

Sara watched as Jake drove away. She sighed, and then jumped, when her Aunt yelled from the other room.

"Whose car was that, Sara? Where have you been?"

Sara cringed and headed in the direction of her aunt's voice. "Just a friend, Aunt Elda. We went for burgers after the game."

"*Hmph.* I see. Well, as long as you're here to do your chores, that's fine."

Sara figured now was as good of a time as any. "Aunt Elda, homecoming is in a couple weeks, and the captain of the football team asked me to go with him. Would that be okay?"

"Really? What is this boy's name, pray tell?"

"Jake Long. His dad is a cop." Sara thought maybe by adding that little tidbit, it would help her chances of going to the dance.

"Yes, I've heard of them. Nice enough family, I guess. I suppose it would be okay."

Sara was actually shocked at her aunt's reply. "Thanks, Aunt Elda!" Now she just had to break it to Ann.

The day of the homecoming dance grew nearer, and Sara had to work a couple of extra shifts at the diner to pay for her dress. She was too busy to go on another date with Jake, but she got to see him every day in school. They were spending every free moment together. After school one day, Sara caught Jake as he headed for football practice, and she was going to cheerleading practice.

"Jake, I hate to ask, but, could you give me a ride downtown to look for a dress for homecoming? You're the only one I know who has a car. It's okay if you don't want to."

'Sure, I can go with you. What about Ann?'

"'That's sweet of you to ask, but Ann is going to walk home after school. She has homework." Sara wanted some time alone with Jake. It seemed as though the only time they spent together was at school.

"Okay. I'll meet you in the parking lot after practice."

"Cool, see you then."

Sara took off for cheerleading practice, glancing back to catch Jake looking at her too. She almost tripped, but caught herself just in time. Jake grinned, and headed for football practice.

When Sara got home that night, she couldn't wait to show Ann her new dress. She found a pretty, spaghetti-strapped, pink dress in the local store. Sara thought it was perfect, and Jake's mouth dropped when she tried it on for him. Sara could not wait for the weekend to get here.

It was another close one, but they won their homecoming game. Everyone was stoked. Jake was flying high. He couldn't wait for the dance that evening. When the cheerleaders ran over to join the team with their cheers and screams, Jake picked Sara up, swinging her around. When he set her back on her feet and looked into her eyes, they were sparkling, and her sweet smile was irresistible. Jake couldn't help himself. He kissed her lightly, and drew back, wondering how Sara would take it.

Her cheeks were a little flushed, but she looked up at him and smiled, touching her lips. *Oh boy, I've got it bad!* Jake thought, as he looked at her beautiful face, falling even harder for the pretty blonde-haired cheerleader.

The homecoming dance was enchanting, with all the decorations, and the band playing. Sara didn't think she could be any happier than she was at that moment. Jake held her close during the slow numbers, and they laughed and danced during the fast ones.

"I don't want this night to end." Jake whispered in Sara's ear.

"Me neither." Sara said, as she rested her head on Jake's shoulder.

They got to know each other better that night, and Sara felt comfortable enough to share with Jake the whole story about her parents' murders. She told him about her father's affair, and the aftermath. Sara also told Jake her dad was a homicide detective, and let him know how she felt when he was never home. Always being called out to another murder. Her mother crying at night as she was left home alone.

Jake was so understanding. Sara was really falling for him. She couldn't help it. "Sara, I want you to meet my parents. I want to show you that not all cop families are like yours. Will you come over for dinner this weekend? Bring Ann too. She deserves to get away from the haunted house and have some fun."

Sara was a bit surprised with Jake's invitation, but she agreed to go. They made a date for the weekend.

She was nervous about meeting Jake's parents, but the minute Sara walked in the door and was enveloped in a hug by Bonnie Long, the nervousness disappeared. Sara loved the Longs from the start. Ann fit right in too. There was a lot of laughter and teasing at the table. When Jake gave them a ride home that night, Sara had to admit that Jake's life was way different than hers ever was. *Maybe a cop's life isn't always bad.* She thought, as she crawled into bed that night.

Toward the end of the school year, Jake and Sara were inseparable. The young couple spent most of their time at Jake's, of course. The few times Jake went over to Elda's, he couldn't wait to get out of there. "Wow, Sara! This place is spooky. How do you sleep here at night?"

Sara would look around and shrug. "I'm used to it, I guess. Besides, I've got Ann."

The summer flew by, and before they knew it, it was Jake's senior year. Sara was feeling down about Jake leaving for college next year. "What's going to happen to us, Jake? Will you still love me when we're not together every day?"

"You know I will, Sara. I'll always love you. Listen, I've been thinking about it, and talked to my parents. I'm going to go to the local college, and then the police academy. Are you okay with that?"

Sara had to be okay with it. She just wanted to be with Jake. "I'm okay, Jake. If we can be a family like your mom and dad, I can handle it."

Jake picked Sara up and swung her around just like he always did, before kissing her softly. "I love you Sara. I want you to always be in my life. I know we're too young to get married right now, but there's something I want to give you." He reached into his pocket and drew out a small velvet box. "It's called a promise ring. Sara, I'm promising that we will always be together, no matter what. Will you wear it?"

Sara slipped the ring on her finger and smiled. "Of course, Jake. I'll never take it off."

Jake never went back on his promise. By the time Sara graduated, they were more in love than ever. The promise ring turned into a beautiful diamond engagement ring. Jake was in the police academy now, and Sara held back her misgivings about him being a cop. Ann was having a little bit of a tough time dealing with their getting married.

Sara felt bad about leaving her alone with their aunt, but she loved Jake, and was going to marry him. "Ann, I'm sorry, but you know I will always be here for you. We're staying in Los Angeles, and I won't be far away."

"But, Sara, I can't stay here alone! Can I go with you?" Ann shrieked.

Sara and Jake talked about Ann moving in with them, but ultimately decided it wouldn't work. There just wouldn't be any room. "I wish you could, Ann, but it just wouldn't work, okay? You will have your own life. I know you'll meet someone someday, and be just as happy as I am. You're my sister, and I love you. I'll always be there for you, no matter what. Always."

3

Jake and Sara's wedding day was perfect. Sara awoke to a bright, sunny day. *Nothing could go wrong on a day like this.* She thought as she headed for the church to get ready for the big day. Her dress was already at the church, just waiting for her to put it on. When she arrived, Ann was already there, carrying her bridesmaid dress.

"About time you got here."

Sara smiled. "Am I late?"

"No. I just figured you would be nervous and awake all night."

"Nope, I slept good. I've been waiting for this for too long to be nervous. I'm just excited."

Sara and Ann hugged, and walked into the dressing room to get ready. There was her beautiful dress. She gently took it off the hanger and fingered the silky smooth material. Sara slipped the gown over her head. Ann buttoned all the pearls down the back. The lace covered bodice fit snugly, accentuating her small waist.

"You look beautiful." Ann had tears in her eyes as she handed Sara a small bouquet filled with daisies. Sara's favorite. Ann had grown to accept her getting married and moving out. She was happy for her.

Sara was glad Ann was there for her special day. Sara wanted a simple wedding. That's just what she planned. There were no frills, just her, Jake, and a small gathering of friends and family. Ann was her maid of honor, and Lacey was a bridesmaid. Even Aunt Elda was there, sitting in the front row.

"I just wish Mom and Dad were here." Sara said with a wistful smile.

"I know. Me too, Sara, but we have each other, right? No matter what?"

Sara hugged Ann tightly. "Always, little sister. Always."

Jake looked so handsome, standing tall next to his brothers, Tom and Sam. As Sara began to walk down the aisle toward Jake, she looked up and silently said a few words to her mom and dad. "I wish you were here, but you are here in my heart, always and forever. I hope you're proud of us." Sara took a deep breath, and kept walking slowly toward her soon-to-be husband. She smiled at him, thinking. *I'm one lucky girl.*

The wedding went off without a hitch, with everyone congratulating the bride and groom. People were still dancing when Sara and Jake left for their honeymoon. It was nothing fancy, just a hotel room in town for the night, but the young couple loved it anyway.

"I'm sorry I couldn't afford to take you on a real honeymoon, Sara."

Sara looked at her new husband, her love shining through her eyes. "It's perfect, Jake. As long as I'm with you, any place is good. Besides, we can always go somewhere later on if we want to."

Jake stopped Sara before she could go through the door. Lifting her, he used the other hand to open the door. Jake carried Sara over the threshold, kissing her as he set her down. "Yes, we will. Now, close your eyes, and don't open them until I tell you to."

Sara closed her eyes tight. "What are you up to, Jake?"

"Just keep them closed a little longer, I'm almost ready...Okay, you can open them."

Sara opened her eyes to the most scrumptious looking meal she'd ever seen. Perfectly cooked steak, baked potato, and a bottle of champagne chilling in a bucket. "Oh, Jake, this looks delicious! You know I love steak. I didn't get to eat much at the reception, I'm starving!"

"I knew you would be. You were so busy dancing, you hardly ate anything. Now sit. I'll wait on you for a change." Jake motioned to the chair.

Sara sat down. "Boy, do I feel pampered. A girl could get used to this."

They dug into the wonderful meal, anticipating what would come next.

Sara woke up and turned to the other side of the bed, reaching out for her husband. The bed was warm, but empty. She sat up and looked around the room. "Jake? Where are you?"

Right on cue, Jake walked in the door. "Well, good morning, sleepyhead!"

Trying to smooth out her long, blonde hair, Sara gave Jake a sheepish grin. "I must look awful. Where did you take off to?"

"Just getting us some breakfast. We worked up quite an appetite last night."

Sara blushed, his comment bringing back memories of their wedding night. "Yes, we did. I think we need to work it up a little more."

Jake nearly dropped the tray of food before setting it down and wrapping his arms around his wife.

Jake and Sara moved into a small house and started their life together. Sara finished her second year of college, and Jake was working for the Los Angeles police department. Things were going pretty well, until Ann called one night and told Sara that their aunt Elda had passed away. Ann was just finishing up her senior year, and they hadn't talked to each other much lately. They both had such busy lives. Sara actually was pretty sad that Elda had died. She may not have wanted them living with her, but she did the best she could.

"I'll be right over, Ann. We will plan her funeral together."

"Whatever. I'll see you later then."

Sara hung up the phone, wondering what that comment was all about. Had she lost touch with her sister that much? *Come to think of it, I can't remember when I talked to her last.* She thought, as she called Jake to let him know what had happened, then left for the old house. Sara was shocked when she walked in. There were people all over the place, drinking and carrying on. "Ann? Ann, where are you at?"

Ann stepped into the room, looking a little drunk, and maybe even high. "I'm right here. What's up?"

"What's going on here, Ann? A party? Really?"

"Just a little, 'Hail, hail, the witch is dead,' party! What's wrong with that? Come join us, sis.”

“No, thank you. Now get these people out of here. We have a funeral to plan.”

⁂

Two years went by, with Sara and Ann growing farther and farther apart. “I just don’t know what to do, Jake. She is hanging out with the wrong people, drinking, and maybe even doing drugs. She’s even talking about leaving Los Angeles.”

“Sara, there’s not much you can do. Ann’s an adult now. She has to make her own decisions. Even if they’re bad ones.”

“I just don’t know. I’m really worried about her.”

Jake wrapped his arms around her, holding her tight. “I know, honey. If you want me to, I could pick her up, try to get her on the straight and narrow after a few nights in jail. A little tough love?”

Sara had to seriously consider that. “Let’s wait with that drastic action. Thanks for the suggestion though. I just don’t know. I’ve had to be the parent since I was eight years old. I’m only two years older than Ann, but I feel like I’m twenty years older.”

Sara couldn’t sleep that night, worrying about Ann. She roamed around the apartment for a while, finally settling on the couch with some hot chocolate. She looked around. *I don’t know if I deserve all of this. A wonderful husband, and a home. Mom, Daddy, what should I do?*

Sara was startled by a loud noise coming from the extra bedroom. She jumped, looking around. “What the heck was that? Jake, is that you?” Nothing, no more noises. Sara stood up from the couch, and slowly crept towards the noise she just heard. “Jake?” Still silence. She moved a little closer to the other room, peeking in the door. Only darkness and silence greeted her. She quickly flicked on the light. “What the…?” Her book was lying on the floor, open to the nursery rhyme, ‘*Hey Diddle Diddle*,’ her dad would always start with when he read to her. “Okay, Daddy, I get it. You are here with us, in your own way. All I need now is for you to tell me what to do about Ann.” Sara picked up the book. Yawning, she went to bed. She fell asleep holding the book close to her chest.

Sara was happy. Jake's job was going well, and she loved her job as manager at the diner she used to be a waitress at. They were even talking about starting a family. Two more years had gone by, Jake was making a name for himself at the Los Angeles police department. He only wished his mom and dad could have lived to see him doing so well. His dad died of a heart attack not long after his mom had died from cancer. Jake always said his dad had died of a broken heart. The higher ups were noticing his work ethic. Jake was approached about joining the homicide division, and he was thrilled. He wanted to be in homicide. Jake knew how Sara felt about that. She told him a long time ago just how she felt about it. How was he going to break it to his wife that he was offered a job as detective in the homicide division?

"Jake, please don't do this! We're perfectly happy the way things are. At least, I am!" Sara pleaded with her husband one more time, trying to change his mind.

 "Sara, this is an opportunity I've been waiting for a long time. I just can't pass it up!"

Sara raised her chin a little. Don't you want a family some day? Have you forgotten that I know what it's like to live in a home with a homicide detective for a father?" She raised her hand up and started counting on her fingers one by one. "Always on call, twenty-four-seven. Getting calls at all hours. Never being there for a birthday, Christmas, you name it! I won't do it, Jake. I won't bring a child into that lifestyle. Jake, my dad basically lost his life because of the job. I know he didn't get killed on duty, but he was with Liz all day, every day. He couldn't help but grow close to her!"

Jake's shoulders slumped a little. "I know that, Sara, but you know I would never cheat on you. No matter what! I really need to do this. Not only for us, but for our future. Please, try to understand. Besides, it couldn't have been all bad. You turned out pretty good."

Sara had to smile at that...a sad smile, just the same. "It wasn't all bad, no. When my dad would read to me from my nursery rhymes book, I was so happy. He would sit on the edge of my bed, reading rhyme after rhyme. I think I know them all by heart. After Ann was old enough, she would lay in bed with me, listening intently to the sound of Daddy's voice. Now look at us, Jake. Ann and I don't even talk anymore. She's in

Portland, doing God knows what! Don't you see, Jake? It was more bad than good in the end!"

Sara turned and walked into the bedroom, shutting the door softly. Jake almost wished she would have slammed it shut. Well, he had made up his mind. He was taking the job in homicide. Sara would come around. She had to.

He took the job in homicide, and he was fitting in nicely. His partner, Tony Scott, was a seasoned detective. He showed Jake the ropes. Their first murder was in the books. Solved, after some good old fashioned police work, along with some great forensics.

Jake leaned back, his feet resting on his desk. Tony walked by and nudged Jake's feet off the desk with his hands. "Time to go to work, buddy. We got a homicide."

All business now, Jake jumped up, put his gun in his holster, and took off. He ended up staying at the crime scene throughout the night, talking to witnesses, and checking over the crime scene. Jake did not get home until late into the next night. He was tired, and in bad need of a shower.

Sara was waiting up, a sad look on her face. "So, is this going to be the norm now?"

"Please, Sara, I'm just not up for this right now. I've had a long day, and we got called to a brutal murder today. I'm tired, and I just want a drink and shower, in that order."

"Sure, Jake. I had a wonderful day too. Thanks for asking." With that, Sara turned and walked away.

Jake let out a long breath. "Yeah, good night, Sara. I love you too."

When Jake got to work the next day, the office was buzzing with business as usual. The murder board had a few pictures of their latest murder victim. There was some writing on it, with different suspects' names, but not much. They didn't have a lot to go on yet. Jake figured this was going to be a long one. "Great, I'm sure Sara will be pleased."

When Sara got home from work that night, everything was quiet. She was growing more and more frustrated every day. "I just don't know how much more of this I can take. Maybe I should go to Portland and find Ann. I could use the getaway. I need my sister." She grabbed her cell phone and dialed Ann's number. Not getting an answer, she left yet another message. "Ann, please call me. I really need to talk to you. I miss you, okay? I want to come to Portland for a while. Please, just call me, okay?" Sara hung up, feeling even more depressed.

Jake dragged himself through the door that night. He was frustrated, tired, and cranky. Sara did not wait up this time. Jake grabbed a drink, and headed for the couch. It's pretty hard to wind down after a long day of interviewing suspects, and getting nowhere with the case. They did get some pretty good tips from some of their confidential informants, or CI's, as they called them. Jake glanced up as Sara came out of the bedroom and sat by him on the couch.

Grabbing his hand, she squeezed it tightly. "I'm sorry for acting this way, Jake. It's just that you know how I feel about you taking this job. It's very hard for me to see you drag yourself in the house late every night, frustrated with how the case is going, and too tired for anything but drink and sleep. I love you, Jake, but I just need to get away from it all. I want to go find Ann. She won't return my calls, and I'm very worried about her. Do you think you could go with me? It could be the honeymoon we never had."

"I wish I could go, Sara. I haven't been in homicide long enough for any time off. Besides, this case is getting closer to getting solved now. We have some tips to follow up on tomorrow. They really sound promising this time."

Sara put her arms around her husband, and hugged him. "Yeah, I guess I knew that. Have you talked to Sam lately? I know he and Ann weren't that close, and Portland is a big city, but maybe he's heard something?"

"I haven't talked to him in a while, but I'll call him soon. I doubt he's seen Ann, but I'll see what he can do on his end."

Sam had stepped out of the family's career path and owned a ranch just outside of Portland. None of the family could figure out where he got the ranching bug, but they supported him just the same. Jake hadn't gotten over to see Sam's ranch yet, but heard great things about it. The Long Ranch, as Sam called it, was set up to help orphans and other troubled children who had a parent, or parents, in law enforcement. Even though Sam wasn't a cop himself, he still couldn't get completely away from law enforcement.

The couple sat quietly on the couch, just holding each other. Sara missed the days when they did this every night. They held each other until Sara could hear Jake softly snoring. Covering him with a blanket, she went to bed alone. Crying herself to sleep, Sara remembered all the nights her mom did the same thing. She fell into a restless sleep, tossing and turning, dreaming of that awful night when her life had changed forever.

Jake woke up abruptly, hearing Sara cry out. "No! No! Daddy, stay with me! Daddy, don't go!"

He rushed to her side, almost tripping over something lying on the floor. He bent down and picked up Sara's book, before running the rest of the way to the bed. Shaking her gently, Jake spoke softly. "Sara, honey, wake up. You're having a bad dream."

Sara kept thrashing around in the bed, her hands grabbing at the air. "Daddy, don't leave me. Please!"

Jake kept trying to soothe her, until Sara finally woke up, sitting up with a start. She was soaking with sweat, and tears were running down her face. He held her tightly. "*Shh*, it's okay, honey. You were dreaming, that's all. I've got you. It's okay now."

Sara never said a word to Jake, just a blank stare. Jake held her until she fell back asleep, gently laying her head on the pillow.

Sara woke up that morning with a splitting headache. *Good grief!* She thought. *What went on last night?* The last thing she remembered was waking up with Jake holding her. When she fell back asleep, she could hear her dad's voice in her head. *I don't feel like I got any sleep, probably because I didn't. Was Daddy trying to tell me something? It was his voice, I know it. What was he trying to say?* Sara just couldn't remember. Shivering, she dragged herself out of bed and headed for the shower. The hot spray cleared her head, and helped wake her up a little. Stepping out of the shower, Sara grabbed for her towel.

Jake startled her, knocking once before opening the bathroom door. He gave her a concerned look. "You okay? I didn't want to leave for work until I talked to you. That dream must have been something else. Were you dreaming about your parents? You kept saying their names."

Sara looked at Jake, wondering how much to tell him. She decided to be as truthful as she could without saying too much. "I don't really remember. I only know, I hope I don't have any more nights like that."

Jake looked at Sara, trying to read her, but she looked away. "Well, I brought you some aspirin. I figured you'd need them."

"Thanks, I do need them." Sara took the aspirin and grabbed her towel. "Well, I better get ready for work."

Jake's phone rang. He took one more look into his wife's eyes before answering. "This is Long. Okay, Tony, I'll be right there." He kissed Sara quickly. "Gotta go, duty calls. Love you."

Jake rushed out the door, not waiting for her reply.

4

olly Jones just got done with a grueling day of being groped, yelled at, grabbed, you name it. She was bone tired and ready to get home to her young son, TJ. TJ was the only reason she kept going after her husband of ten years left her. Teddy Jones could not handle fatherhood, so he up and left them both just one year ago. *What a stand-up guy.* Molly thought. *I guess I can't blame him though. Being a cop was tough enough without bringing a child into the mix.*

Molly jumped, hearing a noise behind her. She stopped, and started looking around. "Always be aware of your surroundings." That's what Teddy always told her. "*Then you should be here to protect us, you big oaf!*" Molly shrugged.

Not seeing anyone in the vicinity, she continued her short walk home. She couldn't shrug off the feeling of being watched, though. Molly kept looking around, as she walked faster. Finally, her house came into sight. She hurried to the door, opening it and slipping through. Molly quickly locked the deadbolt behind her, and breathed a sigh of relief.

She heard footsteps behind her, and turned quickly, still a bit shaken up. Her son was running as fast as he could toward her. "Mommy, Mommy, you're home!" Molly's three-year-old son ran to her open arms.

She picked him up, and hugged him tightly. "Yes, I am home, TJ. Were you a good boy for grandma?"

"He always is." Molly's mother, Tammy, came from the kitchen. "Aren't you, TJ?"

TJ nodded. "Yep! Grandma said if I was extra good, I could stay up and wait for you to come home and read to me."

"Okay, young man! Just this once, it's okay." Molly tried to sound stern, but she secretly loved it when he stayed awake and waited for her.

"Go grab your book, and I'll meet you in your room. Now scoot!"

Molly took one last look out the window, before she turned to her mother. "Was he good, or are you just saying that?"

"He was good. Now, tell me what's got you all nervous. Did something happen at that place you call work? Tell me, Molly, what's wrong?"

Molly could never get anything over on her mom. "It's probably nothing, but I just can't shake the feeling of being watched. It's not work. Just the normal stuff going on there. Nothing new. Like I said, I'm probably just being paranoid."

Tammy frowned, eyeing her daughter. "There's no such thing as being too careful, Molly. Maybe you should quit that job and find something less...dangerous. I don't like you walking home alone from there every night."

"I can't quit, Mom. It's all I could get that had the hours I needed. Teddy is sending his child support, but you know I'm saving that for TJ's education. I'll be fine, don't worry."

He stood close to the tree so he couldn't be seen, looking and listening through the window. "Sure, don't worry, Mom. She'll be fine." He sneered at the sight of her reading to her son. "Enjoy your time together, Molly. It will be over soon."

Jake Long had been in the homicide division for five years now, and he was feeling pretty good—cocky, some would say. Things were going great. Jake felt like he had the world by the tail. He thought Sara was coming around to him working in homicide, and he was sitting at a hundred percent solving rate. He breezed into the office, whistling off-key.

"Holy hell, Long! Quit the whistling, you'll run everyone off!" His partner, Tony, cringed when Jake just whistled louder. "Okay, okay, you win!"

The phone rang. Jake picked it up. "Homicide, Long here. Be right there. Body found at the zoo, Tony. Let's roll." Jake felt the adrenaline pumping, as he grabbed his gun and headed for the door, with Tony at his heels. As they sped to the murder scene, Jake was all business. "The guys at the scene said Doc Miller was already there. No confirmation on who the victim is yet, but he did say it was definitely murder."

Pulling into the zoo, Jake flashed his badge at the guard at the gate. He let them through after pointing the way to the scene. Jake didn't have to drive far before spotting the crime scene tape around the tiger's cage. "I hope that tiger isn't part of the murder. I, for one, won't be going anywhere near it." He cringed a little. "Never liked zoos much."

The coroner, Doc Miller—or Doc, as everyone called him—was bent over a woman's body. He was checking over every inch of her. His keen eyes not missing anything. Doc looked up as Jake and Tony walked over to him. "Hi, guys. How's it going this morning?"

"Well, it's not going too good for her now, is it?" Jake nodded at the woman lying on the ground in front of him. "What's her story, Doc?"

"Well, as you can see, she was strangled with her own bra. That appears to be cause of death, but I'll know more when I get her back to the office. Being wrapped in a blanket, I can't see much of the rest of her body. I'm going to wait until I get her back to the morgue before I take the blanket off. Looks to be twenty-five to thirty years old. Liver temp shows time of death approximately five hours ago, probably around 4:00 a.m. No ID yet. I sent fingerprints to the lab. Hopefully her prints are on file. That's about all I know for now."

Jake knew from experience that was the end of the conversation. Doc didn't like throwing out guesses at the scene. Doc Miller has been a coroner now for thirty years and he knew what he was doing. "Okay, Doc. Let us know when you get her checked over more closely at the autopsy. Thanks, Doc." Jake turned his attention to the officer standing next to them. "Who found the body?"

The officer turned in the direction of raised voices standing by the squad car. "The zookeeper. He's right over there."

"Thanks. Tony, would you check and see if there were any other witnesses? I've got the zookeeper."

Jake headed for the distraught-looking man who was waving his arms around and talking loudly. He kept glancing from the body, to the tiger pacing back and forth in his cage. Jake had seen a few witnesses in his career so far, but this man was a basket case. He nodded to the officer, then turned back to the zookeeper. "Detective Jake Long, homicide. Do you mind if I ask you a few questions?"

"S-sure," he stuttered.

"Please try to relax, Mister...?"

"Grimes. Bobby Grimes."

"Mr. Grimes, I understand you found the body?" Jake kept his voice steady, trying to calm Bobby down.

"Yes, she was just lying there. I thought she was sleeping. Is...Is she dead?"

"I'm afraid so, Mr. Grimes. Bobby, please try to relax. I know what you saw was disturbing, but right now, it's very important that you describe exactly everything you saw."

Bobby took a deep breath, trying to steady his nerves. "Well, I'm always the first one here. I was busy feeding the animals, when I came over to feed Bertha. That's what I call the tiger. I noticed she was very upset and pacing back and forth, back and forth. I didn't know what was going on. She doesn't usually act like that. Animals can sense things, you know. They know when something isn't right. I've seen it time and time again, but little did I know there was a dead body. As I got closer to Bertha's cage, that's when I saw the body. At first, I thought she was just sleeping, because of the blanket, you know. I couldn't figure out how she got in here, you know. The gates are locked up at night."

Jake scanned the area. "I see that, Bobby. There is a high fence around the perimeter, with some thick brush and trees. How do you suppose she got in here, Bobby?"

Bobby got even more nervous, waving his arms faster. "I don't know, man! The gates are locked up tight every night. I do it myself, and I'm always the last one to leave and the first one here. That's why I was so shocked to see her there." He rubbed his chin, thinking. "Maybe the far back gate. It's rusty and old. I can't even open it. But if someone wanted in here bad enough, I guess that could be a way in. I...I haven't been back there in a while."

Jake looked the man up and down. *Could he have done this?* He didn't look like a killer, but they never do. "Well, that's all for now. Don't leave town, Mr. Grimes. We may have more questions later."

Jake turned as Tony approached him. "No witnesses, Jake. Seems our guy is the only one here that early."

"Yeah, so I hear." Jake sighed. "This is definitely not going to be an easy one, Tony. Let's go check out the back gate. Our witness, Bobby, thought it might be an entry point. I'll have the other officers look around for any tracks, or traces of blood, but I doubt they'll find anything."

The two men headed for the rear of the zoo, trudging through the dust, and feeling more and more doubtful about the outcome of this case. Sure enough, the gate had been jimmied open. It was quite a ways from the murder scene. "Had to carry the body a ways...unless she was still alive, and he forced her to walk to her own death. No signs of a struggle though. My guess is, he carried her. Must be a strong guy."

Tony stood up from his examination of the gate. "I'd say so. Definitely quite a walk from here to the scene. No drag marks or footprints either. He definitely carried the body. Must've brushed away footprints too. Do you think she was already dead?"

"Don't know yet. She was wrapped up in that blanket. Doc said he'd let us know what he finds after the autopsy."

By the time they got out of the office, it was midnight. Jake was beyond tired. They didn't find any evidence at the scene. There were too many footprints around the scene from people coming and going, to distinguish between them and the murderer. No DNA found at the scene either. When Jake got home, he was still thinking about the case.

"I sure hope Doc finds something on the body to help us out. Otherwise, it'll be a long and hard case to solve."

"So what's new there, Jake? They all are, aren't they?" Sara walked to him and started rubbing his neck and shoulders.

"I guess so, but this one gives me a bad feeling in the pit of my stomach, Sara. I'm going to grab a quick shower before hitting the hay. I'll be there in a little bit, okay?"

The next week, Jake got a call from Doc Miller. He headed for the

Medical Examiner's office downstairs, hoping Doc had some answers for him. "What've you got for me, Doc?"

"Well, good morning to you too, detective." Doc retorted. "To answer your question, I did find something. The victim's name is Molly Jones. Twenty-eight years old, has a three-year-old son at home. How sad. Anyway, she was strangled, like I said. When I took the blanket off, I found all kinds of interesting stuff, Jake." He pointed to Molly's neck where Jake noticed the bruises. Something else caught Jake's attention, two round burn marks on her neck, just above the bruises.

"Is that what I think it is, Doc?"

"Yes, she was incapacitated with a stun gun. But that's not all I found." Doc Miller pulled back the sheet covering the body.

Jake let out a low whistle. "What the hell?" There were several needles, and a few pins, protruding from the body. "Was she tortured?"

Doc shook his head. "Nope, these were all put in her body post-mortem. Thank God!"

Jake shivered. "What's your take on the needles, Doc?"

"Don't know, Jake. That's your job to figure out, not mine. That's pretty much all I found. No stray hairs or fingerprints on the body. She had no clothes on, but there was no sexual assault. That's it."

"Okay, thanks, Doc." Jake shivered a little as he walked to the elevator. "I'll never get used to this place."

Jake almost collided with Tony as he stepped out of the elevator. "Jake! Just the man I was looking for. You're never gonna believe who the victim is!"

"I already know who she is, Molly Jones. Why?"

"Yeah, Molly Jones, wife of Teddy Jones. Ringing a bell yet?"

"Teddy Jones. *Hmmm.* It does sound familiar. Pretty common name though. Spill it, Tony, who is he?"

"Teddy Jones is a cop. He used to work at LAPD until he and Molly divorced, and he moved to Texas. They have one son. Rumor has it, that's why he left. Couldn't handle being a father, and a cop. Pretty amicable divorce. He didn't want custody, or anything else to do with the boy. Molly lived downtown with her mom, Tammy Locken, and her son, TJ."

Jake blew out a short breath. "Please tell me Teddy isn't in Los Angeles right now."

"Nope, checked his alibi, pretty solid. He was in Texas at the time of the murder."

"Good, I wouldn't want to put away one of our own for this. Tony, Doc found stun gun marks on Molly's neck. You're not going to believe this. There were needles and pins stuck in her body. Who the hell does that?"

"*Whew!* No kidding. What kind of a psycho are we dealing with here, Jake?"

"I don't know, but we need to get him off the streets, fast! Let's go talk to the mother to see if she knows anything."

Talking to grieving parents was the worst part of Jake's job. As they knocked on the door, Tony looked around. "Not a terrible neighborhood. There are worse, that's for sure."

A small woman answered the door. Her eyes red from crying. "Yes, can I help you?"

"Mrs. Locken? I'm Detective Jake Long, and this is Detective Tony Scott. We're from homicide." Jake showed her his badge. "Mrs. Locken, I know this is a bad time. I'm sorry for your loss. Do you mind if we ask you a few questions?"

Tammy opened the door wider. "Please, call me Tammy. Come in, detectives."

"Tammy, we were hoping you could tell us a little bit about Molly. When was the last time you saw her?"

"She had just gotten home from work. She was reading to TJ, her son, when I went to bed. I guess that's the night before she was killed. When she wasn't there in the morning, I just thought she had an errand to run or something. Oh my God! Why would she leave the house in the middle of the night? She would never leave TJ without telling me!" Tammy was shrieking now.

Jake tried to calm her. "Tammy, we need you to try and stay calm. I know you're upset, but in order to catch who did this to Molly, we need your help, okay?"

Tammy took a few deep breaths. "I'm sorry, detectives. How can I help?"

"What about Molly's job? She worked close by, right?"

"Yes, Bob's Bar and Grill right down the street. I told her she should quit that job the minute she said she thought someone was following her."

"*Whoa*, back up. Molly thought someone was following her?"

"Yes, that night when she got home, I could tell she was upset, so I asked her. I have no idea how long this was going on. Oh my! I should have asked her more about it, but she shrugged it off, saying she was being paranoid."

"Did she see anyone following her?" Tony asked.

"No. Like I said, she didn't think it was anything to worry about."

Jake could see there probably wasn't anything more they could do here. "Okay, Tammy, here's my card. If you think of anything—anything at all—please call me, day or night. We'll show ourselves out. Thank you, Tammy. Again, I'm so sorry for your loss." Stepping outside, Jake gave Tony a sidelong glance. "What do you think? Was she being followed?"

"Sounds like she thought she was. Let's head on over to Bob's Bar and Grill, and see what they have to say for themselves."

"Sounds good. Maybe they'll know something. Seems like people have a tendency to tell coworkers things they don't tell their folks."

As they pulled up to Bob's, which was the only thing left lit up on the sign, Jake let out a low whistle. "Wow, from a half decent neighborhood, to a place like this not far away. I hate to judge a book by its cover, but by the looks of this place, I have a feeling we're not going to get much info out of them."

"I have to agree with you there, Jake. No harm in asking, I guess."

Jake and Tony walked into a dark, dank place, where the only light was the one hanging over a torn-up pool table. Letting their eyes adjust, they headed to the bar.

A pudgy, bald man, stood behind the bar, wiping his hands on his greasy apron. "What can I do for you today, officers?"

"Detectives Long and Scott, homicide. Who might you be?"

"Sorry, where are my manners?" The few customers that were there snickered at that comment. "I'm Bob. I own this lovely establishment."

"Okay, Bob. We're here about Molly Jones. I understand she worked for you?"

"Yes, lovely girl. I can't believe she's gone. God rest her soul."

"Did she have any problems with anyone at work? Any customers giving her a hard time? Coworkers?"

"No, sir! Everyone here loved her. Isn't that right?" Bob turned to one of the men sitting at the bar.

He nodded. "That's right. We loved our Molly girl."

Jake eyed the old man at the end of the bar. *Definitely not able to carry a body a long way.* He turned back to Bob. "What about someone she worked with? Can we talk to them?"

"Don't need no help here during the day, as you can see. Just Molly and Janice some nights. Mostly just Molly. Janice only works weekends. They never seen each other much. Barely knew each other. We stick to our own business around here. Nobody saw nothing, officers—I mean, detectives. Before you ask, does it look to you like I have security cameras? Nope, don't need 'em!"

Figures. Jake thought as they turned to leave. "Okay, Bob, if you think of anything else or hear something, let us know." Taking a deep breath as they stepped outside, Tony looked over at Jake. "Damn, Jake! This could be the one we don't solve. This guy seems to be pretty good."

Jake shook his head, sliding his sunglasses down over his eyes. "He may be good, but we're better."

5

"Goddammit, Long! It's been one year, and you haven't gotten any leads on the Jones murder! What the hell is going on? The brass has been breathing down my neck. You've got to give me something I can tell them. Anything!" Captain Burke was getting red in the face. Jake was afraid he was going to have a heart attack.

"Listen, Cap, we have feelers out all over the city. Every snitch we could track down has their ear to the ground. This killer seems to be laying low. No one is hearing any chatter at all. We're stumped, at a standstill, until we can get another lead. Hell, we never had one in the first place. No DNA, no fingerprints, nothing! It's just gone cold."

"Well get out there and find me something I can give the brass to satisfy them for a while. This was a cop's wife, Jake! Part of our family. I want answers and I want them yesterday, understand?"

Jake knew how the captain felt. He and Tony had been working night and day on this case. Nothing was happening. No one came forward with any information. They had hit a dead end. "I know she was family, Cap! Don't you think I'm trying here? I've been here every night 'til midnight. Shit! Sometimes all night. Sara doesn't ever see me. She's wondering if she even has a husband anymore! We're all frustrated and tired, Captain. It's just gone cold!"

Taking a deep breath, Captain Burke ran his hand through his gray hair. "I may have to retire. I just can't handle the political bullshit anymore. We may have to put this one to rest, Jake. You have other murders that need your attention. Murder doesn't take a break just because one doesn't get solved. I'll let the brass know."

Jake couldn't help but notice the way Captain Burke's shoulders slumped, and how slow he got around these days. Maybe Sara was right. Maybe he wasn't right for this job. Jake said as much to Tony when he got there.

"Damn, Jake. If you can't handle one unsolved, maybe you're *not* cut out for this job! You have to shake it off, and move on to the next. This isn't going to be the only murder that you can't figure out, Jake. There's nothing more we can do right now. Until something new comes up, put it to rest."

Jake straightened his shoulders and glared at Tony. "I know that! It's just that Molly's mom calls almost every day, and I have nothing to tell her. It's just so frustrating! Can you imagine how she feels? Next time she calls, I'll have to tell her we're giving up? I just don't know if I can do that, Tony. How do you tell a mother that her only child's murderer is still out there. Enjoying life, while she struggles to raise a boy without a mother? How, Tony, tell me that!"

A week went by, Jake had to admit, the Jones case probably wasn't going to get solved right now. He was not giving up, just setting it aside...for now. Heck, even Molly's mom must have figured the police weren't going to catch her daughter's killer. She had given up calling them. Jake was kind of glad she did. The poor woman needed to move on from this tragedy. He just wished they could have given her the closure she needed.

Jake grabbed a cup of coffee and walked to his desk. He passed by the murder board, looking at the face of Molly Jones tacked onto it. Jake yanked it off, along with the few other clues they had. Grabbing a box, he started stacking them into it, one by one. Closing the lid on the box, Jake wrote Molly's name on it and the date of her murder. Taking the box to the cold case room, he slid it on to a dusty shelf and tapped the box with his hand. "See ya in a while, Molly. See ya in a while."

Jake took one last look around the dismal room. *All these people, so many souls waiting for closure.* He sighed loudly, wondering if they were making a difference at all. Jake lingered a few more minutes, before shaking off the feeling of doom. He headed back to his desk.

Jake and Tony were not called out that day, so Jake took the opportunity to catch up on some dreaded paperwork. He knew it was part of the job, but hated it nonetheless. Before he knew it, it was ten o'clock at night. "Good grief, Sara's gonna kill me! Next thing I know, I'll be plastered all over the murder board!" Jake decided to call it quits for the night, and hurried home. He wasn't surprised to find Sara awake when he got home.

She glanced at her watch then at him. "You're home early. What's up with that?"

Jake cringed at her sarcasm. "Sorry, got carried away with paperwork tonight. I had it stacking up. I couldn't even see the top of my desk."

His humor was lost on Sara. "Sure, I know how that is. Well, good night, Jake."

"Sara, I said I was sorry. I had a rough day, okay? Can we just let it go for tonight?"

Sara turned slowly. "Sure, Jake. Good night."

Jake mixed himself a drink and sat on the couch. "Might as well make myself comfortable." Insomnia came with the job for detectives. He was used to it by now. Jake grabbed a blanket and pillow, picked up the TV remote, and put his feet up on the coffee table. After about an hour of no sleep, and flipping through channels on the TV, Jake decided to call it a night. He folded up the blanket, and headed for the bedroom. Just before he opened the door, he was startled by a noise coming from inside. Jake opened the door slowly, peeking in. Sara's book was lying on the floor again. This time, right by her side of the bed. "*Hmm, Sara must have dropped her book again.*" He picked it up and put it back on the shelf, not thinking any more about it.

Sara could hear her daddy calling out to her. She woke up, startled by the voice. Opening her eyes wide, she could make out a dim figure standing beside her. She closed her eyes, hoping it would go away. When Sara opened her eyes again, the figure was still there. Tentatively, she reached out to touch it. But just when she would get close enough, it would move just out of reach. Daddy, is that you?" The figure started fading away slowly. "No, Daddy, come back! Please, Daddy, don't leave me! Daddy!" Sara closed her eyes, rubbing them with the backs of her hands. She didn't actually see anything, did she? Drenched in sweat, and shaking like a leaf, she thought she may as well get up for the day.

Jake was sitting up in the bed next to her. "Sara, did you have another dream? What the hell is going on?"

"I...I don't know, Jake. Truthfully...I think I saw my dad. Does that sound crazy?"

"Of course not. I'm sure your dream felt very real."

Shaking her head, Sara decided not to tell Jake that what she really meant, was she thought she *really* saw her dad. It was as if he was standing right in front of her. "Sure, that's probably it. I'm going to take a shower before work. You had better get to the office."

Jake was confused by Sara's behavior lately. He couldn't figure her out. One minute, she's happy and smiling, and the next, she's sarcastic and...well, bitchy. He knew she wasn't sleeping well, because she was worrying about Ann. That must be why she was always carrying that book around, and probably why she was having bad dreams. Jake made a note to call Sam soon, to see if he'd found anything out about Ann. That should help Sara's mood...he hoped.

He got out of bed and started getting ready for work when his phone rang. He was surprised to see his brother's name come up on caller ID. Jake smiled. "Hey, what's up, bro?"

Sam's voice boomed on the other end. "Nothing much, Jake. Just thought I'd better see if you were still alive. I never hear from you. How are things there?"

"Okay, I guess. Got a case that's driving me crazy, nothing new. Say, I have been meaning to call you. Sara has been really worried about Ann. Have you found anything out about what she's up to?"

"Sorry, bro, nothing yet. I know she is around here, though. Some of my police contacts have had different run-ins with her. She has had some small amounts of drugs on her, but not enough to hold her very long. I don't think she's doing well, Jake. Probably why she won't talk to Sara. I'll keep looking for her, and let you know what I find out."

Jake scrubbed his hand down his face. "Okay, thanks, Sam. By the way, how's the ranch doing? Mom and Dad would be proud of you, even though you're not a cop. You are still helping the law enforcement community and their families. Sara really wants to come there and find Ann. I wish I could go with her. I miss you, bro."

"Me too, Jake, but tell her not to bother coming here to find Ann. She's in the wind. If I find her, I'll try to anchor her down and call Sara then. Just tell her to stay put for now."

"Will do, Sam. I'll let you go. Don't be a stranger, okay, bro?"

"I should be saying that to you, Jake. Listen, don't let yourself get burned out from this job. You can't save the whole world. Just take it one by one. See ya, Jake."

Sara came into the room just as he hung up from talking to Sam. "Who was that?"

Jake's mouth dropped open when he looked up from his phone to see Sara standing in front of him, wearing nothing but a towel. He almost lost his whole train of thought. "Ah...it was Sam. Yeah, I asked him about Ann."

Sara's face lit up. "Has he seen her? Should I go there? How is she? Jake, tell me!"

"Oh yeah, um, he hasn't seen her yet. His contact at the police department says she's been picked up a couple times for some small drug infractions." Jake held his hand up to stop Sara from panicking. "Nothing major. They held her overnight, and she took off the next morning. Sam is gonna keep us informed if he finds her. He said to tell you to stay put until he contacts us with any information. We just need to wait, Sara. She'll contact you when she's ready."

"I'm not a patient person, Jake. You know that!" Sara took a breath, and the towel moved, nearly slipping all the way off. She pulled it back around her. "I can't just sit around doing nothing, when Ann could be in big trouble. She's my sister, Jake! I feel like I'm letting her down."

Jake couldn't help it, he had to hold her. He wrapped his arms around her, and drew her to him. "I know, sweetie, but there just isn't anything we can do until Ann wants us to. I've seen it over and over again. You just can't force it. She'll come around, I know it, and you'll be there for her. Just like you always have been. It'll be okay, I promise."

Sara breathed in, loving the feel of Jake's arms around her. It had been too long, and she didn't want to let go. They stood like that for what seemed like an eternity, when Jake's phone rang. He slowly had to loosen his hold on her. Jake backed away. "I'm sorry, honey, I have to get that."

"I know, Jake." Sara pulled away, and wrapped the towel tighter around her. "I know."

Jake pulled up to the precinct and parked in the lot next door. He smacked his hands on the steering wheel. "Dammit! Why does the phone ring just when Sara and I are starting to get back to some feelings of normalcy?"

Opening the car door, he shook off the bad feeling he had about his marriage, and put his mind in work mode. It was pretty hard to do that though, when all he could see was Sara standing there, in nothing but that towel. He couldn't stop thinking about his wife, as he rushed up the steps, not watching where he was going. Jake collided with a pretty blonde walking down the steps of the police station. She was looking down at her phone and did not see him either. They both looked up, startled.

Jake grabbed her arms so she wouldn't fall. "Excuse me, ma'am, I didn't see you there. I'm so sorry."

"No, it was totally my fault. I'm sorry!"

When Jake looked up, he was taken aback by a pair of startling blue eyes, peeking up at him behind a pair of black-rimmed glasses. "No, ma'am, it was my fault! Um, I know this is going to sound lame, but do I know you?"

The blonde laughed a little. "It sounds fine, and no, we've never met officially. I'm Dr. Nancy Hall, the clinical psychologist for the police department." She reached out her hand.

Jake shook it lightly. "Jake Long. Well, I guess I could say it's a good thing we haven't met yet! I haven't been in need of your services, Dr. Hall."

"Please call me Nancy, and yes, I guess you could say that, detective." She smiled.

Jake gave her a small salute. "Right, Dr. Nancy. Well, it was nice running into you. Pardon the pun."

She laughed. "Nice meeting you too, Detective Long. I'll be seeing you around, I'm sure."

"Sure thing, Doctor. Bye now."

Jake continued his rush up the stairs, taking them two at a time. When he got to his desk, he asked Tony what the doctor was doing there.

"I don't know, Jake. I think she just comes around every once in a while to see Cap. Not *see* him, just check and see how things are going, I guess."

"Oh, okay. Well, she seems nice enough, I guess—for a shrink!"

"She is good at her job, helped me out when I needed her."

Jake looked at Tony with a puzzled expression. "When you needed her? Do tell!"

"I don't talk about it much. It was my first shooting. The guy drew on me, and I had to shoot to kill. Didn't want to, had to. That's it, end of story."

"Wow, sorry, Tony. I'm glad you got help coping with that. I haven't had to, hope I never do."

"Well, when, and if, you do need her help, take it, Jake. Don't be a stubborn, bull-headed ass. Let her help you."

"Sure thing, Tony. Now, why did you call me, just to shoot the breeze?"

"No, geez, I almost forgot. Captain Burke called a meeting. We better get in there, we're late."

"Any idea what the meeting is about? What's going on?"

"No idea. Let's go find out."

Captain Burke was standing in his usual spot at the podium, as people were milling about. When Cap spoke, he had everyone's attention. "Sit down, people. Now that Long and Scott have graced us with their presence, we can get started." The other cops laughed, glad it wasn't them he was chastising. "I just wanted to tell you this in person before you start hearing rumors through the grapevine. As of the end of the year, I am retiring." Murmurs spread through the room. "Okay, settle down. It's not gonna be for a while yet. I have some things to get in order first, like who my replacement will be. I don't know who the police commissioner will go with, but I want him to stay in house if possible. I just hope someone here will step up and apply for the job. Now get back to work people. Murders don't solve themselves."

Just as if the captain had planned it, Jake heard the phone ringing on his desk. He glanced at Tony and went to answer it. "Homicide, Long here. Okay, we'll be right there. Got a murder, Tony. Just another day in paradise, I guess."

6

Jake and Tony pulled up to the scene of another murder. The yellow crime scene tape stood out in sharp contrast to the plush, green lawns and trimmed hedges.

"Another nice neighborhood. Things like this shouldn't happen to good people, Tony."

"I agree, Jake, but it can happen to anyone. It's our job to find out who did it, and put them away."

Jake nodded. "That's right! Let's get to it then."

Jake looked around, noticing a lot of people milling about. They were curious as to what was going on next door. Jake grabbed the nearest officer. "Make sure you keep any witnesses here. We'll talk to them when we're done inside. Thanks."

The officer nodded. "Will do, detective."

He stood in the crowd, blending in with the other people gawking at the house. "Go ahead, detective, question whoever you want. Nobody saw anything, I made sure of that. After all, I learned from the best." He turned and walked slowly away. No one noticing the stranger in the crowd.

Jake and Tony entered the house, pausing at the door to look over the scene. Jake liked to picture the victim's movements on that day. When he saw what the victim was doing, it helped him picture the perp's movements throughout the house as he prepared to kill. They entered a larger foyer. No signs of forced entry on the front door. To their right was a kitchen, small, but tidy. There were no dishes in the sink, except for one glass on the counter. Straight ahead, was the living area. There was a worn-out recliner, sitting in front of a TV, that was mounted on the wall. The back door was in this room.

Jake checked the door. "Unlocked. I wonder if our victim left it that way. No signs of a break-in here either." There were various pictures on the walls and end tables. Jake picked one up. "Tony, there's a picture here of a man in uniform. Don't even tell me our victim is a cop."

"Okay, I won't tell you that, because I know just as much as you do right now, which is not much."

Setting the picture down, Jake walked toward a narrow hallway. There was a long staircase. Doc Miller was kneeling over a body lying at the bottom. Jake headed for the body, noticing it was sprawled out awkwardly, with arms and legs at odd angles. "Well, Doc, looks like a fall to me. Why are we here?"

Doc looked up as Jake approached. "Well, that's why I'm the doctor and you're not. At first glance, it does look like just a fall. Come closer, I'll show you why you're here."

Jake knelt down so he could get a closer look. "Oh boy, this is the same guy in the picture. He's a cop, isn't he?"

"Yes, he is. Name's Harvey Anderson. He owns the house. A retired cop. Good guy, and good cop, Jake. I knew him personally. He had a few troubles at home, but who doesn't? Anyway, look at his neck and tell me what you see."

Jake knelt lower and took a closer look. "Two circular burn marks. A stun gun? We need to check for licenses bought for a stun gun. Maybe we'll get lucky there. Any other similarities to the Jones murder?"

"No, as you can see, Harvey wasn't strangled. Plus, he's male, and she was female. There is some bruising on his hands. Can't tell if it's from the fall or a fight. I bagged his hands. If there's any DNA, I'll let you know. Looks like there may have been a scuffle at the top of the stairs. Liver temp shows he's been dead four to six hours. That puts time of death around six a.m. He probably died from the fall, but I'll know more after the autopsy. That's about all I've got for now."

Jake stood and nodded, walking up the long flight of stairs. Tony was already at the top, along with the crime scene unit. The investigator was dusting for fingerprints on the walls and railing. "Make sure to dust the back door for prints, looks like point of entry."

Jake understood the importance of forensics in solving murders, so he left him to do his job. "Wow, I can't believe an older person would buy a house with a staircase this long. I got tired walking up it."

Tony snorted, "Yeah, me too. I would have to say he's lived here awhile though, with the family pictures all over. There's a pretty good layer of dust on everything too. Lived alone, I'd say."

Jake looked around, noticing the dusty pictures Tony talked about. "Yeah, looks like it. Not much company either."

Tony looked at Jake and noticed his puzzled expression. "What's bugging you? What did Doc say?"

"Tony, the perp used a stun gun on Mr. Anderson. There isn't any other similarities to the Jones murder, but how often is a stun gun used? Seems odd to me."

"Maybe, but no other similarities to the Jones murder? Was he strangled?"

"No, he probably died from the fall, but Doc saw bruising on his hands. Probably tried to fight him the best he could. Being an ex-cop, I wouldn't expect anything less. I didn't notice any signs of a break-in. Anything appear to be missing?"

Tony shook his head. "There's a gold watch on the dresser, some cash too. Doesn't look like a robbery. There's a gun in the nightstand. Harvey didn't go for that, so he must not have seen it coming. The guy must've been hiding in the spare bedroom, and jumped him from behind."

Jake walked around the crime scene. "Looks like Harvey was in the bathroom. The toothbrush still has toothpaste on it. He probably heard something, walked out to see what it was, and got stunned. Tried to hit whoever it was, and got pushed down the stairs." He walked over to the CSI. "Finding any prints?"

"Nothing yet. Looks like the killer wiped everything clean around the scene. Nothing here, not even the victim's prints."

Jake blew out a breath, running his hand through his hair. "Okay, let's go back outside and question the neighbors. Maybe someone saw something." Jake and Tony noticed that more people had shown up to gawk. They headed toward the officer Jake had talked to earlier. "Do you know who reported finding Mr. Anderson's body?"

"Mrs. Brown over here found the body, but there are a few people you'll want to talk to, Detective Long. Got them right over here."

Jake looked over to where the officer was pointing. "Okay, thanks, Jim. Tony, will you take the group over at the other police car? I'll take the neighbor. Which one of you live right next door to Mr. Anderson?"

A tiny, frail looking, older woman stepped forward. "That would be me. I live right next door."

"Hello, ma'am. I'm Detective Long, homicide. Do you mind if I ask you a few questions, Miss...?"

"You can call me Evie, young man. Evie Brown. What happened to poor Mr. Anderson? God rest his soul. Was it a heart attack?"

"I'm not at liberty to say, Mrs. Brown. Tell me, did you see anything out of the ordinary around six this morning? Anyone hanging around that shouldn't have been here?"

"Please call me Evie. No, I didn't see anything, or anyone, and I'm up at the crack of dawn every day. Harvey and I have coffee together every morning. When he didn't show up at my house this morning, I rushed over to his. Well, he didn't answer the door, so I used my key to get in. We all have keys to each other's house around here. When you get to be our age, you never know what might happen, you know. Anyway, I went in and saw poor Harvey lying at the base of the stairs. I figured he had a heart attack or something, and fell. That's when I rushed out and called the police...Oh my! Did you say you were a homicide detective? Was poor Harvey murdered? Oh my, I have to call my daughter! If she hears this on the news, she'll come running over here, grab my suitcases, and move me in with her. She has five kids! As much as I love my grandchildren, I don't want to live with them. Thank you, young man. You know, my youngest daughter is single. Are you married, detective?"

Jake cleared his throat. "Yes, ma'am, I am. Thank you, Mrs. Brown. If you think of anything else, please call us."

"Call me Evie, everyone does."

Jake could have sworn she winked at him over her shoulder as she walked away. He shook his head as he saw Tony walking toward him. "I hope you had better luck than I did here. All I got was a wink from the next-door neighbor."

Tony laughed. "Not much, I'm afraid. I learned that this is a retirement community, so everyone here is older. Nobody saw anything out of the ordinary this morning. Did you learn of any next of kin?"

"No, Mrs. Brown was too busy trying to give me her daughter's phone number to tell me about Harvey Anderson. Maybe there's something in the house that will tell us if Harvey had any kids." They headed back to the house just as Doc was bringing the body out. "Doc, since you knew Harvey, do you know if he has any next of kin, kids, or ex-wife maybe?"

Doc waved his assistant on, and stopped in front of Jake. "I believe he had a daughter. I don't know her name. Not sure about his wife. I think I heard she passed away a few years ago."

"Thanks, Doc. We'll head into the house and see if we can find something out about the daughter. Let me know when you're done with the autopsy."

"Sure thing. See you later then."

Jake always hated going through the personal belongings of the deceased, but it helped to learn more about them. They found the name of his daughter in some of Harvey's paperwork. "Karen Mason. Looks like she is the only next of kin left. Looks like Harvey left the house and everything he had to her. Could be our first suspect, let's track her down."

After another long night, Jake tiptoed into the house after midnight. He couldn't blame Sara for not waiting up for him. He mixed himself a drink, and plopped down on the couch, rubbing his sore feet. Even with his hard work and long days, he could see his record for murders solved dwindling fast. Jake knew better than to think he could solve every murder that came his way, but he wanted to.

Before he knew it, his drink was empty. He got up to fix himself another. Jake grabbed the remote and started flipping through channels again, not really seeing what was on anyway. All he could think about was this case. They had gotten ahold of the daughter, and she was coming in a couple of days to talk to them. Jake had a few questions for her. "She could be our killer for all we know. I can't wait to talk to her." He mixed another drink and fell asleep on the couch, with the TV on, and remote in his hand.

Two days later, the daughter was there to see them. "I'm Karen Mason. You wanted to see me, detective?"

"Yes, I'm Detective Long and this is Detective Scott. We're sorry for your loss, Ms. Mason. Please, have a seat."

"Call me Karen. Thank you, detectives."

Jake couldn't help but notice that Karen wasn't all that broken up about her dad's death. "Karen, did your dad have any enemies? Maybe from his job as a cop?"

"To tell you the truth, my dad and I were estranged. We only just started talking to each other again about a month ago. I moved back to LA after mom died, and decided to forgive and forget."

"Excuse me for asking, Karen, but forgive and forget what?"

Karen cleared her throat. "Well, to make a long story short, my dad had an affair right under my mom's nose. She walked in the house one day, and found the two of them in their *own* bed." She sighed. "Needless to say, they got a divorce soon after that. I was old enough to make my own decisions, so I moved with my mom to Seattle. She didn't want me to have any contact with my dad, and frankly, I didn't think he cared if he saw me or not. We didn't speak for twenty years. Like I said, when mom passed away, and I got a divorce, I wanted to reconnect with him. So I moved back here. He didn't have any excuses for the affair, but I think he regretted every moment of it. So you see, detective, I won't be of much help."

"If you don't mind my asking, Karen, where were you at the time of the murder?"

Karen was a little taken aback by the question. "You think I killed my father? That's rich! I was in Seattle, packing up some of my things, and cleaning up some loose ends at work. You can check with my coworkers, I'll give you their names. Maybe you should ask his mistress. She probably had more of a motive than me. Dad told me he was going to leave me everything. I don't suppose she was any too happy about that!"

Jake looked at Karen closely. "We will check with your coworkers, Ms. Mason. Now what is this about Harvey's mistress? He didn't break it off with her?"

"I'm not sure if he did or not, she lived right next door! Actually, I think they continued seeing each other after Mom and Dad split. As far as I know, they never married. Her name is Evie Brown. Why don't you ask her where she was that morning?"

Jake's eyes widened at that little tidbit of information. "Oh, we will be asking Mrs. Brown just that. Thank you, Karen, and again, we're sorry for your loss." Jake turned to Tony, eyebrows arched. "I guess someone has some explaining to do. Let's find out what Mrs. Brown's explanation is for not telling us about this affair!"

When Jake and Tony got back to the crime scene, the tape was still up, some of it blowing in the wind. They bypassed the Anderson house, and headed next door. They knocked, and stepped aside, waiting for Mrs. Brown to answer. Hearing her footsteps approaching, Jake stepped closer to the door.

Evie Brown opened the door a crack and peeked out. "Detective Long, how nice to see you!"

"Mrs. Brown, we need to ask you a few more questions about your relationship with Harvey Anderson."

"Whatever do you mean, dear? Please come in."

Jake and Tony entered what could only be called a hoarder's nest. There were magazines, newspapers, and who knows what else, stacked to the ceiling. They followed Evie, with only a narrow path to walk through.

"This is fine, Mrs. Brown. We just have a few questions."

"Not until you call me Evie, detective. Remember?"

"Mrs. Brown—I'm sorry, Evie, why didn't you mention the fact that you and Harvey were having an affair?"

"Well, that was years ago! We stayed friends, but we stopped seeing each other when Harvey's wife found us in our...um, compromising situation. My husband forgave my little transgression, and Harvey's wife left him shortly after that. I didn't feel it was necessary to bring up that old news."

Jake didn't sincerely think Evie was a killer, but he asked anyway. "Evie, did you or someone you know, have anything to do with Harvey's death? Maybe your husband was still holding a grudge against Harvey. If you tell us the truth now, it will look much better for you in the long run."

The friendliness vanished from Evie's face. "Oh my, no! My husband has been dead for many years now. Besides, we were all friends after it was all over and done with. Water under the bridge. What about Harvey's wife? Have you talked to her? She had more of a reason than anyone to want Harvey dead. Why don't you go ask her and quit harassing innocent people."

"Just doing our job, ma'am. We'll show ourselves out." Jake tipped his hat, and backed out the way they came in.

When they got outside Tony was wrinkling his nose and gulping in the fresh air. "Good grief! I don't think I could have lasted another minute in there. I thought I was gonna start gagging!"

"Me too, Tony. Let's get out of here. It looks like a dead end." Jake's phone rang when they got back to the car. Hanging up, he started the car and pulled away from the curb. "That was Doc Miller. The autopsy is done. Let's hope he has some answers. We don't want another unsolved murder on our hands."

The morgue was the same cold, sterile place as always. When Jake got off the elevator, he shivered. "I just don't know how you can stand it down here, Doc!"

Doc Miller looked up from the corpse he was working on. "Get used to it, I guess. It didn't take you long to get here. Well, let's get to it then. Cause of death was blunt force trauma from the fall, like we figured." Doc held his hand up, stopping Jake mid-sentence. "The bruising on the hands was from the fall too, Jake. No DNA, no foreign hairs, nothing."

Jake's shoulders slumped. "You're kidding. Nothing? No clues at all? Here we go again. Well, thanks, Doc. You really know how to brighten a guy's day." He turned and headed back upstairs, feeling another headache coming on. Jake was rubbing his forehead when he stepped out of the elevator.

Tony knew by the look on his face what went on downstairs. "Doc didn't have anything, did he?"

"Nothing! Not one damn thing!" Jake plopped down at his desk. "We are not letting this one go unsolved, Tony! There's got to be something we missed. Let's start from the beginning." Jake stepped over to the murder board. "Number one-no forced entry. Either Harvey left the door open, or let them in. *Two*-it could have been someone he knew. *Three*- stun gun. *Four*-affair. *Five*-left everything to his daughter. She has an airtight alibi. Mrs. Brown is too small to overpower Harvey, even stunned. We're back to square one!"

Jake and Tony spent the rest of the day, and far into the night, pouring over their notes.

Jake headed home after another long day. The house was dark and quiet. The door creaked a little when he opened it. He tried to be quiet, tiptoeing into the house. "This is getting to be a routine. I sure do miss my wife."

Jake needed a shower, but he didn't want to wake Sara. He mixed his favorite drink, and after having a few of those, he dozed off on the couch. Jake didn't hear Sara, crying softly in the other room.

When Jake woke the next morning, he felt like he had been hit by a freight train. He stretched, and looked down at his wrinkled suit. Jake heard the shower just shutting off, and went looking for his wife.

Sara was standing at the mirror, brushing her long, blonde hair. "You didn't come to bed last night. You're making a habit out of sleeping on that couch. Is it more comfortable than our bed?"

"You know it's not. I was just trying to wind down and fell asleep. I didn't want to wake you up. Sorry about that."

Sara wrinkled her nose when he came up behind her and hugged her. "Well, you smell like a whiskey bottle. You'd better shower before you head to work."

"Yeah, I will. Will you be here when I'm done?"

"No, I have to go in early. We hired a new cook, and I have to show him the ropes."

"Okay, I'll see you tonight then. You know I love you, right?"

"Yes, Jake, and I love you, too. I'm not gonna hold my breath on seeing you tonight, though."

Jake got in the shower, feeling much better when the hot spray hit his sore muscles. By the time he got done, he felt more like himself. His phone rang right on cue. Jake looked at the caller ID and saw Tony's name on the screen. "This is Long. What's up, Tony?"

"We got a call from a Detective Marsh in Portland. He got wind of our two stun gun murders, and says he may have some info for us. I'll fill you in when you get here."

"Be right there, Tony. This could be the break we're looking for." Jake felt a renewed excitement for his job, as he hurried to the precinct. He made a beeline for Tony as soon as he walked in to the police station. "I'm here, now tell me what's up."

"Well, like I said, the Portland detective called me this morning. He thinks they may have had a murder there that is similar to ours. Don't get your hopes up, though. The only similarity is the use of a stun gun. The victim wasn't a cop, or related to one. I don't really know why he thinks it's related, but I told him we would take a look at it. He faxed over the paperwork. I put it on your desk."

Jake couldn't help but get his hopes up. If it is the same guy, they could maybe get some clues from this one. It could also mean they have a serial killer on their hands. Jake trotted to his desk and opened the folder Detective Marsh had sent them. Skimming through it, Jake noticed that the victim was a prostitute, a thirty-year-old white female. She was killed ten years ago, and found in an alley. She was stabbed, not strangled, and a stun gun was used at some point in the attack. That was the only thing similar to the Molly Jones and Harvey Anderson murders. Jake felt a little dejected.

"I don't really see why Marsh thought this was our guy. Just because of the stun gun? Not much here to go on either. If it is our killer, he must've started in Portland, and moved here for some reason. I don't know, Tony. They didn't get anything off her body to help us out."

Tony shrugged. "Yeah, that's what I thought too. It was worth a shot, though. I think we should keep the file with our other two murder books though. You never know."

"Yeah, let's get to work on the Anderson murder. It seems nobody cared about him when he was alive. Let's show him we care about his death. I'm not gonna let this one go, Tony."

7

Another year gone, Jake found himself back in the cold case room. He slid another box—this time, with Harvey Anderson's name on it—onto the shelf.

Getting more and more frustrated, Jake let out a long breath. "I don't blame Captain Burke for retiring. This could make a person go crazy. There's one killer—maybe two—out there, and we are no closer to finding them than when we started."

Jake turned and left the room, sadness enveloping him. He wondered where Tony was when he got back to his desk. He was always there earlier than Jake. Rubbing his neck, he glanced over at Tony's desk. It was neat as a pin. His was covered with paperwork, a stale coffee cup, and a couple of old trophies from high school. Jake shook his head. *Why I'm keeping those, I don't know. Reliving the glory years, I guess.* Jake looked up when he heard his name called. Tony was standing at the captain's door, motioning to him with his hands. "What are you doing, Tony? I was wondering where you were. What are you doing in Cap's office?"

Tony opened the door. "Come in here, Jake. I have something I want to tell you. Sit down, please."

Jake was confused. He noticed the empty desk Tony was sitting on. "So, Cap is gone. I honestly didn't think he would actually do it. Cap said he wasn't going to leave until he found someone to replace him. Who did he get, Tony? Do we know him? I hope he's a decent guy. I don't work well with assholes—present company excluded, of course."

Tony laughed. "Yeah, I get it. I've got something to tell you, so I'm just gonna come out and say it. I put in my application for captain a while back. I didn't say anything, because I didn't think I would get it anyway. Well, the police commissioner called me in yesterday. I got the job, Jake. You're looking at your new captain."

Jake jumped up and grabbed Tony's hand, pulling him in for a short hug. "You sneaky devil! You could have told me. I didn't even know you were considering the job! I'm happy for you, Tony. Really, I am. You're a good cop, and a good friend. What's gonna happen to me? Am I without a partner now?"

"Maybe, for now. Can you handle that?"

"Sure thing, I probably will work better alone anyway. No complaining about my driving. No yelling about my coffee cups in the car. Yeah, I can handle it."

Tony smiled at Jake. "You'll just have me yelling at you as your boss now. Can you handle that too?"

"I think so. You're a good guy, Tony. Congratulations on your promotion."

"Thanks, Jake."

When Jake left Tony's new office, the phone rang on his desk. He answered on the third ring. "Homicide, Long here."

Jake peeked his head into the new captain's office. "Got another one, Tony. I guess I'll head out on my own."

"Well, hell! No way, Jake. I need to be in the action. Doesn't say anything in the rule book about the captain not being able to help out his subordinates."

"I kinda hoped you'd say that. Let's roll."

Tony grabbed his gun and badge. "Where are we headed?"

Jake started the car, and squealed out of the parking lot. He grinned at his new captain. "LA Park. A hiker found a body. Hope you wore your comfortable shoes, we may have a walk to reach the body. We'll see when we get there."

"You mean *if* we get there!" Tony cringed when Jake peeled around a corner, sirens blaring. They pulled into the park, looking for the other police cars. Tony got on his radio to find out exactly where to go. "It's at Bamboo trail, kind of a quiet spot for a murder."

Jake drove along Bamboo Drive toward the museum. "Bamboo

is a relatively short hiking trail. Maybe we lucked out and won't have to walk too far." They pulled up next to a police car near the trail. "What have we got?"

"Hey, Jake. Got a body just down the trail. Hiker found it around ten o'clock this morning. The body is just off the trail, about a hundred yards in."

"Okay, thanks. Let's go, Captain!" They took off, hiking a short way down the trail. Seeing the yellow tape, Jake stopped. "Well, here we are. Same stuff, different day, I guess. This is an out-of-the-way place. Looks like Doc is here already, as usual." Jake stopped the nearest policeman. "What've we got here?"

"Body halfway down the incline. Hiker found it this morning. No idea who it is yet. Doc Miller is down there." He pointed just a short way down the trail.

"Okay, thanks. Where's the guy who found the body?" The cop pointed to a man on his hands and knees, throwing up in the bushes nearby. "Um…I think we'll question him in a little bit, maybe after we talk to Doc Miller. Make sure he doesn't go anywhere."

Tony looked from the witness to Jake. "You're kidding, right? I don't see him moving too fast."

"Well, yeah, but you never know. Does you making captain allow you to be a smart-ass?" Jake shook his head. "Don't answer that. Let's go find Doc."

Jake and Tony walked the short distance to where Doc Miller was examining the body. "Hey, Doc! You okay down there?"

"I'm fine. I'm tougher than I look, Jake. Besides, he's not that far down here, almost like the killer wanted him found. Looks like a young male, in his twenties. He's been dead about four hours, probably early morning. I'm having a little trouble checking over the body closely in this environment. I might have to wait until I get him back to the morgue to tell you much. I can see he's got one shoe on and one off, and it appears the foot is missing. Okay, I found his wallet here. ID says he is Martin Parker, twenty-four years old, from LA. As you can see, the boy was walking on the trail, probably ambushed, and pushed, or dragged, down here. The foot was removed down here. A pretty sharp instrument used to remove it, probably a scalpel. Haven't found the foot anywhere, so the killer must have took it with him."

Jake looked around the area. The crime scene unit was combing the brush, looking for clues. "Taking a trophy from his kill, I suppose. Pretty bold, killing right out in the open like this. He must have been fairly certain nobody was around. Took some time to cut the foot off, even with a scalpel. What do you think, Tony?"

Tony had been talking to the CSI down the path. "Crime scene unit haven't found anything yet. No sign there was much of a struggle here. Doc, any head trauma? How did he get him down there?"

"Not sure. I'm gonna take the body back to the medical examiner's office and do an autopsy right away. I'll let you know as soon as I know what happened."

"Sounds good, Doc. Let's get the body hauled out of there, so we can check the scene closer."

Doc nodded, and motioned for his assistant to help. They got the victim in the body bag, and hauled him out of there. It took some doing, but with Jake and Tony's help, they finally got the body to the van, and headed for the morgue.

Jake slid down the embankment on his heels. "You know, it's not too far down here, but still pretty steep. Our killer—or killers— must be young, and pretty agile, to work on cutting the foot off down here." He turned to the CSI. "Did you swab the blood over here yet?"

"Yep, we'll check the DNA, but it's probably the victim's. Could be the killer cut himself, too. We'll know that when we check the blood."

Jake climbed back up the embankment, grabbing Tony's outstretched hand for help. "Thanks, Captain. Let's go see if our witness is done puking up breakfast."

Tony shivered. "Please stop. I'm gonna be next if he's still throwing up."

Jake laughed. "I didn't realize you had such a weak stomach. No wonder I always go to the autopsies alone. All this time, I thought you were just confident in my abilities, but really, you just couldn't handle it. Learn something new every day, I guess. I think I may save that knowledge, in case I need some leverage down the road."

"Go ahead, I'll just deny it anyway. It won't do you any good."

When Tony and Jake got to him, the witness was still pale and shaky, but upright at least. "I'm Detective Long. This is Detective Scott. What's your name, sir?"

Shakily, the man looked up and wiped his mouth with the paper towel someone gave him. "I'm Dan Crocket. I walk this trail every day. Never saw anything like this, though. Never want to again."

"Mr. Crocket, did you see anyone else on the trail this morning? Anyone looking suspicious to you?"

Dan shook his head. "Nope. I like to go early in the morning, when there's no one else here. Don't like people—I mean, I like to be alone, you know. It gives me time to think. I'm an accountant, and you can understand why I like to be alone to clear my mind."

"Sure, I understand, Dan." Jake nodded. "So, tell me exactly what you saw here."

"Well, as I walked down the pathway, I was feeling pretty good. Beautiful morning, you know. When I got to the bend there, I noticed some tracks in the dirt. It didn't look normal to me, so I stopped and looked around. I thought maybe someone had fallen off the trail and was hurt. That's when I saw the body down there. So, I went down to try and help, you know. Once I got there, I could see it was too late to help him. Then I noticed his foot was gone, and...well, I think you know the rest of the story."

Jake glanced over at Tony. "Yeah, I think we got the rest. So you didn't see or hear anything at all? No branches breaking, no one up on the trail ahead of you?"

"No, it was dead silence. I was totally alone—except for the dead guy, of course. I always start my hike at the cafe, and if I feel up to it, I go all the way up to the observatory. I didn't get too far this time, though."

"Well, that's all for now, Mr. Crocket. If you think of anything else, let us know. Thank you."

Jake turned to Tony after Mr. Crocket left. "I don't think he had anything to do with this murder, judging from the puking part. Maybe when Doc gets the autopsy done, he'll have some answers. Let's get back to the office and find out just who Mr. Parker is."

Jake drove a little slower on the way back to the police station. He was all business now, done giving his new captain a hard time. Tony went straight to his office when they got back, as he had captain business to attend to. Jake sat down at the computer, typing Martin Parker into the police database. "Okay, let's see, Martin Parker is twenty-four years old. No outstanding warrants, no run-ins with the police, and no record. Pretty clean-cut kid, it looks like to me. No apparent reason to get murdered, just because you wanted an early morning walk. Parents are Larry and Marilyn Parker. Oh boy, his dad's a cop. Wait until Tony hears this. A cop's son was murdered."

Jake printed out the info and headed for the captain's office. He knocked and walked in. "Captain, I thought you had better see this right away. Martin Parker is a cop's son. Larry Parker, do you know him?"

Tony shook his head. "No, I don't know him. Jake, I see kind of a pattern going on here. I sure hope I'm wrong."

"I do too, Tony. Let's not panic quite yet. We'll wait and see what Doc Miller has to say."

"Yeah, I doubt we'll hear from Doc today. Why don't you go home to your beautiful wife? Get out of here early for a change."

"I might just do that. Thanks, Tony." Jake took his friend's advice and called it a day. He surprised Sara by picking up takeout from the Chinese restaurant.

She looked happy to see him when he walked in carrying supper. "Jake, what's this? What are you doing home so early? Not that I'm not happy to see you. I am."

"Well, you'd better be. If you weren't, I'd be worried. We are at a standstill with the investigation until Doc's autopsy, so I blew out of there early. Hey, guess what? Tony applied for captain without me knowing, and he got the job! Isn't that something?"

"Wow, that's great! Good for him! How do you really feel about it? Are you really okay with it?"

"Yeah, I am. If anybody deserves it, Tony does. He's a good guy, and a great cop. I think he'll make a great captain. Now, let's eat before it gets cold."

They enjoyed a nice meal, and some great quality time together, something they hadn't done in a long time. Jake helped with the cleanup, enjoying seeing Sara happy.

"We need to do this more often, Jake."

He put his arms around Sara's waist and drew her to him for a kiss. "I can think of one other thing we need to do more often."

Sara had to agree with that. She took Jake by the hand and led him to their bedroom. Jake slept soundly that night, not hearing Sara up in the middle of the night. She went into the bathroom, trying to untangle her hair. Splashing cold water on her face, she looked in the mirror. Haunted brown eyes stared back at her. *What's going on with me? I can't sleep, and I cry over absolutely everything. I may need to see a doctor, make sure everything's okay. I know I've been under a lot of stress lately. That's probably it.* She crawled back into bed, and was immediately engulfed in Jake's strong arms. Cuddling closer, she fell into a deep sleep.

Jake woke up with his arm asleep. Sara's head was laying on it, and he didn't want to wake her. He carefully slid his arm out from under her head, and went into the bathroom. He rubbed his arm vigorously, trying to get the feeling back. Jake wanted to just stay home with Sara, but he already had his mind on the young man who was murdered and mutilated yesterday morning. Sighing, he started up the shower. By the time he was done, Sara was awake, and had the coffee brewing. "*Mmm*, that smells great!" Sara smiled up at Jake as he kissed her softly. "Last night was amazing, Sara. I love you."

"I love you too, Jake. Now shoo, before I make you stay home from work."

He grabbed a banana, and took off for work, before he decided to play hooky and stay home. Jake knew he could'nt do that. It was his job to figure out who did this to Martin Parker, and he was going to do just that. Jake did not wait for Doc Miller to call him. He went straight down to the medical examiner's office when he got to work. "Okay, Doc, tell me you have some good news."

"I wish I could, Jake. I do know what killed Mr. Parker though. He was given a shot of a drug called propofol. It's normally used as an anesthetic, but this boy was given three times the amount needed to just put someone to sleep. He was given enough to make sure he was dead. That was cause of death, but look at his neck."

"I don't think I have to. Stun gun?"

"Yes...Jake, was he a cop?"

"He was a cop's son, Doc. This is no coincidence. Something is going on here. Even though the cause of death is different, the other similarities can't be denied. Is that it, Doc? No evidence? DNA on the body? What about the missing shoe and foot?"

"The only thing is that the foot is gone, cut off with a sharp instrument. Could be our killer is in the medical field. Propofol isn't easy to come by, unless you work in a lab or hospital."

"That's a start, Doc. Closest thing to a lead we've had so far. I have to go let Captain Scott know what we've got here. I don't know if he'll agree with me or not." Jake rushed into Tony's office. "Tony, you're not going to believe this! Martin Parker was given a lethal dose of propofol, which is what killed him. But get this, a stun gun was used first, and he's a cop's son! Tony, I think we have a serial killer on our hands. There are just too many similarities to ignore the fact that all three victims were incapacitated with a stun gun. They were all in law enforcement, or related to someone in law enforcement."

Tony sat up straight in his chair, rubbing his chin. "Jake, it very well could be a serial killer, but it also could be a coincidence. Why would the guy kill them all differently? That doesn't make sense either. I don't think we should jump to conclusions here. We need more evidence before we treat these murders like a serial. What else did Doc have to say?"

"He said the drug that was used to kill Martin is pretty hard to come by. Doc suggested our killer may work in the medical profession, or know someone who does. I'm going to start calling hospitals in the area, and see if any propofol has gone missing. I still think these murders are related, but I'll hold off on that theory for now."

"Sounds good, Jake. Let me know what you find out about that drug. Someone must know something. I think this guy may have screwed up. Let's hope so. If it is the same person that killed these three people, we've got a problem. We need to find out what's going on here, Jake, and fast."

Jake could not shake the feeling he had about these murders. He worked late into the night, calling every hospital in the Los Angeles area. So far, nothing. Not one hospital was missing any propofol. Jake felt he was on the right track, but he wasn't getting anywhere with the propofol. Either this guy knew enough about the drug to get it in the black market, or he covered his tracks so well, that no one noticed it was missing. Jake was frustrated even more, after he learned from the victim's dad that Martin wanted to be in law enforcement. Just like he was. He said that Martin jogged the Bamboo Trail every day, getting in shape for the police academy training.

When Jake got home, he was still wired from the frustrations in this case. From all three cases, actually. He still had to disagree with Tony. These cases were related somehow. He just had to figure out the *who* and *why*. Jake mixed himself a drink and loosened his tie, trying to relax. He could hear Sara softly snoring in the bedroom. "Well, at least one of us is sleeping." After four or five drinks, Jake finally fell asleep, sprawled on the couch.

Sara woke up not feeling well again. *I guess it's time I make a doctor's appointment to see what's going on with me. Probably nothing a good vacation wouldn't cure.* She had to laugh at that. They still hadn't went on a honeymoon, after seven years of marriage. Sara noticed that Jake wasn't in their bed again, so she walked out to the living room. She found him on the couch, snoring away. Sara took the empty drink glass out of Jake's hand, and covered him with a blanket, letting him sleep a little longer. His lifestyle was getting to be too much for her. They go from a wonderful evening together, to not ever seeing each other. Seemed like a vicious circle to her. "I love you, Jake, but I just don't know how much more I can handle."

8

He stood by the apartment complex, waiting for his next victim. *This one could be a challenge. At least, I hope so. The others have been too easy. Timing will be everything for this one. He carries a gun, after all.* He had to laugh to himself at that one. *Lot of good that'll do him. This one is special. He deserves everything he gets. Maybe your partner will be with you. I could kill two birds with one stone. Ha ha! I suppose you're with her right now. That's okay, have your fun. It'll be the last time you do!"*

It had been three weeks since Martin Parker's murder. Jake wasn't getting anywhere on the propofol lead, so he decided to shelf that for now. He looked into Martin's life a little more closely. The kid was smart, top of his class. He was close with his family. He had two older brothers, both policemen, and his dad was a cop. He had no girlfriend, or significant other. Just a clean-cut kid wanting to follow in his father's footsteps. *No reason to die, that's for sure.* Jake thought. *I can't find any connection to the other two murders, other than the relation to police work, and the stun gun. Maybe I'm wrong about this being a serial killer, but I just can't shake the feeling that's just what it is.*

Jake had been at the office late every night, pouring over the case files and various notes he had written on the case. He hadn't seen Sara for more than an hour at a time in the last three weeks. Jake felt bad about that, but he had to figure these murders out, before someone else got killed by this maniac. He just had to hope Sara understood that.

Sara got home later than usual that night. She was tired. She really just wanted her husband to hold her for a little while, and tell her everything was going to be okay. Of course, Jake wasn't home. She hadn't seen much of him for the past three weeks. Sara had seen the doctor earlier that day, and she didn't like the news that she got. Well, it wasn't that she didn't like it, as much as she didn't like the timing of it. Things weren't going well between her and Jake right now, and she didn't need this complication. Sara needed to make a decision of what she was going to do very soon. She just didn't know what that would be. She looked in the mirror, pressing her hands on her flat tummy. *I'm going to do what's best for us, little one. I promise.*

Jake finally got home about one in the morning. Sara was waiting up for him, which was unusual. "Hey, sorry I'm so late again. It's been a rough month so far. I've been trying to gather some clues together with these cases, but it's just not happening. Are you okay? You look a little pale."

"Well, actually, I'm not, Jake. Can you sit down for a minute? There's something I need to tell you."

Jake was only half listening. "Sure, but can it wait until after I shower? I smell like I haven't showered in a week. Maybe I haven't, I don't know. I promise I'll only have ears for you then, okay?"

Sara smiled sadly. "Sure, whatever you need to do, Jake. I'll be in the bedroom when you're done."

Jake leaned down and kissed her. "I'll hurry, I promise." Jake got to thinking about the murders as he showered. He figured if this guy was targeting cops, any one of them could be next. Or a member of their family. He had to find the connection. He stepped out of the shower and grabbed his towel. *If I can't figure this out, someone else is going to die at this guy's hands, I just know it.*

Jake grabbed a clean T-shirt and sweat pants, then headed for the case files he brought home with him. Paging through the Molly Jones file, he started with the facts they already knew. Molly was the ex-wife of a cop, killed at the zoo, and covered in pins and needles. Jake read through the whole file, then picked up the next, Harvey Jones. Harvey was a retired cop, stunned, and pushed down a flight of stairs in his own home. Then there was Martin Parker, son of a cop. He was killed on the trail, stunned, and dragged down the embankment, missing a shoe and a foot. Jake looked at the clock after he read through the last file. It was after four in the morning. "Oh man! I forgot all about talking to Sara. She's gonna kill me!" He rushed into the bedroom. "Sara, look, I'm sorry..."

Sara had her back to him, and was pretending to be asleep. She had no desire to talk to him now—or ever, for that matter. She had made her decision. Obviously, Jake could only think about his job. She hated to say *I told you so*, but had to admit, she had known for a while now that this time was coming.

Jake did not sleep much at all after that. Between worrying about these cases, and Sara, he finally fell into a fitful sleep at five. He didn't even hear Sara leave for work that morning. He wanted to talk to her, but overslept. He only woke up because his phone was ringing at nine o'clock. He cleared his throat, and answered the phone. "Long here. Yeah, Tony, what's up? Okay, I'll meet you there."

Jake didn't have time for more than a cup of coffee before he rushed off to another murder. This one was at an apartment building on Overland. Jake squealed to a stop in front of the tall building. "Wow, nice place." He got out of the car, and ducked under the crime scene tape. "What've we got this time?"

Tony was standing by the reporting officer at the scene. "This one is bad, Jake. Come and take a look for yourself."

Tony led him over to the wall surrounding the building. There was a body posed on the wall, tied there with barbed wire. Jake let out a whistle. "Wow, you weren't kidding! What the hell?" Jake stepped closer to the body. "Why is he so broken up? Where's Doc?"

Tony shook his head. "Doc got caught up in traffic, he'll be here any minute. Can't tell you much about this until he gets here and checks over the body."

Jake stepped carefully, not wanting to disturb the scene. He knew how particular Doc was about the crime scenes. He sure didn't want to start this day off with the wrath of Doc Miller coming down on him. "The body appears posed, but the only blood I see is some running down the wall. Not much blood though. I bet he wasn't killed here."

"Well, I'll be the judge of that. Now back away from that body, Jake. You do your job, and I'll do mine." Doc Miller walked toward the body carefully, glaring at Jake.

Jake backed off, hands in the air. "Sorry, Doc. I didn't touch anything, I'm just looking."

"You know better than to touch anything, Jake. I have sharp

instruments in here, you know." Doc tapped his medical bag. "You may lose a digit or two if you touch the body before I do. Now let me get to it."

"Sure thing, Doc. I'll just be over here, patiently waiting."

"Well, you won't have to wait long. I can already tell you that he didn't die here. There's not much blood." Doc waved his assistant over. "Help me get the body down and see if he has any identification on him. Hopefully that will give these detectives another crime scene to investigate."

The two men carefully cut the barbed wire, lifting the body down to the ground. Doc immediately felt around, looking for an ID. "Here we go. Name's Ryan Sands, thirty years old. Jake, he's got a badge. He's a cop. Address is the building right here, twelfth floor apartment 1232. My bet is that's the original murder scene. Jake, how does this keep happening to law enforcement, and why?"

I don't know, Doc, but I aim to find out. Any idea on cause or time of death?"

"Well, cause is questionable, but judging from the damage to the body, probably a long fall." Doc took the victim's liver temperature. "Time of death, approximately five hours ago. Around 5:00 a.m."

"Okay, thanks, Doc." Jake walked over to the officer who was first on the scene. "Any witnesses? Who called this in?"

"No witnesses. An anonymous caller reported the body, but the building manager just came out. I've got him waiting for you over here."

Jake looked where he was pointing. "Good, we're going to need to get in that apartment pronto. Thanks."

The building manager was standing alongside the squad car, and stepped forward when Jake approached him. "What's going on here? Why all the police cars?"

Jake shook the man's hand. "Hello, I'm Detective Long. Are you the manager here?"

"Yes, I'm Andy Brock. Nice to meet you detective."

"Same here, Mr. Brock. Is there a Ryan Sands who lives in this building?"

"Yes, Mr. Sands lives on the twelfth floor. Nice man. I was glad to have a policeman living here. Kind of helps with the crime in the building, you know. Why, did something happen to him?"

"Mr. Brock, I'm going to need you to take me to his apartment. I assume you have keys to all of the apartments?"

"Yes, I do. I'll grab the keys and meet you at the apartment. I believe it's 1232."

We'll just tag along with you if you don't mind. Tony, will you join us here?"

"Sure thing, Jake. Lead the way, Mr. Brock."

When they got to the apartment of Andy Brock, Jake stepped inside, while Andy got the set of keys for apartment 1232. Andy lived on the first floor, the perk of being manager. "Did you see or hear anything odd this morning around five o'clock, Mr. Brock?"

"Um...no, I'm usually sleeping then. I'm not an early riser, detective, but some of Ryan's neighbors may have been awake then. I'm afraid the building is almost empty, though. It's scheduled for demolition in a year. This is one of the oldest buildings in this area. The city is in the process of buying out the tenants. They want to raze the building and put in a parking lot, can you believe that? So, the only neighbors are on the other side of the building. There is only about ten hold outs. Ryan was one of them."

Tony and Jake let Andy lead the way to Mr. Sands' apartment. The elevator took them to the twelfth floor. Jake noted that there were security cameras in the lobby. "We're going to need to see the security tapes from this morning, Mr. Brock."

"I'm afraid they are inoperable right now. The owner of the building didn't feel the need to keep them in working order, considering the demolition and all."

They had reached apartment 1232. Jake stopped in front of the door. "We'll take it from here, Mr. Brock. You can wait in your apartment. If we need anything else, we'll get in touch with you."

"Oh, okay. Are you sure it's okay to go in there? I mean, I don't know how Ryan would feel about me letting you in his apartment."

"Trust me, Mr. Brock. It'll be fine." Jake grabbed the key from the stunned apartment manager. "Thank you for your time."

Mr. Brock backed off, doing what he was told, heading to the elevator.

Jake took the key and slowly inserted it in the lock. When he opened the door, the detectives entered the apartment with their guns drawn. "Police, anyone here?" Silence greeted them. "All clear in here!" Jake yelled from the kitchen.

"Clear!" Tony also yelled from the bedroom. As soon as they entered the living area, Jake knew this was definitely the original scene of the crime. There was a big picture window overlooking the courtyard. The glass had been broken out, and there was blood on the remaining glass in the frame. Tony got on his radio and called for CSI to come up to the apartment. "We've got a broken window and blood up here. Looks like the victim was pushed, or jumped, out of the window."

Jake stood at the broken window and looked down. He could see Doc straight down from the apartment window. They were getting ready to load up the body. "Quite a fall from here. Twelve stories, not a chance of survival from that far. What do you think, Tony? Suicide or murder?"

"Looking at the scene, I'd say murder. There is definitely signs of a struggle. Looks like our victim tried to draw his gun. It's right over there. I'll have CSI dust it for prints, along with anything else that may have gotten touched by the perp."

Jake looked around. "Nothing else has been disturbed. Our perpetrator must've been waiting in the apartment for Sands, or right outside the door." Jake stepped out of the apartment, checking around the door.

"Nothing here." Stepping back in, he noticed something. "Wait a minute. Look at this, Tony." Jake pointed to a mark on the wall behind the door. "He definitely jumped Sands from outside the door. Looks like the door flew back and hit the wall here. So, if he was pushed out this window, why take the time to pose the body like that? He took a huge chance of getting caught by spending the time to do that."

Tony nodded. "I can't believe that a trained cop wouldn't notice someone following him, too. Mr. Sands must've been distracted by something."

"Yeah, unless it was someone he knew, and he invited them up here. Let's not jump to conclusions. We still need to question the few people left in this building, and see what Doc has to say."

"I agree. CSI is here. Let's let them do their job, while we start knocking on doors."

Mr. Brock was right. There weren't too many people left in the building, and those that were here never saw or heard anything. Jake and Tony left the crime scene and headed back to the office. It was already dusk by then, and they still had a lot to do.

Jake thought he'd better call Sara and let her know what was going on. He wasn't going to be home anytime soon. When Sara didn't answer, he tried her cell phone. She didn't answer that either, so he left a message. "Sara, we caught another murder. I'll be late getting home. Call me if you need to. I love you."

Jake and Tony worked into the night, putting together the little bit of evidence they had gathered at the scene. By the time they were done, it was another day, and Jake hadn't gone home. He hadn't heard from Sara either, which worried him a little. He couldn't think about that right now, though. He had a murder to solve.

Jake always kept an extra change of clothes at the office, just in case. He grabbed one of the shirts out of the drawer of his desk, and headed for the bathroom. Throwing some cold water on his face, Jake slipped on the shirt. He went out the door of the bathroom and straight to the elevator that would take him to the morgue. He knew Doc was always early, and he didn't want to wait on this one. If Doc wasn't done with the examination of Ryan Sands' body, Jake was going to stay down there until he was. Sure enough, Doc was already there when Jake walked in. "Doc, tell me what you've got."

"Jake, since when do you rush down here before I'm even done? I'll call you."

Jake shook his head. "Since this is the fourth murder in as many years, and probably from a serial killer. That's why I didn't wait for your call. Tell me what you've got so far...please."

"Okay, since you asked nicely. I'm actually almost done. Mr. Sands died from trauma from the fall. The body was badly broken up, almost every bone was broken. You're right about one thing, I think it's the same perp on all four murders. He did use a stun gun. Also, we ran a blood test. Mr. Sands had double the legal alcohol limit in his system. He was inebriated. Very much so, in fact. I'd say that's why the killer got the better of him. That and, of course, the stun gun. Jake, look what I found stuffed in his mouth." Doc showed Jake a photograph he had straightened out. There was a man and a woman standing close, heads together.

"There's our victim but who is the woman?"

"No idea. That's your job to find out."

"All right, I will. This could be the only lead we've got. Thanks, Doc."

When Jake got upstairs, he went straight to Tony's office. "Tony, we've got a serial killer for sure. Hear me out. Four people, all incapacitated with a stun gun, and all involved in law enforcement somehow. I don't know why our killer doesn't use the same method of killing, but I know it's the same guy, Tony. Look what Doc found stuffed in Sands' mouth." Jake took out a copy of the picture. "I need to find out who this woman is. She could be our only lead."

"Well, I think I already have an answer to that question, Jake." Tony pointed to Jake's desk. "You have a visitor."

Jake looked over at his desk and gasped. He looked from the woman sitting there, to the picture in his hand. "Holy cow! That's her! Who is she, Tony? Never mind, I'll find out for myself." Jake rushed over to find out who was sitting at his desk. She stood when he got there. He did notice that she had been crying. "Please sit down, ma'am. How can I help you today?"

"I'm Melissa Towner. I am Ryan's partner. We have been working together for three years now. What happened? I heard he jumped out of a twelve-story building. Is that true, detective? I know Ryan would never commit suicide."

"Ms. Towner, when was the last time you saw or talked to Ryan?"

"Mrs. Towner. Call me Missy, everyone does." Jake's eyes widened a little at the *Mrs.* part of that statement. He figured from the picture, that they were a lot closer than just partners. He kept that to himself for now. "Is there somewhere more private that we could talk, detective?"

"Of course, I'm sure the captain won't mind us using his office. Right this way."

Tony started to get up to leave, but Missy motioned for him to stay. "You may as well stay and hear this too, captain. To make a long story short, Ryan and I have been seeing each other for about a year now. My husband and I grew apart and...well, you know what the life of a cop is like. I planned on leaving my husband, so Ryan and I were going to be together. Before you ask, my husband is overseas with his work. He didn't have anything to do with this. Listen, I just saw Ryan last night. We went out for a nice supper, and drinks afterward. We went to my place for a while. He had a little too much to drink, so I dropped him off at his apartment around four-thirty this morning. So, are you gonna tell me what happened to him, or do I have to wait for the local news?"

"Ryan was murdered, Mrs. Towner. Did you see anyone lurking around the apartment building when you dropped him off?"

"No, we had a small argument, so I just dropped him off and left. Oh my gosh! If I would have gone up with him, or at least waited for him to get in the door..." She started sobbing, wiping her eyes with a tissue.

"You can't blame yourself, Missy. I'm sorry for your loss, ma'am. If you think of anything else, will you let us know?" When Missy left, Jake turned to Tony. "Wow! Okay, I don't even know what to think now. She may have killed him, or maybe her husband did. I'll check his alibi. Or, we have a serial killer. What do you think?"

"She seemed genuinely broken up about Ryan's death. I don't think it was her. The husband, very possible, if he's in town. Work related? Maybe, maybe not. All I know is, my head is spinning. You go home and get some rest, Jake...and a shower, please. We'll start fresh in the morning."

Jake sniffed the air. "Are you saying I smell bad, Tony? Thanks for the heads-up. Come to think of it, Sara still hasn't called me back. I better get home, if I have one to go to."

Jake walked through the door, flowers in one hand, and bottle of wine in the other. The house was dark, and very quiet. Something was off. "Sara, I'm home...Sara?" No answer. Setting the goodies on the kitchen table, Jake flipped on the light. His eyes were immediately drawn to the white envelope propped up on the table. He opened the envelope, sitting down to read the letter inside.

"Dearest Jake. I want to start out by saying I love you. I really do. But I just can't do this anymore. I have tried for seven years, and I just don't have the strength anymore. I knew when you took this job that it would be a struggle, but I was willing to try. Problem is, I don't think you were. Please don't try to find me. I need space, Jake, from this, and from you. You'll be fine, I know it. I will have my lawyer get in touch with you soon. Sara."

Jake's arms went limp, and the letter floated down onto the table. "Oh hell no! This is not happening! Not now, Sara! Not now!"

Jake swiped the letter onto the floor, and laid his head in his hands. He stayed that way until he could make his way to the empty bedroom. "She really did leave me. Dammit, Sara! How could you?"

9

Sara drove most of the night, before stopping at the nearest motel. She was tired, and sad. She hoped and prayed that she was doing the right thing, leaving Jake like that, with just a note. She knew if she had talked to him face-to-face, he would have talked her out of leaving. Sara knew it was the cowardly way out, but she just couldn't face him, probably never will be able to. Better to cut ties altogether. She checked in, and barely took time to wash her face before falling into a restless sleep.

Sara dragged herself out of bed the next morning. She nibbled on a few crackers, trying to quell her upset stomach. Grabbing her cell phone, she dialed Ann's number. No answer again. "Ann, it's me again. Listen, I'm on my way to Portland. I really need you right now. Please call me." She hung up and stared at her phone, debating about what to do now. *I wonder how Jake is doing? Should I call him?*

Her phone rang in her hand, startling her. It was Jake. "No, Jake, I can't talk to you right now." Sara pushed ignore and started packing up to leave.

"Dammit, Sara, answer the phone! I'm not going to give up on us that easy." Jake stared at his phone, willing her to answer. When he heard Sara's voice on the other end, he breathed a sigh of relief. "Sara—" but all he heard was "Please leave me a message." Jake threw his phone onto the bed, not bothering to leave another message. "Well, if that's the way you want it, I'll go with it for now. But you will talk to me, Sara, sooner or later."

Jake got to the office with a chip on his shoulder the size of Texas. He definitely wasn't in the mood for the news that he got when he walked in the door. Tony was waiting for Jake at his desk.

"Jake, I just got a call from the commissioner. He's coming here personally to talk to us about the serial murders. I need you to gather up what evidence we've got, and meet us in the conference room."

"Why the hell is he coming down here for that? Does he think we're not doing our jobs? Is he bringing a babysitter with him too?"

"Relax, Jake, he's just doing his job. He's getting pressure from the mayor and the public. They want answers, and we're not giving them any. What's wrong with you? You act like you lost your best friend!"

"Yeah? Well, maybe I did, Tony. Maybe I did."

Tony raised his eyebrows. "What do you mean by that?"

"Sara left me, Tony. Just up and left without a word. She left me a 'Dear John' letter, of all things! She couldn't even tell me face-to-face. Just a note! I tried calling her all night but she won't even answer her phone. I don't have any idea where she's at or where she is going. Nothing!"

"Oh man! I'm sorry, Jake. That's rough. Do you need some time off? Maybe to go look for her?"

Jake let out a long breath. "Thanks, Tony, but I'll be okay. Obviously, she doesn't want to be found, and I just need to work. It's all I have right now. Just give me a minute, and I'll meet you in the conference room."

When Sara reached Portland later that day, she still had not heard from Ann. *What do I do now?* She thought. She took out her cell phone and stared at it. Taking a deep breath, Sara scrolled through her contacts. Finding the number she needed, she dialed before she could change her mind. When Sam answered, she paused, wondering if she could trust Jake's brother with her secret.

"Hello, this is Sam. Hello?"

Sara knew she had to trust Sam; there was no one else. "Sam? It's Sara."

"Sara! How are things in Los Angeles? Is my big lug of a brother treating you all right?"

"Sam, I need your help, but you have to promise me you won't tell Jake."

"Um, what's going on, Sara? Are you okay?"

"Actually, no, I'm not. I left Jake, Sam. I'm in Portland, and I can't find Ann. Can I trust you, Sam?"

"You know I'm here for you, Sara. You can trust me, but you have to tell me what's going on. What happened?"

"I don't want to get into it over the phone, Sam. Can I come out to the ranch? I really don't have anywhere else to go."

"Of course, Sara. You know you're always welcome here. Should I come and pick you up?"

"No, just give me directions, I'll find it. Thanks, Sam."

When Sara pulled in to the sprawling ranch, she was impressed with the setting. A large red barn sat in the center of ten smaller buildings. A large corral was next to the barn, with about ten horses milling about and munching on hay. She pulled up to the main house, taking in the huge deck surrounding the log home. Sara was kind of surprised with the size of the ranch. Sam must be doing okay for himself.

Speaking of Sam, he appeared in the doorway with a grim look on his face. He stepped out onto the deck and down the steps. When Sara opened her car door and stepped out, Sam engulfed her in a big hug. "Sara, it's great to see you. You look beat. Come on in." He grabbed her suitcase from the back seat and led the way into the house.

Sara looked around the spacious home. "Wow, Sam! This is really nice. Life must be pretty good for you."

"It has been good, Sara. Lots of help from people who believe in the same things I do. Do you need anything? Water? A beer? Make yourself comfortable. I'll take your bags to your room."

"I'm fine, Sam. I just need to sit for a while." She sat down on the plush leather couch, loving the feel of the soft material. Sara almost dozed off while she waited for her brother-in-law to return. She jumped a little when he came in to the room.

"Sorry, Sara. Where are my manners, you probably need to rest after that long drive. You look beat."

"I am tired. Do you mind if I take a little nap before the third degree?"

"Sure. You don't need to tell me anything until you're ready to. I won't pressure you, I promise. I'll show you to your room."

Sara got up off the couch and gave Sam a hug. "Thanks. I really do appreciate you putting me up while I'm here. I promise I'll tell you the whole story when I come back down. Remember, you promised not to call Jake."

"I remember, but if he calls me, I can't promise I won't at least let him know you're all right. Deal?"

"Deal. I'll see you in a little bit." Sara hoped that Jake didn't think about calling Sam until she had a chance to explain things.

By the time Sara woke up, it was dark. She was surprised when her stomach growled. She hadn't felt much like eating for a while now. She found her way into the kitchen, where Sam was waiting for her.

"The cook left you a sandwich. It's in the fridge." Sam opened a beer for himself, and gave Sara a delicious-looking ham sandwich. "Would you like a beer?"

"No, thanks. Do you have milk? I will take that."

"Sure, you can't run a place with kids around without having milk." Sam grinned.

Sara couldn't help but smile back. "Tell me again exactly what you do here. I know you help kids and families of law enforcement, but what do you do for them?"

"Well, if they need a place to go when the parent or loved one is injured or killed in the line of duty, they come here. I don't know if you noticed, but we have about ten horses right now. The kids do their own chores, taking care of feeding, or brushing the horses, even cleaning stalls. We have about ten outbuildings that serve as places for the families, and the hands I've hired, to live in. We are working on building more, and getting more livestock. We have trail rides and camping. We just try to keep everyone busy so they can heal. When they feel they are ready, they go back home. Some of them stay here indefinitely. I've even hired some on. It's been very rewarding."

Sara was sincerely impressed with how Sam turned out. No surprise there, he had a great upbringing. Thinking about that made her miss Jake even more. She decided to tell Sam the truth, and let him judge her how he saw fit. She took a bite of her sandwich, nibbling on it to make sure it wanted to stay down. "I think that's great, Sam. Your parents would be so proud." With a loud sigh, Sara thought she may as well tell Sam everything. "I guess you're wanting to hear why I've come for this impromptu visit."

"Take your time, Sara. You can tell me when you're ready."

"Well, there's no time like the present." She took a deep breath. "I just couldn't do it anymore, Sam. Jake was never home—and I mean *never*. He is drinking quite a bit. The job is really getting to him. He's got cases he can't solve, and it's really working on him. He was bringing work home with him too! I tried, Sam. I really did but I just couldn't *try* anymore."

"I understand, Sara. Really, I do. I know how Jake can get when he gets a burr under his saddle. But shouldn't you at least talk to him? Let him know how you feel?"

Sara was shaking her head before Sam even finished talking. "I tried that too. He didn't even give me a chance to talk. He stayed up all night reading through case files instead. There's something else, Sam. I found out I'm pregnant. I told Jake I wasn't going to bring a baby into our lives if his job interfered. It is doing just that. I'm not raising a child in that atmosphere. I told Jake as much before he took that job. I meant it then and I mean it now."

Sam was shocked. "First of all, congratulations on the baby. Second, you know Jake would be thrilled if he knew. He has the right to know, Sara. You have to tell him about the baby."

"I can't talk to him right now. I'll think about it, but for now, please don't say anything. If you do, I'll just leave here and go where no one can find me."

Sam threw his hands up. "Okay, okay, I won't say anything...for now."

"Thank you. Now, I really need to find Ann. Can you help me with that?"

"I'll do everything I can, Sara. I've had some feelers out, but so far, nothing. I'll check with them in the morning to see what they've found."

Yawning, Sara nodded. "Thanks. Thanks for the delicious

sandwich too. I think I'll hit the hay. See you in the morning."

Sam stood when Sara got up from the chair. "Good night, Sara."

Two weeks went by, without a word from Sara. Jake was trying to keep his mind on work, but it was hard. He kept trying to figure out where she might be when it finally hit him. *Ann! She had to be looking for her sister.* Excited now, Jake grabbed his phone and hurriedly dialed Sam's number. After the third ring, Sam answered.

"Hey, Jake."

Jake did not pull any punches. "Is Sara there with you, Sam? Have you seen or heard from Ann, or her? Tell me, Sam, or I swear I'm going to come there and strangle you. I mean it!"

"Hold on a minute, Jake. Yes, Sara is here. She doesn't want to talk to you right now, and I promised I would respect that. You need to do that too. We found Ann, and she is here too. We're helping her straighten out her life. She's doing pretty good, considering. Give Sara some space, Jake. She might come around."

Jake drew in a breath. "Thank God she's with you and okay. I've been worried sick. Why won't she talk to me, Sam? I don't understand what's going on!"

"She needs some time to be with her sister right now. I'll try and talk her into calling you, but for now, we need to respect her wishes. Leave her be."

"What about me, Sam. I don't care what her wishes are, I'm coming to Portland. I'm not giving up that easily."

"I didn't think you would, Jake."

Two days later, after some finagling with work, and throwing some clothes in a bag, Jake pulled into Portland. He went straight to the diner that Sam had told him Sara worked. He spotted Sara standing behind a podium, looking beautiful as usual. He made a beeline for her.

Sara looked up and spotted Jake coming toward her. She had to look twice, but yes, it was him. She quickly stood directly behind the podium, trying to hide her burgeoning stomach. "Jake, what are you doing here?"

"I came to see my wife, and I'm not leaving until you talk to me. Can you take a few minutes for that?"

Sara's hackles rose at that. "I'm working, Jake. If you needed to talk to me so bad, you had every opportunity while I was home. There's really nothing more to say anyway. I think you know why I left."

"I do know, I just don't understand. Don't you love me anymore? I love you, Sara. I always will."

Sara spotted the owner walking over to them. "Jake, you need to leave. Go home. I really am fine here. I have Ann and Sam here. I don't need anything else."

"Fine, I'll leave for now, but I'm not giving up on us. Tell your lawyer not to bother sending divorce papers, I won't sign them!" He turned and stormed out of the restaurant.

Sara looked down at her hands, trying to make them quit shaking. "I love you too, Jake."

Sara gave birth to a beautiful baby girl six months after she got to Portland. She named her Jenny. Jenny had her daddy's blue eyes and her mom's blonde hair. She looked so much like Jake, Sara had to hold back a sob when she looked at her. Even though Ann decided to move back out to the ranch, she was by her side when Jenny was born. So was Sam. Sara couldn't help but wish Jake was there, holding her hand. She definitely felt guilty for not telling Jake about Jenny, but in her heart, she felt she was doing the right thing. Someday, their daughter would meet her daddy, but for now, this was for the best.

Three years went by without the serial killer striking again. Jake didn't know if he had left town, or ended up in jail for some other crime. But, he knew in his gut that the killer wasn't done. He had a specific mission, and Jake felt like he wasn't going to quit until he achieved his goal—whatever that was.

Jake still had not heard from Sara either. He tried to keep tabs on her through Sam, but he was not saying much. As far as he knew, Sara hadn't changed her mind about leaving him. Her lawyer sent divorce papers for him to sign. Jake sent them back without signing them.

Sara wasn't getting off that easy. She could bring the papers in person, then maybe he would sign them. But not until she looked him in the eye and said she didn't love him anymore. Jake was back to solving murders, but the ones that kept him awake at night remained elusive. Not much had changed in his life. He worked pretty much all the time, and when he was home, he drank until he passed out on the couch. Jake couldn't bring himself to sleep in their bed alone. Tony was worried about him, but he was the only one. All Jake had now was his work.

Two more years, and still nothing from the serial killer. Jake went to Tony one day to get his opinion on the case. "Tony, this guy can't be done with his vendetta against cops yet. What do you suppose he's been up to?"

"I don't know Jake, but I do agree with you. He's not done. Probably got sick, or is in jail. A lot of times, they screw up somewhere down the line, and get arrested for a different crime. Either way, I have a feeling he'll be back, sooner, rather than later. Now to change the subject, how are you doing? Have you heard anything from Sara?"

"Not a word. Sam says she's fine. She got a small house in Portland. Sara and Ann are growing close again, and Ann has been clean for five years now. So that's good news. I wish Sara would have stayed with Sam though. I don't like the thought of her in the city alone."

"Sara can take care of herself. Sam is keeping tabs on them, right?"

Jake nodded. "Yes, he is. If it weren't for him being there, I would've been there long ago."

"Well, you know I'm behind you if you need time off. Anytime you need, just ask. You know, maybe you should talk to Dr. Hall. I know you say you're alright, but it wouldn't hurt to have someone to talk to."

Jake was shaking his head before Tony was even done talking. "I don't need a shrink! I'm fine, Tony. Thanks for the vote of confidence."

"This has nothing to do with my confidence in you, Jake." Tony shook his head. "Forget it, just know she's there if you need her."

"Sure thing. I'm sorry I blew up. I know you're only trying to help. Thanks for being such a good friend. I think I will take you up on that offer sometime soon though. It's past time I went to Sara. She obviously isn't coming back to me."

The killer was growing restless. He was itching to get started again. He listened to her this time, but it's been long enough. He wasn't going to wait any longer. "That damn Detective Long probably thinks I'm done. Little does he know, I'm not going to be done until I get revenge on those who did us wrong. I made a promise and I'm going to keep it!"

His phone rang, startling him. He grimaced when he looked at the caller ID. "Hello, how are you doing?" he answered meekly.

Her voice came over the line loud and clear. "The question is, how are *you* doing? Why haven't you come to see me? Are you doing what I told you to do? You'd better be. You know I'm always right. Especially in these matters. I've been helping you for too many years for you to screw it up now!" He held the phone away from his ear as she screeched into the phone.

"I'm doing just as you said and waiting for the precise moment. You know I'm not very patient. I can't wait much longer."

"You need to keep the cops guessing. By now, they probably have figured out that one person has done all of these murders. If you wait, they'll be even more confused, wondering if they're right. You know I'm right. Just keep listening to me. Have I ever led you astray, darling?" Her tone changed dramatically.

"No, you haven't. I'll try to stay focused on the final prize but it's hard, Mama. I'll be good, I promise."

"That's my good boy. Now, come and see me soon, and we will figure out together what our next step is. Good-bye, son."

10

Jenny was a beautiful, rambunctious six-year-old girl. She was super smart. At least Sara thought so, but she could be a bit biased about that. Things were going well. Sam kept his promise, and didn't say anything to Jake about his daughter. Sara was definitely having second thoughts about not telling him. She knew a little girl should have her father around, but deep in her heart, Sara knew he wouldn't have been there for Jenny anyway. He wasn't there for her when she needed him the most.

She had Ann, and Sam was there if she needed anything major, but they were doing okay on their own. Sara was home every night to read to Jenny out of the book she had kept all these years, she made sure of it. Jenny loved her nursery rhymes just as much as Sara did, and she let Jenny know that the book would be hers someday. Sara told her daughter all about when her father would come home from a long, hard day, and read to her and Ann out of the very same book. They were a happy little family, and Jenny was a well-adjusted little girl. That is, until Jenny turned twelve years old.

One night, Sara was startled awake by Jenny's screams. She rushed into her room, and found her little girl thrashing about on the bed, crying out. She knew right away what was wrong. After all, Sara had the same thing happen to her. Too many times to count. Sara couldn't quite make out what Jenny was saying. All she could do, was try and comfort her as best she could. Sara held her and rocked her, remembering what those dreams were like. If Jenny was hearing the voices in her head like she did, she may need to find some help for her.

Sara wasn't at all sure what Jenny's dreams were about. When Jenny told her about them, Sara decided they definitely needed some help. She was hoping her daughter would have been spared this affliction, but evidently, she wasn't. If Jenny's dreams were anything at all like her own, they would come more frequently the older Jenny got. It was time for a phone call. Sara was not going to let her daughter go through this alone.

Jenny was nervous and excited at the same time, if that was possible. She was so ready to have someone she could actually talk to about these dreams. She felt that they were a lot more than. Just dreams though. She could actually hear people calling out to her. Sometimes, she wasn't even asleep.

When her name was called for her appointment with the doctor, Jenny looked at her mom and grabbed her hand. "Mom, I really think I should go in alone. At least, this first time. I know you're worried, but I'll be okay. I just think I need to do this alone, okay?"

Sara reluctantly agreed. "If you're sure. But if you need me, I'll be right out here. I'm not going anywhere, okay?" Jenny nodded and smiled, as she disappeared through the door. Sara wondered where her little girl had gone. This wise, soon-to-be teenager, had taken her place.

So, it was finally time for his next kill. He could hardly wait. They sure did make a good team, her picking some of the victims, and him just taking care of some on his own. Just because he wanted them dead. He got to choose how they would be killed—that was a fun part—but the best thing was carrying out the murder. A person needed so much planning, and a cunning mind. The cops had been stymied now for over ten years. They would never catch him. Long wasn't smart enough; not as smart as he was. His ultimate goal was coming soon, but first things first.

Mary Sax was home alone, as usual. Her husband, Leon, worked in the drug enforcement agency, so he wasn't home much. He was set to retire soon, so they were looking forward to moving to the retirement community. This big old house was getting to be too much for them to keep up. The older couple didn't need this much space anyway. Especially now that the kids had grown up and moved away. Mary was cleaning up the kitchen after eating a light meal, when she thought she heard a noise outside. Looking out the window, she didn't see anyone out there. Mary shrugged. "Must be squirrels, or cats in the trees out there." She peeked one more time before getting ready for bed.

⚜

This one is going to be too easy. He thought. *Oh well. What Mama wants, Mama gets. I'll do what I'm told...for now.* He waited until just the right moment, and struck just before dawn.

⚜

Jake dragged himself out of bed and went into the bathroom. Looking in the mirror, he saw two bloodshot eyes, and a scraggly beard, staring back at him. *Oh boy! You don't look so hot, Long. Well, a shower and shave should help with that...I hope.* He turned the water on as hot as he could stand it, and got in.

Jake heard his phone ringing the minute he stepped out of the shower. He knew who it was before he even answered. No one called him anymore, except for work. "Long here." He listened as dispatch rattled off an address. "Okay, I'll be there pronto." He hung up and went to get dressed. *No rest for the wicked.*

Jake pulled up to an older neighborhood in LA. He opened his car door, and looked around. He saw the usual, neighbors gawking, and police officers scattered about. The coroner's van was already there, of course. Jake noticed there was a distraught man sitting in the nearest squad car. He headed that way first, greeting the officer standing near the car. "Hey, Neil. What have we got here?"

"Hi, Jake. Victim is inside, an elderly woman. You'll have to see this to believe it! Husband of the deceased is in the squad car. He found the body. Name's Leon Sax, works for the DEA. He said he came home from a long stakeout, and couldn't find his wife, Mary, so he started looking around. He found her...well, like I said, you have to see it to believe it."

Jake nodded, a little confused. "Okay, I'll talk to Mr. Sax after I see the victim...I guess."

He headed into the old house, stopping in the doorway to ask the CSI if he'd found anything. "No prints that I can see. Must've been wiped clean again."

"Again?"

"Yeah, well, you need to talk to Doc over there to get the details."

He pointed to a large living area. There was a huge fireplace in the center of a wall, surrounded by two recliners.

Jake could barely see Doc's legs poking out from under the fireplace. "Ah, Doc? What the hell is going on here?"

Doc bent down, looking at Jake over his wire-rimmed glasses. "Got a doozy, Jake. Woman stuffed up into the fireplace chimney. We can't get her down until someone gets here with some kind of hammer or chisel. She's stuck up there with mortar, of all things. Someone took their time on this one. Did you talk to the husband yet? I guess he's a drug enforcement agent. Anyway, from the part of the body that I can see, which is the head and shoulders, she has stun gun marks on her neck. I'm fairly certain it's our serial, Jake. I'm not sure of the cause of death yet. That's about all I've got until the autopsy."

Jake shook his head, exasperated. "Well, I guess I'll talk to the husband. I'm sure he must have some enemies from his work at the Drug Enforcement Agency. Maybe he has an idea of who did this to his wife." Jake turned and headed back outside to talk to the husband. He shook the man's hand. "Mr. Sax, I'm Detective Long, homicide. I'm sorry for your loss. Do you mind answering a few questions for me?"

The older man looked at Jake through tear-stained eyes. "Sure. I don't think I'll be of much help though. I've been on stakeout for days. Haven't even talked to Mary all week. I can't remember for sure when the last time was that I spoke to her."

He sighed. "Long, did you say? I've heard of you. You got all the serial killer murders. Heard you were a good detective. You gonna figure out who killed my wife? She didn't deserve this. I was set to retire next month. We had an apartment picked out in a retirement community. We were ready to downsize and get out of this old house. My Mary, she wanted me to retire last month, but I wouldn't do it. Just had to bring down one last criminal."

The older man shook his head. "Listen, son, take my advice. Family is more important than this job. Don't be like me and wait until it's too late. Keep your wife and kids close. I wish I would have done that. If I would've retired last month, like Mary wanted me to, I would have been here. This would have never happened."

"I understand, sir. If you don't mind my asking, what made you think to look for your wife in the chimney? Were you on stakeout alone?"

"No, my partner was with me. I'll get his contact info for you. Don't waste your time on investigating me for this, Long. I would never hurt my Mary. To answer your first question, after searching everywhere for Mary, I noticed some dirt falling from the chimney, so I crawled underneath it and when I looked up...well, that's when I saw her." Leon's voice cracked when he talked about his wife. Jake didn't feel like the man killed her.

"Mr. Sax, do you think this could have anything to do with your job? Someone you put away maybe wanting some revenge?"

The old man thought for a second, then shook his head. "I think if someone wanted revenge on me, they would have taken me out, not Mary. The drug cartels don't work that way."

"Okay, Mr. Sax. Again, I'm sorry for your loss, sir."

"Thank you, son. Just find the son of a bitch who did this!"

"I'll do my best, sir. You can count on that!" With that said, Jake turned and went back to talk to Doc. The carpenters had arrived, and were just getting the body out of the chimney. Jake whistled. "Okay, you definitely don't see that every day."

"No, thank God for that." Doc was checking the body closely now. "Stun gun was definitely used. Petechial hemorrhage shows possible strangulation. Time of death around 5:00 a.m. I will call you when I know more."

"Okay, thanks, Doc." Jake pretty much already knew there weren't going to be any fingerprints or other evidence at the scene, so he left and went back to the office.

Of course, Tony was waiting for him at his desk. "I don't know if I can stand it, Jake! Sitting here on my thumbs, while you're out where the action is. Fill me in on what you've got so far." When Jake told him it was another murder from the serial killer, Tony cussed a blue streak. "I knew it was too good to be true that this guy died or something. I wonder why the ten-year hiatus?"

"Well, when we catch him, we'll ask him that. In the meantime, let's see what we've got so far, which isn't much, I'm afraid."

Jake's phone rang early the next morning. It was Doc Miller. He was already done with the autopsy. Jake went straight to the morgue when he got to work. "Hey, Doc, you find anything we didn't already know?"

"Not really. Our victim was strangled, like I said. The killer used his own hands with this one. Stun gun was used too, although why he felt the need to do that, I don't know. This woman wasn't going to put up much of a fight. I didn't find any evidence on the body. Damn Jake, this guy is smart! I looked very closely at the bodies in these cases, there's nothing there!"

"I know, Doc. We will get him. He's bound to screw up sooner or later."

❧

Sara woke up in the middle of the night hearing a muffled scream. She ran into Jenny's room, only to find her daughter wide awake and sitting up in bed. "Mommy, someone was standing next to my bed. I saw them!"

Sara rushed to Jenny's side. "Tell me, Jenny. Who did you see?"

"It was a man. He was tall. I was so scared, mom! He kept trying to say something, but it was like I just couldn't quite hear him, you know?"

Sara held her daughter tight. "As a matter of fact, I do know Jenny."

She thought it was time to share with Jenny the things she had seen and heard. She also told Jenny about her parents, and how they died. She described what her father and mother looked like, and asked Jenny if that could have been who she saw.

Jenny thought awhile, then shrugged. "I don't know, Mom. It could have been him, I guess. I won't be so scared next time if I know it's Grandpa. Will you grab me my notepad, please? Doctor Gray says I should write down everything I see and hear during my visions."

"Visions? Just what is he telling you that he thinks this is? Not just nightmares, obviously."

"He says I could be seeing people who need help getting to the other side. They are asking me to help them. Dr. Gray said I should embrace my gift, not fight it."

Sara nodded, noting that she needed to have a talk with Dr. Gray. She wasn't sure if she wanted him encouraging Jenny's gift or not. "I know you like Dr. Gray, honey, but do you really want to keep pursuing this? Wouldn't you rather he help you overcome these dreams?"

"Mom, if these people need help, then who am I to tell them no? I really want to help them, any way I can. You understand, right, Mom?"

"I understand, honey. I'll help any way I can, too." Sara hugged Jenny. "Well, good night, sweetie. Try to get some rest now. You have school tomorrow."

"Good night, Mom. I love you."

11

It was finally time, time for the kills he'd been waiting for. "Mama, I'm so glad you're finally ready for this one. It's the one that we've been waiting for all these years. Maybe you can come home after this. What do you say, Mama?"

"Darling, I know this is the one you've wanted all this time. You do understand why we waited, don't you? I needed you to take care of things, because I couldn't do it. I wish I could have helped you more, but they wouldn't let me out of here. Going home is my dream, Billy. When this is over, maybe you could get me out of here. I would love that! We just need to trick Dr. Bell into believing I'm getting better. I can do that. You just figure out how you're going to kill her. I'm counting on you, Billy, and I want to hear every last detail."

Billy grinned. "I already have this one figured out, Mama. You're going to love it. It's the best one yet."

Jenny was so excited. She was busy telling her mother all about cheerleading tryouts, and how she made the squad. "Mom, only two freshman made it, and I'm one of them! I can't believe it!"

Sara smiled at her beautiful fifteen-year-old daughter. She thought back on her cheerleading days: cheering Jake's name as he passed for another touchdown. Him picking her up and swinging her around, before placing a soft kiss on her lips. Sara put her fingers to her lips, remembering the feel of Jake's lips on hers. She was missing him so much lately, probably because Jenny reminded her so much of Jake. Sara had fought with herself about telling Jenny about her father. She had just told her that he was dead. That's all Jenny has known since she was old enough to understand. She hated lying to her, but Sara didn't know what else to do. Jake had proven over and over again, that his job as a detective, was his life. He just didn't have room for her in his life, let alone a rambunctious and spunky daughter.

She was brought back to the present by her daughter's squeals of happiness. "Well, I always knew you could do it, Jenny. You're not only beautiful, but also very smart, and talented. How could anybody resist picking you for cheerleading?"

Jenny jumped up and kissed Sara on the cheek. "Oh, Mom, you're always saying that. I love you, Mom!"

"I love you too, sweetie. Now, go get washed up for supper, it's almost ready."

"Okay. Oh yeah, I almost forgot. Can I stay at Misty's tonight? We have to practice our cheers, and she wanted me to just stay with her. Her mom said it was okay. Can I, Mom?"

Sara couldn't believe how mature her daughter was. She was growing into a lovely woman. "Sure, that would be okay. I'll give you a ride over after supper."

"Thanks, Mom!" Jenny jumped up and ran for the bathroom to wash up.

Jake had given Sara ample opportunity to come back to him. Maybe he should just sign the damn divorce papers and let her go. He called Sam and told him he was coming back to Portland; this time, with papers in hand. He had given up.

Billy arrived in Portland just in time to eat at his favorite restaurant. He had some reconnaissance to do before the big event tonight. He thought he could plan better on a full stomach. "Been a while since I've been to Portland. Gotta love this town!" He took a bite of his burger, enjoying the juicy flavor.

After supper, Sara dropped Jenny off at her friend's house. She decided to call Ann to see if she could meet her for coffee.

Ann actually answered this time. "What's up, Sara?"

"Hi, Ann. I was wondering if you wanted to meet for coffee? I haven't seen you in a little while, and I'm alone tonight. Jenny's at a friend's house, and I'm already bored. What do you say?"

"Sure, I can meet you. When and where?"

"How about you come over to the house? Around eight?"

"Sure thing. I'll see you then."

Billy grinned, watching, and listening to her talk on her phone. *Ah, these people just make it too easy for me. Kill two birds with one stone tonight, I guess.* He whistled and sang to himself as he walked away.

Sara decided to bake some cookies, since she had some time before Ann got there. She had been thinking more and more about Jake, Jenny, and herself, lately. She was going to talk to Ann tonight and get her opinion, but she had pretty much made up her mind. She was going to tell Jake about his daughter. He wouldn't be at all happy, she knew that. Jenny wouldn't be too happy either, but she would deal with that when the time came.

Sara hugged her sister extra hard when she got to her house later that night. "I miss you, Annie. I know I'm being selfish, but I wish you would have stayed living here with me. How are you doing?"

Ann hugged Sara back. "If you mean, have I fallen back into that rut, the answer is no. Sam has been great, letting me move back out to the ranch. It helps to stay busy, and I really enjoy helping those kids. Life is good, Sara. Really good. How about you? You doing okay?"

"I am, which brings me to why I asked you here. It's part of the reason, but I really just wanted to spend time with you. So I would like to ask your opinion on something else. I really want you to tell me the truth about how you feel, okay?" Ann nodded. Sara just blurted it out. "I think it's time Jenny and Jake learn the truth. I really feel that now that Jenny's older, she should get to know her father, Annie. What do you think?"

"What do I think? I think it's about time, Sara! Past time, to tell you the truth! When is this going to happen? Soon, I hope."

"Yes, soon. Like, maybe tomorrow, or the next day. I haven't decided for sure yet. I'm really nervous, Ann. Am I doing the right thing?"

Ann jumped up and hugged her again. "Well, hallelujah! Yes, this is definitely the right thing to do. Do you need me here when you talk to Jenny? She's not going to be too happy, and neither will Jake."

"I know, but I can handle it, Annie. Now that I've made up my mind, I feel good about my decision. Let's have our coffee, okay? I even baked cookies."

"Cookies? You know I won't turn them down!"

After Sara poured their coffee, she grabbed a plate of cookies. They sat beside each other on the couch. The two women laughed and talked until midnight.

"Ann, why don't you stay here tonight? You can have Jenny's bed for the night. I really don't want you driving all the way back to the ranch."

Ann tried to stifle a yawn. "I am tired. Maybe I will stay."

"Oh yeah, you want to stay, Ann. You look tired." Billy had to chuckle at his luck. He set about getting ready for the big one. "You really should learn to shut your windows, Sara. There are bad people lurking about."

Sara and Ann talked late into the night. By the time they went to bed, it was two in the morning. Sara fell into a deep sleep, feeling good about her decision. She woke up suddenly, smelling smoke, and hearing the fire alarms going off. *Am I dreaming? Thinking about the past, or was this real?* She sat up, sniffing the air. No, it was real. She smelled smoke.

Trying not to panic, Sara jumped out of bed and rushed to her bedroom door. "This can't be happening again! Ann! Annie!" She felt the doorknob, it was still cool to the touch, so Sara swung the door open. The smoke was thick in the hallway. "Ann, wake up! The house is on fire!" She made her way to Jenny's room, feeling the wall in order to know where she was going. Sara looked behind her, watching the flames engulf her bedroom. She had to hurry. She heard Ann coughing. "Ann, I'm coming!" Sara got to the bedroom door and flung it open, finding Ann huddled in the middle of the bed, crying, and holding her hands to her ears.

Ann started screaming when she saw Sara. "No, no, no! This isn't happening! It can't happen again! No!"

"Annie, it's okay. I'm here now. I'll get us out of here." Looking around, Sara spotted the nursery rhymes book she kept all these years. She picked it up and handed it to Ann. "Hold on to this, Annie, It'll keep you safe. I'll keep you safe, I promise." Sara grabbed Ann by the hand. "Come on, let's get out of here."

The smoke was getting thicker now. Sara could feel the heat on her face and arms. She couldn't see her hands in front of her face. Sara choked back the feeling of panic that was threatening to engulf her. "Ann, we need to crawl over to the window, okay? We have made it through this once, we can do it again. Let's go." They got down as low as they could, and felt their way to the nearest wall. It was hot to the touch. Feeling around, they couldn't find a window. "Ann, listen to me. There's not a way out here. We need to get over to the other side of the room." Sara kept Ann in front of her, and they slowly felt their way to the other side. Sara reached out in front of Ann. She could feel the glass of the window. She slowly slid it open, helping Ann crawl up and out the window.

Ann gulped down the fresh air, coughing and choking. She held out her hand and reached for Sara. Sara was reaching out her hand to Ann just as the roof caved in right above her. The last thing Ann saw was Sara getting covered with debris, disappearing right before her eyes. The last thing she heard, was Sara's screams.

Billy stood near the house, watching his handiwork. He couldn't even describe how excited he was, watching the two women desperately trying to get out of the burning house. He breathed deeply, loving the smell of the smoke. The sight of the yellow-red-and-blue flames licking into the night sky. *They weren't going to get out, no way.* He heard the sirens blaring, and turned to leave, taking one last look at the burning house.

Ann couldn't move; she was frozen to the spot. She couldn't believe what she was seeing. She called out to her sister, but there was nothing but smoke and flames. When Ann started coughing and couldn't stop, the fireman came up to her and placed an oxygen mask on her face. She ripped it off. "My sister! My sister Sara, I think she's still in the house!

Please, help her." Ann clung to the book, screaming at the fireman until no sound would come out. All she could do was cough, and cry, as she sat helplessly in the back of the ambulance.

When the fireman came back to where she was sitting, Ann could tell by the look on his face, it wasn't good news. "Where is my sister? Did you find her?"

The fireman and ambulance crew looked at her with sympathy in their eyes. "I'm sorry, ma'am. Your sister didn't make it out of the house. Is there someone we can call for you?"

Ann was numb. All she could think was. *This couldn't be happening to them again.* She could only think of Jake and Jenny, and how they would feel when they heard the news. The only person who could help her was Sam. She had to call him first. She choked out a reply between sobs. "Yes, please call Sam Long. He lives out at the Long ranch. He'll know what to do."

Jake found out from Sam where Sara lived. Even though it was the middle of the night, he was going straight there. He needed to get this over with, before he changed his mind. Glancing down at the divorce papers he had signed, he sighed, and started his car. Jake had to pull over for a fire truck and two police cars to pass him. "Wow, must be a bad one."

He put his car in drive. As he got closer to the address Sam gave him, he could see a house burning. "No, this can't be it!" He stopped his car and got out, stopping a policeman. "Excuse me, do you know who lives here? Is it Sara Long? I'm a detective from Los Angeles. Tell me, dammit!"

"I'm sorry, sir. We can't give out that information." The man hurried away.

Ann thought she must be dreaming when she heard Jake's voice. Standing up from the ambulance, she looked around. There was a tall man talking to a policeman nearby. It was Jake. Ann called his name. "Jake, is that you?"

Jake turned at the sound of Ann's voice. "Ann! What's going on? Do you and Sara live here? Where is she?"

"I don't live here anymore, Jake. She...um, lives alone, but I was spending the night. Jake, I don't know how to tell you this, but Sara is gone. She didn't make it out of the house." That's all Ann could get out before she collapsed, sobbing, and coughing.

Jake was confused. He couldn't believe it. *Sara was dead? No way!* "This can't be happening! How did this happen?"

Ann stood, Jake helping her up. "I don't know, Jake. I really don't know."

Jenny sat straight up in bed, gasping for air. "Mama? Mama!" She grabbed her cell phone and looked at the time, four a.m. Something was wrong, she could feel it. She quickly dialed Sara's number. "Come on, Mom, answer the phone." It went straight to voice mail. Jenny knew that wasn't right. Her mom answered her cell whenever and whatever time Jenny called her. She hung up and dialed her Aunt Ann's cell. Same result, no answer. "Okay, now I know something's wrong."

Waking her friend at four in the morning because of a feeling she had, may sound strange to some people, but not to her. She shook her friend awake, and told her she had to go home right away.

"What are you talking about, Jenny? It's four in the morning!"

"I know, but something is wrong, I know it. Please, will you get your parents up and see if they'll give me a ride home?"

"Okay, okay, I'll get them."

Jenny was beside herself with worry when they pulled out of the driveway, heading toward her home. "Please hurry. I just know something's not right."

The closer they got to her house, Jenny's fear grew into an all-out panic. They could see the smoke, and the flashing lights from the fire trucks and police cars. When they pulled up beside the ambulance, Jenny opened her car door and jumped out. She started to run toward the house, when she was stopped by a policeman.

"Hold on, you can't go near the house."

Jenny tried to wrestle away from him. "That's my house! Let me go! I have to find my mom!"

The officer held tight. "What's your name?"

"I'm Jenny Long, I live here. Please let me go!"

That's when Jenny heard a familiar voice. "Jenny? Jenny what are you doing here?"

Jenny turned, and saw her Aunt Ann sitting in the back of the ambulance. "Ann! What's going on? Are you okay? Where's Mom?" The officer let her go, and she ran to Ann and hugged her tight. "Ann, where's my mom? Is she at the hospital?" Jenny backed off, and frantically looked around. "What is going on, Ann?"

Ann jumped down from where she was sitting and grabbed Jenny by the hand, pulling her away from the burning house, and people standing around. "Jenny, honey, I'm so sorry." She started sobbing. "Jenny, your mom didn't make it out of the house. She sacrificed her life to save me...again! I wish it was me and not her, honey. Really, I do."

"No! There's got to be some mistake, Ann! Did they find her? Maybe she is hiding somewhere in the house, trying to get away from the fire. They'll find her alive, I know it!"

Ann shook her head. "Jenny, listen to me. They found Sara's body already. She's gone, sweetie. Listen, I know this is a bad time, but there is something else I need to tell you."

Jake walked up to them right then. Jenny turned to face him. "Who are you? Are you a fireman? What happened to my mom?"

"*Your mom?* You mean Sara? She was your mom?" Jake looked from Jenny to Ann, searching her face for an answer.

"Jenny, this isn't how your mom wanted this to be, but under the circumstances, you need to know. This is your dad, Jen. He's not dead. Sara was going to tell you. We talked about it tonight before the fire. Jake, this is Jenny, your daughter."

They stared at each other, not knowing what to do. Jake reached for Jenny tentatively, but she pulled back. "Get away from me! You're not my dad! I don't even know you. Get out of here!"

Jake pulled away. "Fine, I'll leave, but I will be here when you are ready to talk to me. Ann, you know where to find me." With that, he left.

Ann and Jenny were clinging to each other, crying, as Billy watched from the crowd. *Dammit! How did she get out of the house? They*

were both supposed to die in that fire. Hmph! Well, there's always a next time, I guess. He turned, walking away slowly so as to not draw any attention to himself.

❧

Sam left the ranch as soon as he got the call from the police. He was shaken at the news of Sara's death, but he knew he had to hold it together for the sake of Jenny and Ann. He drove as fast as he could, without speeding too much. When Sam pulled up to what was left of the house, he spotted the girls holding each other. He ran straight over to them, putting his arms around them both. "Ann, are you okay? Has anybody said what happened here?"

"No, Sam, I'm not okay. Sara is gone! I don't know what happened. All I remember, is smelling the smoke, and Sara coming into the room. I guess I panicked because I sort of froze up, you know. Sara guided me to the window and helped me out first. When I turned around to help her, she just disappeared. I'm so sorry, Jenny."

Sam looked over at Jenny. She seemed shell-shocked. He waved at the first responders. "Can you come over here and take a look at my niece? She may need some help." The first responder took Jenny by the hand, and gently led her over to the ambulance. While they looked her over, Sam left Ann to watch over Jenny, and strode over to where the firemen and police were gathered. "Who is in charge here?"

A man in a uniform stepped forward. "That would be me, sir. Chief Percy. Who might you be?"

"I'm Sam Long, sir. Brother-in-law to the victim, Sara Long. Can you tell me what happened here?"

"We won't know until the arson squad gets here. It's still too hot to enter the house. Probably won't know anything until later in the day. Why don't you leave your name and number, I'll call you when they know more."

"Come on, chief, you must have an idea of what happened here. Can you at least tell me if you think it's arson?"

The chief took off his hard hat, and ran his hands through his hair. "Well, don't quote me on this, but it may have been arson. We smelled gasoline when we entered the house, trying to get to the victim.

Like I said, we'll let you know for sure later on."

"Okay, thanks, chief. I'm going to take the girls out to my ranch. If you need us for something, that's where we'll be. I'll leave my phone number with the police." Sam headed back to where Ann and Jenny were standing. "Come on, girls. I'm going to take you home to the ranch. There's nothing more we can do here."

Ann pulled Sam aside. "Sam, Jake was here. Evidently, he came to see Sara. This is what he drove up on. Jenny got here right then, and I had no choice but to introduce them. I hope I did the right thing. Jenny wouldn't have anything to do with him. He left to go back to Los Angeles, I presume."

"Well, that saves us from having to call him. I think it'll be okay. They just need some time. I think we all do."

Jenny didn't want to leave, but she silently followed along, as Ann and Sam led her to his pickup.

"Wait a minute, I almost forgot." Ann turned, and ran back to the ambulance. She came back holding the nursery rhymes book. "Jenny, this is yours now. Your mom wanted you to have it. This book has survived two fires now. Sara handed it to me right before she..."

Jenny held on to the book, but stayed silent. Sam was worried about her, and Ann. It was going to be a long day.

12

J ake got back to LA in record time. He didn't feel like stopping anywhere, so he drove straight through. He had a daughter! Why didn't Sara tell him? The girl, Jenny, looked to be about fourteen or fifteen years old. He was going to give her some time before he contacted her, but he was still in shock. *Sara was gone!*

Jake was beginning to feel like his life was heading somewhere he didn't want it to go. Not only was Sara dead, this serial killer was getting to him more and more each day. They just weren't getting any clues at all to his identity. Jake was just going through the everyday motions. He would wake up, shower, go to work, and repeat that day after day. Murder didn't stop just because Jake wasn't on top of the world. People were being killed. He would solve them one by one, but the serial killer remained elusive. They kept the murder board up in the conference room with the pictures of all of the victims. No suspects, no clues, no DNA, nothing. Jake would walk by the board, and study the faces of all five victims, vowing to bring this person to justice.

His phone rang just as he got to work. He saw Sam's name come up on the screen. "Sam! It's about time you called! I've been trying to be patient, but it's been two weeks!"

Sam hesitated. "Jake, I know that, but we've all been in shock here! None of us can believe she's gone. Jake, Sara saved Ann's life before the house caved in on her. Ann is having trouble with that. Not to mention what Jenny is going through. The coroner wouldn't release the body until he was sure of cause of death."

Jake didn't even know what to say. He just sat there in stunned silence. "Sam, can I call you back? I just can't talk right now. I need to figure out what to do." Jake paused, before he finished. "I do know this much, I'm coming to Portland for sure. Even if Sara and I haven't talked in fifteen years, I need to be there. Just let me get things in order here. I'll call you soon."

As a police detective, Jake dealt with death every day, but this was different. He always held out hope that Sara would come back to him, even after all these years. Now she was gone. He went straight to Tony's office when he hung up the phone. He not only needed a friend right now, he needed his captain to give him some time off. He couldn't believe the irony. All Sara ever wanted was for him to take some time off to be with her. Now, there he was, taking time off to attend her funeral. She had to die to get him to use his many vacation days he had acquired over the years. He suddenly felt very old. Jake had never questioned his love for his job until this very moment.

Tony looked up as Jake knocked. "Come on in, Jake. What's going on? I can tell by the look on your face something is wrong. Sit down."

"Something is very wrong, Tony. Sara was killed in a fire a couple of weeks ago. I should've told you sooner, but I wasn't sure what I was going to do. I need some time off to go there and see for myself what went on, and to arrange her funeral service. The coroner just got done with her body, and I need to be there. Tony stood, and came around his desk to hug his friend. "I'm so sorry, Jake. Do you know any details? How did the fire start? What happened?"

"I don't know the answer to that. I need to talk to the fire inspector myself. Tony, what are the odds of her dying in a fire, when that's how her parents died? It just doesn't seem right to me. I really need to be there, Tony."

"Whatever you need, Jake. Take as much time as you want. We'll hold down the fort here. You take care of things in Portland. Just keep in touch, okay? I want to be kept in the loop."

Jake got up from his chair, and shook his friend's hand. "Will do, Tony. I'll let you know what I find out."

Sam waited for Ann to wake up so he could talk to her. They needed to break the news to Jenny that Jake was coming to Portland. Sam knew Jake would come. He was surprised that he hadn't already been here. Ann still looked rough when she walked down the huge staircase in Sam's log home. He didn't want to put more pressure on her, but they needed to talk to Jenny soon. Jake was probably almost there already. He decided to give Ann an hour or so before he bombarded her with that news.

"Good morning, Ann. Did you get any sleep at all? I know I didn't. I think the shock is wearing off. I still can't believe this actually happened. Is Jenny awake?"

"Good morning, Sam. I'm doing better, and no, I didn't rest very much. Jenny isn't awake yet. I just don't know what to do about Jenny, Sam. We need to talk to her about her dad right away. That was the last thing Sara said to me before the fire. We had a long talk, and she was going to tell her about Jake. Jenny needs to accept the fact that Jake is her father. She is going to need him now."

"Well, you beat me to the punch in bringing that up. I was going to give you a little time before I told you, but, I talked to Jake. He is on his way here. So yes, we definitely need to talk to Jenny."

"Talk to me about what?" Jenny walked in just in time to hear the last of the conversation.

Ann was startled when she heard Jenny's voice. "Oh, you're awake. You doing okay? Well, that's a stupid question, I guess. I don't think anything will ever be okay again. How are you feeling this morning?"

"Oh, I'm still in shock, I guess. I still can't believe it. Aunt Ann, what will happen to me now? I know I'm only fifteen, but do I have a say in what happens to me? Will I have to go into an orphanage or something? I'm scared."

Ann hugged her niece. "I won't let that happen, Jenny. You'll always have me, and your Uncle Sam. Always remember that."

"Thanks, I will need you. I don't have anyone else right now." Her voice broke when she finished her sentence.

Ann cleared her throat. "Jenny, will you come and sit down for a minute please? We have something we need to talk about."

Jenny looked at Ann and Sam, confused. "What is it? Did you find something out about the fire?"

Sam hunched down beside Jenny and held her hand. "No, honey, we haven't learned anything knew. This isn't about the fire, really. It's about your mom...and your dad."

"My dad? Why bring him up? Mom told me he died before I was even born. Is this about that guy who showed up at the fire? Don't even go there. He isn't my dad. My dad is dead!"

Sam stood and moved over by Ann, putting his arm around her shoulders, encouraging her to tell Jenny the truth. Ann felt stronger with Sam by her side, so she took a deep breath. "Jenny, honey, the night that your mom died, we talked a lot. Mostly about you, but some about your dad, too. Sara wanted you to know something. She wanted to tell you herself, but as we all know, she couldn't." Ann grabbed Sam by the hand, and he gently squeezed it. "Jenny, your dad isn't dead. He's very much alive, and lives in Los Angeles, California."

Jenny looked almost as shocked as she did when learning about her mom's death. "No! Mom wouldn't do that to me. She never lied to me. No matter what, we always told each other the truth. I don't believe you!"

Sam stopped her from running off. "Listen, Jenny, I know you've been through a lot. I wish we could have waited awhile before dropping this bombshell on you, but it's true. Your dad isn't dead. That was really him that you met the other night. As a matter of fact, he is on his way here right now. Jenny, there's something else. Jake didn't know about you, either. Sara didn't tell him about you. She was only trying to protect you. She didn't want your feelings to be hurt. Jake is a detective and he is married to his job. He loved Sara very much. I know my brother, he would've loved you too, and he still will. It's just that his job makes it very difficult to have any relationship. He works all hours of the day and night. There's a lot of stress involved with being in homicide too, and I mean *a lot*."

Jenny started shaking like a leaf. She couldn't stop shaking. Ann grabbed a blanket from the couch and wrapped it around her shoulders. "Honey, I know this is a lot to take in, but you have to know that your mom loved you more than life itself. She felt it was better that you didn't know about Jake. Because of his job, not because he's a bad person. That's why she had decided to tell you now. She felt you were old enough to make your own decision about wanting to meet Jake. I'm going to tell you right now that we will stand by your decision. If you don't want to see him, we can work something out. I can tell him you're going to stay with me or something. But I'm going to tell you, he'll fight tooth and nail to win your love. I'm so sorry we had to lay all of this on you now, but Sara wanted you to know. I'm following through with what she wanted. The rest is up to you."

After sitting in silence for quite awhile, Jenny came out of the shock that she was in. The more she thought about it, she had to admit that she actually was happy to learn her dad was still alive. She wasn't all alone now, she had a dad! She could kind of understand her mom's reasoning behind keeping this from her until now. Jenny was much more able to cope with her dad's job now than when she was younger. After thinking about it for a while, she decided it might be okay to give him a chance. After all, it sounded like she didn't have a choice anyway.

"Although I don't agree with you all keeping my dad and me apart, I kind of understand. But what's my dad going to think about having a fifteen-year-old daughter in tow? Is he going to accept me as his? I don't know how I am supposed to feel. This is going to be an interesting day, that's for sure."

Jake didn't stop too many times on his way to Portland. He stayed in contact with Sam, letting him know how far away he was. Jake was a little tired when he pulled into Sam's ranch, but he still had to take time to look around when he got out of the car. Sam was walking toward him when he went to the trunk to grab his luggage. He grabbed his brother in a bear hug. "Sam, it's been too long, bro. I sure do miss you!"

"Me too, Jake. I'm so sorry our reunion had to be for this reason."

"Yeah, it sucks big time, but I am glad to see you. Your ranch is fantastic! How did you manage all of this?"

"I've had a lot of help over the years, from a lot of people. We started out small, and built it up to what you see right now. I'm not done yet, though. I'm planning on building more if I can. I'll show you around after awhile, but let's get you settled in first. You must be exhausted."

"I'm okay. I'm used to not getting any sleep. I really want to call the fire inspector, but I guess it's too late now. I'll wait until morning for that. Let's get my bags inside, then I want a cold beer, and a tour, in that order."

Sam put his arm around Jake as they walked to the house, catching up along the way. When Jake stepped into the house, he let out a low whistle. "Wow! The inside is just as impressive as the outside."

"Thanks, bro, I appreciate it."

"So do I." Ann walked up to Jake, hugging him. "Sam has been great to me, I'll always appreciate that."

"It's good to see you, Ann. Are you doing all right? This is unbelievable, but I am happy that you got to spend time with Sara before she died."

"So am I, Jake. She was so much help to me. I don't know what would've happened to me if she wouldn't have come here."

"Well, I'm glad she did. Now, let's grab that beer and go look around this joint."

"Let's do that." Sam grabbed Jake's bags and headed upstairs. "Come with me, we'll take your bags to your room first."

Jake made himself at home. After splashing some water on his face, he hurried back downstairs. He heard voices in the kitchen so he headed that way. When he stepped through the doorway, he was taken aback a little when he saw Jenny standing at the sink. He wasn't sure what he was supposed to say to her so he settled for hello.

Jenny nodded, "Hello.... Listen, I'm sorry about the other night. I was just in so much pain, and I honestly didn't know you were even alive. I promise I didn't know, or I would have insisted on meeting you before this. My mom must have had her reasons for not telling us, but I can't understand what they would be."

"I know Sara was doing what she thought was best for you, but it just wasn't right that she kept us apart for so many years. I know I wasn't there when she needed me, and I probably wouldn't have been there for you, either. I just wish Sara would have given me a chance."

"I'm not gonna lie, it's hard to think that Mom felt she had to keep us apart, but that is water under the bridge right now. I do want to get to know you, if that's okay with you."

Jake reached out tentatively and hugged his daughter. "I want that too, Jenny. Let's start slowly, and just try to get to know each other a little bit, okay?"

"Sure, I'm going back to my room now. I'll see you all later."

Jake looked over at Sam and tried to smile. "Want to show me around?"

As the two of them walked outside, he breathed in the fresh air. "Well, Sam, here we are. It's unbelievable how things change. I really wonder if Sara would ever have told me about her. I just don't know."

"I think she meant it when she told Ann that she wanted to tell you. She didn't say things she didn't mean."

The two men stood on the deck, letting the sounds of the animals on the ranch surround them. "It's been a long day, Sam, I think I'll just go to bed. Tell Ann good night for me, will you?"

After Jake went to bed, Sam and Ann sat out on the porch talking. "I think that went okay, don't you?"

"I do, but there's still that other thing we need to talk to Jake about. The sooner, the better. Jenny's abilities could change his decision whether or not he wants to have her move in with him. I don't want Jen getting her hopes up, only to have them dashed. What do you think, Sam?"

"Well, we'll let him deal with one thing at a time for now. I have a feeling Jake will take it in stride, just like he does everything else. They're both handling things pretty well so far. Let's take our time with these other things."

Jenny didn't come back downstairs until evening the next day. When she saw Jake sitting at the kitchen table, she asked tentatively. "Do you want to see the horses?"

He wasn't going to turn that down, so off they went. Jenny took Jake straight to the horse pen. There were horses of all different colors and sizes milling about, munching on fresh hay. Jake propped his foot up on the lower rung of the fence, looking down at his daughter. "It still hasn't sunk in that I have a daughter. I missed out on so much of your life, Jenny. Your first steps, school plays, Christmas. I'm so sorry that I wasn't there for Sara when she needed me most...and for you."

Jenny grabbed a handful of hay and fed it to the nearest horse, petting his soft nose. The horse snorted and spit out some of the hay, as he eagerly snatched it out of Jenny's hand. "I know, but you couldn't have known I was even born. You can't blame yourself."

"So many times, I wanted to come here just to talk to Sara, but

I thought I was doing the right thing in leaving her alone. I kept telling myself she just needed space, and that she would come around eventually. The more time that passed, the easier it got to ignore, I guess. The months turned into years—and I know it sounds crazy, but time just flew by. I missed so much of your life. Did any pictures of you growing up survive the fire? Anything at all?"

"No, nothing, except mom's nursery rhymes book. That thing is invincible. It's survived two fires."

Jake had to chuckle at that news. "No way. That book was very important to your mom, Jenny. It's all we have left of her now. Keep it close to your heart."

"I will do that."

Jake and Jenny stood like that for a long time, just listening to the croaking frogs and the sound of the horses eating their hay. Finally, Jake broke the silence. "I promise I'm going to find out what happened to your mom, Jen. It's the least I can do for her, and you."

"I believe you, Jake, or Dad. What should I call you? What I really want to know is, what happens to me now? Do I have to leave my friends and move to Los Angeles? Do you even want me to?"

"You can call me whatever you want to. I would love it to be Dad, but Jake is fine too. Of course I want you to stay with me, don't ever question that. Would that be okay with you?"

Jenny thought about it for a minute. "I think so, but can we take some time to decide for sure? I've had a lot to take in these past few days."

"I have a job at home I need to get back to, but I'm not going anywhere. I'll stay here until you make your decision."

When they finally went back into the house, it was dark and quiet. Jake said good night to Jenny, and headed up to his room. It wasn't until then, that he realized he never did get a beer. He was sure that his life would be changed in more ways than just his drinking. Jake fell asleep, thinking about Sara raising their daughter alone all this time. She did a great job from what he could tell. Tomorrow, he was going to find out if that fire was an accident or not. Then he would set about burying his wife.

13

The day was bright and sunny. Jake woke up feeling pretty good. He usually needed at least three aspirin before he could get going in the morning. *"Hmmm...I could get used to this. Well, I'd better get used to it anyway. I have a daughter to raise now. I still can't believe it."*

When he shut the door to his room, Jake could hear people talking downstairs. He headed toward the sound of the voices. Sam, Ann, and Jenny, were already in the kitchen, eating breakfast, and talking. Sam looked up at his brother when he entered the room.

"You're going to have to start waking up earlier in the morning if you want to hang out with us, Jake. We already have the chores done. I'll let it go this time, being you were up so late. But from here on out, you can do your share around here."

Jake scoffed at his brother's comment. "What the hell time do you get up? It's only seven a.m." He glanced over at Ann and Jenny, who were holding back a smile. "Does he always act like this, or is this just for my benefit?"

Ann couldn't help but laugh. "He's pretty much always this way. We call him the slave driver. Always standing there with a whip in his hand, telling us what to do."

Ann and Jenny burst out laughing at the look on Sam's face, then everyone sobered up, remembering why they were all there. Jake looked at each person there.

"You know, Sara loved to laugh. She had a very distinct laugh, that made everyone else do the same. It's okay to laugh. Besides, I believe Sam is a slave driver. I've known him all his life, he never changes."

Sam shook his head, glaring at Jake. "Right, well, if I'm that bad, maybe you should get to work then! Break time is over!" He yelled, pretending to crack a whip over his head.

They all laughed at that, but they all got quiet again, feeling guilty about laughing at anything. When the phone rang, everyone sobered up fast. Sam answered, putting it on speaker phone, when he saw who it was.

"Chief Percy, you're on speaker. I have Jake Long here with me. He's Sara's husband, and a homicide detective in Los Angeles."

"Nice to meet you, Detective Long. I'm sorry for your loss. Sam, I told you I would call when I learned more from the arson investigators. They finished their investigation of the fire last night. It was definitely arson. Gasoline was used as the accelerant, so the house burned very quickly. I'm amazed anyone got out alive, Miss Olsen is very lucky."

Ann hung her head. "I don't feel very lucky Mr. Percy, my sister died in that fire."

"I know Miss Olsen, and I'm very sorry. I didn't mean anything by that. Anyway, our medical examiner said that he is done with the autopsy, and ready to release the body. You can come in this afternoon and visit with him. If you want to talk to me in person, I'm available any time. That's about all I have for now."

Jake spoke up, wanting to make sure the man knew how he felt. "I will definitely want to talk to you chief, and I want to see the house. My brother Sam and I will leave shortly, so we will see you in about an hour."

"If you're sure that's what you want to do. I'll meet you at the house, detective. Goodbye then."

Sam hung up the phone, and looked at Jake. "Are you okay bro? Are you sure that you want to go to the house? We don't need to do that."

I need to see it, Sam. I know it won't bring Sara back, but maybe I'll see something the arson guys missed. After all, I am trained for this. You heard him, it was murder. Someone wanted Sara dead, probably Ann too. Maybe even Jen. Which reminds me, we need to keep our eyes open for anything strange going on here at the ranch too. Have you vetted all of your workers? Background checks, things like that? If not, get it done."

Jake looked over at the girls. They looked like they were shocked to hear him talking about murder, with their names brought up in the same sentence.

"I'm sorry to scare you two, but this is necessary. You may be a target now. You need to be extra careful. Don't go anywhere alone, you hear me?"

Ann spoke first. "Wow! You sure know how to scare a person! I can't imagine anyone wanting to hurt us, but we do hear you Jake. We'll be careful, but, I feel safe on the ranch. Nothing is going to happen to us here."

Sam stood, grabbing his cowboy hat. "I'll make sure of it, Jake. But right now, we need to get to town, and start trying to figure out who started that fire."

Sam took Ann by the hands. "Listen, do what Jake says, okay? Keep Jenny with you at all times. I'll talk to the hands, make sure they're armed, and assign someone to stay with you two. You'll be okay."

Turning, and walking to the door, he waited for his brother. "Let's go, Jake."

Jake nodded to Ann, and hugged Jenny. "I'll take care of you, I promise. I told you I would find out who did this, and I meant it. We'll be home tonight, hopefully with some answers to our questions by then. In the meantime, be careful, and stay with your aunt."

The two men strode out of the room, while Jenny and Ann started cleaning up breakfast dishes. Ann looked out through the window. She could see Jake and Sam talking to Booker, the foreman. No doubt filling him in on the situation.

She sighed. "Well, it looks like we are going to be prisoners in our own home for a while. I have no doubt that Sam and Jake will find this evil person, but it may take a while."

Jake and Sam reached what was left of Sara's house, just as Chief Percy pulled up. Jake couldn't believe his eyes when he looked at the structure in front of him. There wasn't anything left of it. Just a few beams here and there. Along with a pile of rubble on the ground. Jake knew he wasn't going to get anything for evidence from the sight of the fire. He strode over to the chief, wanting some answers. They shook hands when Jake introduced himself.

"Nice to meet you in person, chief. Wow, looking at this mess, I can see that there is nothing left as far as evidence goes. How on earth did you decipher that it was arson? Did you find anything at all? A gas can maybe?"

Chief Percy was shaking his head. "No sir. No gas can, or anything else for that matter. Our arson investigators are very good at what they do, detective. They find things that are lost on the rest of us. Whoever did this, hid himself very well. We questioned the neighbors, no one saw a thing. If there was any evidence as to who did this, it burned up in the fire. I'm afraid this killer knew what he was doing. He has probably done it before. I haven't talked to the medical examiner yet. He may have found something on the body. If you want to follow me, I'll take you there myself."

Jake nodded, taking one last look at the place where Sara lost her life. They walked back to the pickup they were driving, and left the scene. They drove in silence, pulling up behind the chief, in front of the police station. Getting out, Jake had to admit, his nerves were on edge just thinking about seeing Sara like this. He wasn't sure if he could do it, but he felt like he had to. He glanced at Sam, knowing his brother understood. "Would you give me a minute, please?"

"Sure thing, Jake. Take your time." Sam did understand. He knew that this wasn't going to be easy, but it was necessary. He would let Jake go down to the morgue in his own time. Seeing Sara like that wasn't something either one of them wanted to do. Sam waited outside in the hall while Jake went into the men's restroom.

Jake splashed cold water on his face, looking into the mirror. "I sure could use a drink right about now." He held out his hand, rubbing it when it started to shake. "Shape up, Long. You're done with that, remember?"

When Jake came out of the restroom, he spotted Sam talking with a tall, gray-haired man. He rubbed his hands together, and headed in their direction. Sam turned as Jake approached. "Hey, Jake, you doing alright?"

"I'm fine. What's going on here?"

"This is Doctor French, the medical examiner. Doctor, this is my brother, Jake. He is Sara's husband."

The doctor looked at Jake with sympathy in his eyes. "Nice to meet you Jake. I understand you are a detective?"

"Yes, I am. In Los Angeles. Doctor, can I see Sara now?"

"Are you sure you want to do that detective? It's not pretty. I'm afraid there's not much to see anyway. She was burned pretty badly."

"I'm sure. Let's go, please."

The doctor led the way to the morgue. Jake could feel, and smell, the sterile environment, before he even stepped foot inside. He shivered, which didn't go unnoticed by Sam.

"Jake, you don't have to do this. They already identified Sara by her dental records. Doctor French said that there was no evidence on the body. Let's just let her go."

Jake took a deep breath. "I need to do this, Sam."

They walked into the morgue, and Jake saw a body, covered with a white cloth. Just like he had so many times before. This was very different from all of those other times. This was personal.

"Could I have a few moments alone, please?"

Sam and the doctor nodded in agreement, and left the room, giving Jake his privacy. He slowly pulled back the cloth, gasping at what he saw. Jake quickly covered her back up, and held back a sob. "I'm so sorry Sara. Sorry you had to die like this, but mostly because I wasn't there to protect you. I promise you, I will keep our daughter safe. Ann too. I only hope you didn't suffer. I love you, Sara. I always will."

When Jake was done, Sam followed him back out to the car. "Well, what now bro? Any ideas on where to go from here?"

"We need to go to the local funeral home first, and prepare Sara's funeral. I know what she wanted to do. I'll arrange things here. You don't have to go with me if you don't want to."

"No way, Jake. I'm with you all the way. You're not doing this alone, so don't even try getting rid of me!"

"I was hoping you would say that. Let's get to it then, and Sam, in case I haven't said this. Thanks, for everything. Taking care of Sara, and Ann, Jenny too. I'm glad you were here. I just wish I would have been."

"I know you would have done the same for me, Jake. That's what family is for."

Jake nodded. "Not to change the subject, but speaking of Ann. Is there something going on between you two? I noticed you held her hands a little longer than was necessary this morning."

Sam smiled. "Well, not that I wouldn't mind, but neither one of us needs that right now. We are good friends, but, who knows what may happen down the road."

"Well, I'll support you either way. I just want you both to be happy."

"Yeah, well, that's a long way down the road, if it happens at all."

They pulled up in front of a large, brick building.

"Well, here is the nicest funeral home around. I've dealt with them many times with the families of the police officers I've had out at the ranch. They are the best, Jake. They will treat Sara right."

Jake looked at the brick building and sighed. "Well, let's do this, then."

It didn't take them long to make the arrangements. Sara's remains were going to be flown back to Los Angeles, and buried beside her mother and father. It's what she wanted. Jake decided to have the service here in Portland, so Ann and Sam didn't have to travel all the way to Los Angeles. Any friends that Sara made here could say their goodbyes also.

It still hurt him to think that Sara had a whole other life, away from him. She raised their daughter for fifteen years. Not telling him about her. Jake didn't know what Jenny was going to do yet. But he was going to try very hard to persuade her to come to Los Angeles with him. He only hoped it was enough.

The day of Sara's service was cloudy and rainy. Kind of like everyone's mood. "This is fitting weather for a funeral." Ann said. "Kind of like how we feel today."

Jake looked up at the clouds, and nodded. "Yes, it is. Come on, let's go say our goodbyes."

There weren't a lot of people there. Some from the ranch, that had met Sara. Some from work. Some of Jenny's friends, and their families.

Jake didn't know any of them.

He looked around the room after the service, wondering how he let himself get to be such a stranger to his own wife. He had let the years pass without talking to her, just because he was so damn stubborn. They were both stubborn.

They were just walking out the door, when a man stopped them. He was just one of the many strangers at the church.

"Mr. Long, I'm so sorry for your loss. Sara was a wonderful girl." He shook Jake's hand, and turned to Ann and Jenny, doing the same. Jake got a bad vibe from the man, but tried to shake it off. He resisted the urge to wipe his hand off where the man touched it. "Thank you, Mr—"

"Oh, I'm sorry. My name is Billy. I've known Sara for a while now. Not well, but I just wanted to pay my respects."

"Well, thank you, Billy. I appreciate your condolences. We'll just be on our way now. Excuse us."

Billy glared after them, whispering under his breath. *Too good for me are you? We'll just see about that now, won't we?*

Jenny was so tired by the time they got back to the ranch, she could barely keep her eyes open. The trip home was very solemn and quiet. Everyone in their own thoughts. When Jake pulled up to the house, he turned to talk to his daughter after Sam and Ann left the car.

"I know it's been a rough day, Jenny. But have you thought any more about what you want to do now? There is plenty of room at my house for you. You'll have your own room, and the high school is nearby. I promise you, we'll come back here to visit whenever you want to. I'm not going to make that mistake again. If there's one thing I have learned from all of this, it's that family is important. Time is too short to spend apart from the ones you love. What do you say?"

Jenny stifled a yawn. "Can we talk about it in the morning? You're right, it's been a very long day, and I just can't think straight right now. I do want to get to know you better, and this is my chance to do that. But, I was thinking, what about Ann? Will she be okay without me?"

Jake couldn't get over how mature his daughter was for her age. "Ann will have Sam, I think she'll be fine. But, if she wants to, we could probably work something out for her to come with us. We'll see what she says about that."

"Okay, well, I'm beat, so I'm going to go to bed. Goodnight, Jake, I mean Dad. I still have trouble with the fact that you're alive. It just makes me so sad that my mom thought she had to keep us apart for so many years."

"I know, but she had her reasons. Goodnight Jenny. Sweet dreams."

Ann and Sam were sitting at the kitchen table when Jake came in the house. Jake grabbed a beer out of the fridge, and sat down next to them. "It's just one beer. I'll be fine, so don't start. Well, long day, huh?"

"Yes, it was. Jake, has Jenny made her decision yet? I know she is a minor. If you give your consent, she could stay here if she wanted to. What is she going to do?"

"She's going to sleep on it, but it sounds like she is coming home with me. I'm very happy, but a little scared too. Ann, do you want to come with us? Even if it's just for a little while? I could sure use the help."

"I'll think about it, but you'll be fine. Jenny is a very special girl. She is not a problem to have around. She seems to have adjusted to everything very well so far. There is one thing you should know about before you go home, though. I'm not sure how to say this, but...well. Jenny has been seeing a psychologist. What that means is, he's been helping her cope with a gift that Jenny was born with. Jake, she can hear voices of people who have passed on. She can sometimes see them, too."

Ann held her hand up, stopping Jake from saying anything. "Listen, I know it's hard to believe, but she really does have a gift. Sara had it, and so does Jen. Sara decided to get her help with it, rather than try and suppress it. How do you feel about that? Do you still want to take her on?"

Jake was shocked. He didn't really believe in that hocus pocus, mumbo jumbo. "*Ummm...*Okay, I must say, this is a bit troubling. I remember Sara having dreams, but she never said anything to me about this gift. I don't think we should be encouraging Jenny to think this stuff is true. But, I do know someone in Los Angeles who can help. She's the psychologist for the police department. If anyone can help Jen, she can. I'm not agreeing that this stuff is real, just that Jenny should have someone to talk to if she needs to. We'll have to agree to disagree about the rest of this stuff."

"Somehow, that's just what I thought you would say. I can understand what you're saying. But you need to stay open-minded at least, agreed?"

Jake nodded. "Agreed."

When Jen went to bed that night, she hoped she could sleep soundly. She didn't want to be bothered by the people who begged her for help almost every night. She decided to make a plea, hoping it worked.

"Please, I know you all need my help, but tonight I need to rest, okay? Just for tonight. I promise, I'll try to help you another day, if you let me be for one night."

Jen sighed, hoping that worked. She hugged the book close, and thought of her mom, as she drifted off into a deep sleep.

Jen was unaware of the people who watched over as she slept. Taking care of her, even as they refrained from talking to her that night.

14

Jake stayed in Portland for another week. Just getting to know his daughter, and doing some well-needed healing himself. He was shocked at how easy it was to just relax. He couldn't believe he wasn't chomping at the bit to get back to his job, but it was never far from his mind. It was wonderful though. Jake and Sam got closer too. He was getting up early and helping with chores, loving every minute of it.The fresh morning air was just what the doctor ordered to clear Jake's head, and get him back on track.

The morning of August fifteenth, Jake woke up early, as usual. He spotted Sam in the corral with the horses, pitching hay. The horses were whinnying, and running in the corral, waiting for Sam to get done. Jake took a deep breath, loving the smell of the horses, mingled with the scent of the hay. He sure was going to miss this place. It had been great for his health—both mind and body—being here. He headed in the direction of the horse barn. "Morning, Sam. You're up extra early today."

"Yeah, just getting ready for the annual trail ride at the end of the month. Do you think you'll still be here? It's a great time."

"Probably not, Sam. This has been a great break from the stress of the job, but I need to get back to work. This serial killer is still out there, and it's just a matter of time before he strikes again. I just can't, and won't, rest until I catch him. Plus, we still don't know what happened to Sara. It's really hard to sit back and let the Portland police department handle this. I need some answers, and they have no clues yet. Maybe if I catch this serial, I can come back here and focus more on Sara's killer. I'm going to be right in the middle of Sara's murder investigation if they can't find her killer, whether the Portland police want me to or not. I have a strange feeling that this killer is connected to me somehow. But, for now, it's time for me to get back to Los Angeles. Not that I don't want to stay, I could definitely get used to this. Have I told you how proud I am of you? So is Tom."

"Well, thanks, Jake. Have you talked to Tom lately? Does he know the details on Sara's murder?"

Jake nodded. "Yes, I called him before the funeral. He said he couldn't make it here then, but I know if I needed him, he would be there. Anyway, I need to go talk to Jenny about going back to Los Angeles. I think we should leave in a couple days. Thanks for your hospitality, Sam. I really needed it."

"You're welcome here any time, Jake. You and Jenny. I wish you good luck with solving those murders. If you need me for anything, you call me, okay?"

Jake hugged his brother. "I will, bro. I will."

Jake and Jenny packed up the car, and took off for home two days later. Jenny was a bit apprehensive, but excited too. She didn't mind change. Actually, she was kind of ready to get out of Portland. All that was left here were bad memories now—not counting Ann and Sam, of course. She had said her goodbyes to all of her friends. She and Ann stayed up talking until the wee hours of the morning. Jenny was going to miss her the most. They had grown close, and she really tried to get her to come with them to Los Angeles. Ann thought Jenny and Jake should get to know each other without interference from her, so she decided to stay with Sam. It was just the two of them now, Jenny and her dad, starting a new phase in their lives.

Jenny turned to Jake as they drove down the road. "Dad, tell me about your job. I want to know what to expect when we get home."

Jake didn't really know how to respond to that question. "What do you want to know exactly? I'm not sure how to explain it in so many words. I guess I'd say it's more of a calling than a job. Some would call it an obsession. I call it passion. Homicide detectives—all police officers, really—are passionate about their work. I guess you could say we are sympathetic toward the victims, but you have to stay aloof, too. In a nutshell, it's a difficult job, that consumes your life. That's why Sara left me. I was consumed by it." He glanced over at Jenny. "I'm going to try to change that, Jenny, but I can't promise anything. You're going to have to be patient with me, okay?"

"I'm okay with everything you said. It sounds interesting and challenging to me. Maybe I should be a cop someday. I think I'd be good at it, what do you think?"

"I'd be very proud, and happy if you did that, Jen. But let's take one day at a time for now, deal?"

Jenny nodded, and leaned back in her seat, closing her eyes. "Deal."

Jake sighed, thinking that this was not going to be easy for him, or for Jenny. He had a lot to learn about raising a fifteen-year-old daughter. Jake wasn't at all sure how he was going to go about it. He began a mental list. It's only a month before school starts. First thing Monday morning, he was going to have to go to the high school, and get Jenny registered for the school year. Then, he had to figure out how he was going to juggle his job, and a fifteen-year-old girl. Maybe he needed to talk to Nancy Hall himself. Jake ran his hand through his hair. He glanced over at his daughter, peacefully sleeping now. Jake knew they had some rough times ahead. He just hoped they could get through them. Jake figured he'd better contact Dr. Hall soon. Maybe she had some advice for him on raising Jenny. He thought he'd better let Jenny talk to Dr. Hall about her supposed gift too. Jake wasn't going to bring that crazy idea up with Jenny or the doctor though. He just wasn't willing to accept the notion that Jenny could see dead people. It just sounded crazy to him. Jenny needed to get over the idea of this so-called gift she had. Maybe Doctor Hall will help with that.

He turned the radio up a little, and concentrated on his driving the rest of the way to Los Angeles. Jenny had slept most of the way. She woke up just as they pulled into town. "Wow! This is a big city, Dad. You lived here all of your life, right?"

"Yes, I have. You're mom and I met in high school. We both grew up here." They pulled up in front of the small house. "Well, this is it. Here's your new home. It's not much. Certainly not like Sam's spread, but it's home, nonetheless. What do you think?" Jake watched Jen closely, as he opened the door to the house.

Jen stopped and looked around as she entered. Like any typical teenager, she was pretty vague with her answer. "Looks okay. Where is my room? I'm tired."

"Right this way." Jake gestured toward the far bedroom. He flicked on the light. "It doesn't look like much right now, but you can decorate however you like."

"Thanks. I already have some ideas on what I want to do." She reached up and hugged Jake. "I'll see you in the morning then. Good night."

"Night, Jen. If you need me, I'm right next door. The bathroom is right down the hall."

Jen clung to the book, falling into a restless sleep. She tossed and turned, hearing voices in her head. She woke with a start, sitting up in bed. There was a person standing beside her bed, fading in and out. She shook her head, then rubbed her eyes, trying to clear up her vision. She could make out long hair. The figure was wearing pajamas, or something long and flowing. Jen could almost see the vision's mouth moving. Her arms were straight out in front of her, pointing at something. When Jenny looked to where the apparition was pointing, all she saw was the nursery rhymes book, which had fallen on the bed when Jenny woke up.

"What?" She screamed. "It's just this book. There's nothing else there!" The apparition was starting to fade out now. "No, wait! Don't go. Who are you? I want to help you, but I don't understand what you're trying to say. Are you my mom?"

It was gone now. Jen lay back down, exasperated and confused. She lay there for a long time, trying to settle her thoughts. "I need to tell Dad about this. I think I just saw Mom!" She jumped out of bed and hurried to the next room, but slowed her footsteps the closer she got to her dad's room. She was having second thoughts. What if he didn't believe her, or worse yet, thought something was wrong with her? Was something wrong with her?

She turned, and slowly walked back to her room, a sadness coming over her. She didn't know where to go from here. Jen wanted to help these people—really, she did—but she had no idea how, especially all on her own. She was going to call Dr. Stone tomorrow and see what she should do.

Jake called Tony the next morning to let him know that he was back and ready for work. He just needed a couple of days to get Jenny enrolled in high school, and settled into the house. Tony agreed, and told

Jake to take as much time as he needed.

When Jenny came out to the kitchen, Jake was on the phone to the principal of the high school. He hung up the phone. "Good morning, sleepyhead. I was talking to the high school principal on the phone. We can get you enrolled today, isn't that great?"

"Um...yeah, cool. Dad, I need to make a phone call first, okay? I need to call my doctor in Portland. I, um, have some questions I need to ask him. I'll just be a minute, then we can go."

"Is this about these dreams you've been having? If it is, I have a suggestion. I know someone here in Los Angeles that you can talk to if you want to. She's the psychologist for the police department, Dr. Nancy Hall is her name. She can help you get rid of these dreams. If you want me to, I can call her right now."

Jenny was surprised at his words. "I guess that would be okay. I do need someone to talk to. How did you know about my visions?"

"Ann told me about them. I know they're not real, but you can talk to Dr. Hall about all of that."

She turned away from him, tears starting to fall. She knew he wouldn't understand. Jenny suddenly felt very alone.

After getting the tour of the high school, and grabbing a quick lunch, Jenny felt much better. She decided it was as good of a time as any to call Dr. Hall. "Dad, can we call the doctor now? How well do you know her? Will I like her?"

"Sure, we can call her. I don't know her well, but Tony has talked to her. He said she's great. Hold on, I'll get her number from Tony. I really want you to meet him, by the way. He's a great friend, and my captain." Jake got the number and set up an appointment for Jenny for one o'clock the next day.

She was happy to have someone to talk to now. "Can we go to the store? I want to pick up some paint and other stuff for my room. Also, some food for that bachelor pad of yours."

Jake cringed. "Yeah, good idea. Maybe we can stop by the station too, so I can introduce you to everybody. I think I'm going back to work tomorrow. Are you okay with that? Do I need to be there for your meeting with Dr. Hall? Never mind, I'll come and get you and give you a ride."

"It's okay, I can call a taxi. Just give me the address. You know, I am old enough for a car now. I have my license."

"What? Oh boy, what have I gotten myself into! Seriously though, we'll have to practice some driving in this city. Then we'll think about getting you a car."

"Okay, but I have driven in Portland. I think I can handle Los Angeles."

Jake laughed. "We'll see about that."

Jenny was up with her dad the next morning. "I wanted to see you off to work. Dad, did Mom do this? Sitting here at the table, talking to you before work?" She grabbed a piece of toast from the table, munching on it while she talked.

"Yes, she did. Every day. Unless I got called into work in the middle of the night, which happens all the time. We had a good marriage, Jen. I loved your mom very much. I guess we drifted apart because I was never home. I never stopped loving her, I promise you that."

Jake's phone rang right on cue. He looked at Jenny and shrugged. "It's the office. Long here." He was walking out the door and waving at Jen as he talked. "Be right there."

Jen had a great talk with Dr. Hall. She trusted her from the beginning. Jenny told the doctor all about her visions, and her feeling that one of them was her mom. So far, it only happened at night. Dr. Hall explained to her that is probably because her mind is more susceptible while it is resting. Jenny hoped that soon the people would come to her anytime, not just at night. She wanted to help them with whatever they were asking her to do. She was very surprised at how receptive the doctor was to her gift. Jenny felt that Dr. Hall actually believed her. Jenny genuinely liked her.

After her appointment, Jenny decided to walk around Los Angeles a little bit. She liked the city, especially the weather. She took a deep breath, and set about doing some exploring on her own, before calling Jake to come and get her.

Life certainly didn't pull any punches for Jake with this

murder. It was bad, a murder-suicide. The good thing was—if there was such a thing—it was pretty much an open-and-shut case. It looked like the husband shot his wife, then turned the gun on himself. There was definitely nothing good about that, but it was an easy one to solve. That made Jake's job easier.

By the time Jen called, he hoped he was done for the day. He decided to take his daughter out for supper, instead of them having to eat his awful cooking. He knew Jenny learned to cook at the ranch, and she loved it. But this night, he wanted to take her somewhere he and Sara loved to go. Jenny jumped in the car when he pulled up. He still couldn't believe he had a daughter—and a beautiful young lady at that. He was going to have to keep a close watch on those high school boys, that's for sure.

"Well, how was your day?" she asked when she hopped in the car.

"Same old, same old. How was yours? How did your appointment with Dr. Hall go?"

"It was actually pretty good. I really like her. She told me all about how you two ran into each other when you met. That was hilarious! I also called Ann today. She is doing pretty good. She and Sam are keeping busy at the ranch. I miss them already."

"I know, sweetie. We'll go visit them next summer, I promise. Maybe go on that trail ride Sam bragged about. Now, we are going out for supper. I hope you like Chinese food."

"I do like it. Sounds great to me."

Billy was trying really hard to be patient again, but he messed up his last kill when Ann got away. He knew that her luck would only last so long, and he was eager to get back to it. He was busy planning his next chance at killing Ann. It really did take a lot of planning to be as good as he was. Billy was proud of his cunning, outsmarting the cops over two states now. His mama was working on getting out of that hellhole and coming home, so he wanted to make her proud. All of his kills have been special and meaningful in some way, to both of them. He was going to see her tomorrow, and they were going to plan another one. He couldn't wait. He already had an idea how he was going to do it. He just needed names, and Mama had them.

⁂

Jenny went to bed feeling pretty good about her life. She was going to like the high school. Her dad talked about getting her a car, after she proved to him she could drive in Los Angeles. Yawning, she crawled into bed and thought about all the times her mom did the very same thing right here in this house. It made her sad, but it was also comforting. She was going to paint her room tomorrow, and hang up the new curtains they bought. Everything was good.

Jake sat on the couch with the remote in his hand, wanting a drink. He was paging through the files on the serial murders, just like he did almost every night. He was hoping he would see something they missed before. All of the victims were cops, or related to a cop. Some were men; some were women. One strangled; one pushed down a flight of stairs. One drug overdose, and one pushed from a twelve-story building. Then there was poor Mrs. Sax, stuffed into a fireplace chimney, of all things. None of them knew each other. Jake couldn't find any connection between any of them. There was no evidence at the scenes. There had to be some kind of a connection other than law enforcement. Jake just needed to find it, and he wasn't going to quit until he did. He had to admit this guy was good. Jake wondered why the killer took long breaks in between kills. Probably to keep the law guessing. Well, it was working. They were stumped. This guy has to mess up sometime, and Jake was going to be there when he did.

15

Billy arrived at the hospital early for his daily visit with his mother. He was very excited for this particular visit. He was going to learn the name of his latest target.

Life was good. Everything was going forward like clockwork. The final goal was in sight, albeit a little bit different now. Or extended, however you wanted to put it. There was a slight change of plans when Ann escaped, but that was just a minor glitch. Nothing was going to stop them. Not the cops, not the doctors, no one.

Billy whistled as he checked in at the desk and got his visitor pass. He took his time walking to her room, thinking about his plans for this kill. Billy couldn't wait to share his thoughts with his mother. He got to her door and knocked, listening for her familiar, scratchy, voice.

"Come in, son. I know it's you. I could hear your footsteps in the hallway."

He opened the door, and stepped inside the bare, cold room. "Hello, Mother, how are you feeling today?" Billy leaned down for his peck on the cheek.

"I'm not doing well at all, Billy. Doctor Bell is getting wise to my tricks, I'm afraid. He is not going to sign off on my release from this hell hole! I want out of here! You have to do something, darling, I need you."

Billy was surprised at his mother's pleading, it wasn't like her at all.

"What can I do mother? Do you want me to take care of him? Is he next?"

"No! If that happened, I would have to start all over with a new doctor!" She looked at Billy with a glazed expression on her face. He could tell he was losing her. was losing her. "I'm fine, I tell you! Let me out of here!"

"Mother, it's me, Billy. You've confused me with someone else again. Mother, do you remember why I'm here?" He had to straighten her out long enough to get the name of the target. "Stay with me Mother."

A blank stare was all he got from her. "Dammit! Mother, talk to me!"

At that moment, a burly male nurse stepped in to the room.

"What's going on in here, Billy? I heard yelling."

Billy was a little intimidated by the big man, but held his ground. "Nothing, we were just discussing some things, and she blanked out. Have you been giving her new medication or something? She is getting worse instead of better. Why is that? I want to see Doctor Bell right now."

"He isn't in today, and you need to settle down. You're going to upset your mother. She needs to stay calm. Maybe you should leave now."

Billy panicked. He hadn't gotten what he came here for. He wasn't going anywhere. "I'll quiet down, I need to stay with her for a while yet. I just need to sit with her, be with her." He hated groveling, but it was necessary sometimes. "Can I just sit here until she comes to again?"

The nurse thought for a moment, and gave his consent for Billy to stay, leaving them alone in the room.

"Mother, you need to come back to me now. Remember our plans? I need a name. Come on, mother, talk to me." Still nothing, no sign of recognition. "Well, I guess I know why Dr. Bell saw through your act. We need to work on that. But for now, I'll go and leave you alone." Billy leaned over and gave her a quick kiss on the cheek. "I'll see you tomorrow then."

⁂

Jenny was fitting in at the high school, making new friends, and doing well. She just always felt like she was a little different than everyone else. At Portland, she didn't have a dad, and now, she didn't have a mom. It seemed like the only people that she could talk to, were the ones that showed up at random times, wanting her attention, Doctor Hall, and Ann, of course. Her dad had made it abundantly clear that he didn't believe her. He wanted nothing to do with her gift. Jenny kept it to herself, but kept her journal of everything she saw and heard. Doctor Hall agreed with her doctor from Portland about keeping a journal. It helped her understand what was happening to her.

Jenny and her dad were getting along okay, for the most part. That is, when she actually saw him. He wasn't kidding when he said he wasn't home much. When he was there, his head was buried in files from work. Jenny just left him alone, and she did her own thing. Which consisted of homework, and talking to Ann on the phone. She really missed the ranch, and all of the animals. Jenny was beginning to wonder if she had made a mistake, moving to Los Angeles. She really did like the city, it's just that she wanted to get to know her dad, and that wasn't happening. She never saw him.

When Jen called Ann after her homework was done, she shared her feelings with her. "I'm feeling really lonely here, Ann. Dad is never here, and I haven't made any really close friends yet. Everyone here is either into playing sports, or partying, and I'm bored. I wanted to try out for cheerleading, but I didn't get a chance to talk to my dad about it, so I missed tryouts. Did I make a mistake moving here? Nothing is going like I thought it would."

"I know it's hard, Jen. Your mom went through the same thing with Jake. I totally understand what you're going through. You need to talk to Jake, let him know your feelings, before it's too late. Don't give up yet. Do you want me to talk to him?"

"No, I will do it. Maybe he'll be home tonight, and I can talk to him then. Sometimes, I think I need to be a victim myself for him to notice me. It's like I'm not even here."

"Don't even say that as a joke, Jen. It's not funny, not even one little bit. Do I need to come there, or what?"

"I'm sorry Ann, I was just kidding. I'll talk to my dad tonight, I promise. Then, I may decide to move back to the ranch, we'll see. Well, I'd better go, I'll talk to you tomorrow. Good night, I love you."

"I love you too, sweetie. Good night."

Jake did come home earlier than usual that night. He knew that he hadn't been spending much time with his daughter. He was falling into the same old rut that he had with Sara. He made a vow that he wasn't going to do that. Yet here he was, repeating past mistakes.

Jenny was happy to see him. He got a hug, which was something he really missed. Jake talked through misty eyes. "I'm sorry I haven't been here for you, Jen. I promised you I wouldn't do that. And here I am, going back on that promise. I will try harder, I promise."

"I know you're busy Dad, but I have to admit, it's good to have you here now. To tell you the truth, I don't know if I can go on like this. I want to get to know you, but you're never here for that to happen. Do you really want me here, or should I go back to Portland?"

Jake was taken aback by that question. "No, definitely not! I want you to stay here. Do you want to go back there? Is that what you really want to do?"

"Not really. I like it here, it's just that it seems like I'm always alone."

"Well, that's going to change right now. Let's go out and do something fun. Anything you want. Just name it."

Jenny thought for a moment. "Okay, I want to go to my mom's grave. I have a plaque I made in school that I would like to put there. Then, I want you to let me drive around Los Angeles for a while. Oh yeah, and burgers after all of that. How about that?"

"Sounds like a plan to me. Let's go!"

Billy went back to the hospital the next day, hoping his mother would be more coherent. He got lucky, Doctor Bell was there when he arrived. His mother was very sharp, answering all of the doctor's questions, precisely and accurately. Billy stepped into the room just as the doctor was finishing up.

"Well, hello, Dr. Bell. How are things going in here today?"

"Billy, so nice to see you. Your mother is always looking forward to your visits."

"Yes, I enjoy our visits very much, too. Will she be able to go home soon?"

"I'm afraid not, Billy. She had a bad episode yesterday, I can't clear her quite yet. If she continues to make progress, like she did today, I'll certainly consider it."

"Well, she seems good to me right now. I think she is more than ready to go into my care."

Doctor Bell shook his head. "Well, I'm afraid that's not so, Billy. I'll make that decision myself. Until then, she'll be staying right here. Now, if you will excuse me, I have more patients to see."

Billy was not happy, but he let it go for now. "Yes, goodbye Doctor."

Billy waited until the doctor got down the hall, before he spoke to his mother. "*Hmmph*...he certainly thinks highly of himself! Someone should knock him down a few pegs! Anyway, how are you today, Mother? You look well."

"I'm good, but have you taken care of who I told you to? I'm waiting to hear the details. It's all I have to look forward to these days."

"Mother, you fell asleep before you gave me names yesterday. Don't you remember? I didn't get anything done. Will you tell me who it is now? I've been waiting all night."

"What? I fell asleep? Must be this damn medication they have me on. I hate it! I barely remember anything, anymore. Well, after some computer time, I found the perfect people again. Gotta love the Internet! These two are definitely on the hit list. Not only are they partners, but they are married to each other. Do you believe that? Back in my day, that would never have happened! They don't deserve their happiness. We need to show them that it's just wrong, being married to your own partner. Just isn't right I tell you! They'll learn the hard way. Their names are Jack and Susan Martin. Just take care of it for me, will you? You can tell me all about it tomorrow, just don't get caught Billy. If that happens, you're on your own. I can't do anything to help you from here. I think I'm doing good enough to get out soon, don't you?"

"Yes, Mother, I do. I will handle everything. Don't worry, I won't be getting caught. They're too stupid, and I'm too smart, for that. I have a great plan for this one. I'll do a little more research, and surveillance. Then, make my move, at just the right time."

Billy stood to leave. "I'll let you know the details tomorrow, okay? I'd better get started, so I'll see you tomorrow. Goodbye, Mother." He couldn't wait to get started on this one. It was the first time he was going to do two people at one time. This could take some planning. He knew he was up for the challenge though.

❧

Jack and Susan Martin were a good team. In police work, and at home. They had the night shift. They were just biding their time until they would get promoted to working the days. The young couple had only been out of the academy for two years, but had shown great promise in their chosen field. They pulled up in front of the coffee shop, needing the caffeine for their all-nighter. Jack went into the coffee shop, while Sue waited in the car. It was a nightly ritual of theirs. Suddenly, the radio crackled to life, calling them to duty. "Unit 1230, you're needed to respond to Ash park. Just got a 911 call, two campers were accosted on the trail."

Sue picked up the mic and responded. "Ten-four, 1230 responding to the scene."

Jack was just coming out the door, holding two coffees, when Sue waved at him to hurry.

"We just got a call out. Dispatch said that two campers were attacked at the park. Out on the high trail. Hope you wore comfortable shoes."

Jack handed her the coffees, and then started the lights and sirens. "I did, as a matter of fact. Let's go, duty calls."

The park was pretty quiet when they arrived. No other police cars, no sign of the campers.

"Well, number one, why would people be hiking the high trail in the middle of the night; and number two, where are they? This seems odd to me, keep your eyes open for anything unusual.

Sue grabbed the flashlight from the back seat, and started up the trail. "Copy that. You just watch my back, and we'll be okay. Let's head farther up the trail, and see if anyone is there."

The two cops were walking carefully on the narrow trail, calling out for whoever it was that called 911.

"Police! Is anyone there? I don't like this at all, Jack. I'm about ready to turn around. I'm thinking this a crank call. What do you think?"

She turned around to look at Jack, just as she felt a burning sensation in her neck. She went down, dropping her gun and flashlight, as she grabbed at her neck. Without the flashlight, it was pitch black outside. Jack couldn't see his hand in front of his face. He came up behind Sue just as she went down.

"Sue! Are you alright? What happened? Sue, answer me!"

There was no response. Jack turned in a circle, clicking his flashlight on, desperately searching for his wife. A sharp pain in his neck incapacitated him long enough to drop to his knees. Jack kept ahold of his flashlight, and the beam landed on his wife, lying on the trail. He keyed his radio. This is Unit 1230. Officer down! I repeat, officer down!"

Jack crawled over to her, feeling for a pulse. As he reached for Sue, he was stunned again, losing his balance. The last thing he saw, was his attacker bearing down on him. Jack couldn't make his limbs respond. He was helpless, the stun gun totally incapacitating him. The next thing he knew, his wrists were being bound. His attacker then tied the rope to his wife's hands. Jack could feel the man lifting , and dragging them closer to the edge of the cliff. He could hear his grunts, smell his sweat. The next thing Jack could feel was his body hitting trees, rolling down the steep cliff. Then, everything went black.

Jake was really losing his patience, or what little he had left, anyway. If they didn't solve these serial killings soon, he knew the killer would continue his quest. This guy wasn't going to stop on his own.

Jake thought he and Jenny were getting along very well. Ever since their talk, and their night out, things were going good. He decided that he was going to get her a car for Christmas. She did a good job driving in Los Angeles. Jake was going to surprise Jen with a little car as soon as he could get away to do some shopping. It made his stomach hurt a little, to think that just last year, he didn't even know that he had a daughter. Now, he was going car shopping for her. Life sure has its ups and downs, that's for sure.

Jake was just getting ready for bed, when his phone rang. He sighed, and answered it just like he always did. "Long here." It was dispatch, there was a double homicide in the hills over Los Angeles. No sleep for him tonight. "I'm on my way."

Jake peeked into Jenny's room before he left. She was sound asleep. He wasn't going to wake her, so he left a note on the kitchen table, telling her that he got called out.

Jake pulled into the park, looking for the familiar flashing lights of the police cars, and the coroner's van. He spotted them just off the road, in a parking lot next to the trail. There was one car sitting in the lot with no lights flashing. He wondered what that was all about. Pulling up to the nearest car, Jake got out, and made a beeline to the officer standing nearby.

"Well, what have we got here, Don?"

"You're not going to like it, Jake. The squad car here, belongs to LAPD officers, Jack and Sue Martin. Husband and wife team. It sounds like they responded to a call on the trail next to the campgrounds. Last anyone heard from them, was an officer down call. By the time the next squad car got here, they were nowhere to be found. After some searching, we found a flashlight up on the trail. There are two bodies down the cliff. We're presuming it's the two officers. Doc is down there now. You can reach the bodies by following the trail down. There are flood lights set up, so you can find your way."

Jake sighed loudly. "Okay, thanks. I'll find out the rest from Doc."

He looked at the police car as he walked by, wondering who could have blindsided two trained police officers. How in the world could that have happened? Jake carefully made his way to where the crime scene tape surrounded an area that was pretty dense with trees and others foliage. He picked his way down the hill, to where Doc was standing over two bodies.

"Well, what have you got for me Doc? We're going to need hiking gear for this job pretty soon."

"Yeah. Well, it's definitely the two police officers, husband and wife. Looks like they were thrown from the trail about one-hundred and fifty feet above us. Looks like our serial killer struck again. Stun gun marks on both victims. He had to stun the male twice. He may have messed up this time. He tied them together with a rope. I bagged it, and sent it in with forensics. Maybe we'll get some DNA off of it, if we're lucky. I won't know the cause of death until I do a complete autopsy, but I'm guessing the fall killed them. We're just getting ready to remove the bodies now."

"Okay Doc. Wow, I hope we can get something off of the rope. That would be a good start, anyway. I'm going to head up to the sight of the struggle. Being cops, I'm sure they tried to defend themselves. Hopefully, you can find something on the bodies."

Jake turned, and looked back at the two young people, who were just starting their lives together. He shook his head, trying to shake off the sadness that was threatening to bring him down. When he got up to the top of the trail, two CSI's were searching for clues. Looking around, all Jake saw was some scuff marks, and a lot of tracks. There was a flashlight lying on the trail, but nothing else. He knew the answer he was going to get before he even asked, but he had to ask anyway.

"I don't suppose you're finding much up here. Did we get lucky this time?"

The CSI looked up at Jake and shook his head. "Nothing here. The flashlight is standard police issue, and there's no way of getting any evidence from this dirt. Too many tracks to count. I can't figure out why these trained police officers would come up here in the middle of the night. Seems obvious to me that no one should be up here at that time of the night."

Jake bristled at the man's comments. "Those two were doing their jobs, that's all. They responded to a call, and felt obligated to investigate. I'm sure they were suspicious when they got here and didn't see anyone around. I don't suppose there was anyone here to see anything?"

"Nope. The responding officer to Jack Martin's distress call, didn't see anything. No vehicles, or campers, anywhere around. Sorry Jake, can't help you much I'm afraid."

"That's what I figured. Let me know if you find anything at all."

Jake turned, and looked over the cliff, where the two officers fell to their deaths. He shivered a little, as he turned to go back down the trail. Doc was just loading up the bodies when Jake reached the parking lot. Everyone there was very solemn. These two had lost their lives in the line of duty. Jake wasn't going to rest until he caught this guy. His daughter was going to have to be very understanding until this guy was behind bars.

16

It was early morning by the time Jake got back to the office from the crime scene. He headed straight to his desk and dialed Jenny's cell phone.

She answered just before the answering machine picked up. "Hi, Dad. Are you okay? I got your note."

"I'm fine, sweetheart, just tired. I was just checking in, making sure you were up and ready for school. Do you need me to give you a ride? I can come and get you if you want me to."

Jenny laughed. It reminded Jake of Sara. They had the same kind of laugh. "Don't be silly. I can walk. It's only a few blocks away. I'm fine. You just need to take care of yourself. Did you eat any breakfast?"

Jake looked down at the cup of coffee in his hand. "I will. I just walked into the office, so there's not much to choose from, I'm afraid. Anyway, what do you want for supper tonight? I can pick something up on my way home."

"*Hmmm.* How about pizza? I've been craving a good pepperoni and sausage pizza lately."

"Sounds good. I'll be home by six if everything goes good here. If you have your homework done, maybe we could play a game of rummy after supper." Jake looked up as Tony approached his desk. "I have to go, Jen. Have a good day at school. I'll see you tonight. Love you."

"Love you too, Dad. See you later."

Tony spoke as Jake hung up the phone. "Sounds like you and Jenny are getting along well. That's great."

"Yeah, we're still learning a lot about each other, but basically, we're doing okay. As long as I'm home once in a while to spend time with her."

"I hear ya. My kids barely know me. Well, the reason I'm bothering you, is to let you know that Doc is done with the autopsies. He was here all night. I'm almost afraid to go down there. That's why I'll just leave that to you."

"Gee, thanks, Tony. We all know the real reason why you don't want to go down to the morgue, but I'll leave that for another time."

"Shut up and get to work, Long. Let me know what you find out from Doc."

"Will do." Jake stopped in at the restroom, splashed some cold water on his face, and changed his shirt, before going down to talk to Doc. He looked in the mirror, and said a silent prayer that Doc found something they could use this time.

As Jake stepped into the room, he saw two bodies lying on the autopsy tables, covered with a white cloth. The memories of seeing Sara just like that threatened to bring him to his knees. Jake shook it off. "Please tell me you've got something, Doc."

"Actually, I do." Doc Miller was excited, and this made Jake excited.

"What? What is it, Doc? Don't leave me hanging."

"I found some skin cells on the rope that the killer used to tie the victim's hands together. I sent it to the lab. They are working on a DNA profile right now. The two victims died from the fall, and like I said, the stun gun incapacitated them. They didn't have a chance to fight back, Jake. They couldn't move. I can't imagine the fear that they must have felt. Just lying there helplessly, while this madman threw them off of the cliff like a couple of rag dolls."

"I know. It had to be bad, knowing that this guy had complete control over you. Finally though, maybe we can at least have a clue to who this guy is. Now let's hope his DNA is in the database. This evil SOB has to have committed another crime somewhere. This is great, Doc!" Jake ran over and hugged Doc Miller, whooping as he got in the elevator.

Doc shook his head. "I hope your excitement is warranted,

Jake. I really do."

Jake was beyond excited when he walked into Tony's office. "Tony, he finally did it! The bastard screwed up. We got his DNA, Tony. I feel like it's just a matter of time, now. We got him, I just know it!"

"*Whoa*, hang on Jake! I know that's good news, but we still need to do our job. Beginning with notifying the next of kin. I'm sorry to bring your mood down, but I'm leaving that to our lead detective, which is you. Good luck."

"Oh man! I really don't want to do that. It's the worst part of the job. Do you have info on the families?"

Tony handed over a piece of paper. "It's all right here. Why don't you go spend time with your daughter after that and do some Christmas shopping. Clear your mind."

"I may do that. I wanted to buy Jen a car, so I need to go to the bank and see how much of a loan I can get. She's not getting anything fancy, that's for sure."

Notifying the next of kin is not a fun part of the job. When the victims are one of their own, it's personal. Jake vowed to all of the families of the victims that he would find whomever did this, and he meant it. They were all involved in law enforcement somehow, being a wife, mother, son, or daughter. They were all important. These two murders made seven people this crazy, evil person has taken away from their families. Maybe eight, if Sara turned out to be one of those people. Was she killed because he was the lead investigator in this case? Did her murder even have anything to do with this serial killer? If so, that made eight people he has killed, which could mean that Ann, Jenny, and himself were one of those families. He knew how they all felt, even though he wasn't at all sure Sara was one of them. The 'modus operandi,' or MO, was not the same as the other murders. No stun gun was used, as far as they could tell. Her body was too badly burned to be able to see that for sure. As far as Jake knew, he had only killed in LA, but who knows.

Right now, he had to tell a family that they would never see their loved ones again. These people knew what had happened before Jake even opened his mouth. They were cop families, they just knew. They were very distraught, so Jake left them to their grief.

Jake drove to his bank after that to see about a loan. He got approved for a twenty-thousand-dollar car. He figured he should be able to get her a pretty good used car for that. So here he was, car shopping for his daughter. He found one at the second dealership he went to. After signing the paperwork, Jake asked the salesman if he could bring his daughter the day before Christmas Eve to pick it up. He wanted to surprise her. It was all arranged.

Jake had some time before he picked up pizza and headed home. He called Tony on his way back to the precinct. "Tony, have you heard anything from forensics? Any match on that DNA?"

"Good grief, Jake! You know it's way too soon for any results. It'll probably be weeks before we find out anything. How did the notifications go?"

"As good as can be expected. They were heartbroken. Even if they knew getting killed in the line of duty was always a possibility, it didn't help in coping with a loss like that. Well, I'm coming back in for a while. Jen is meeting with Dr. Hall this afternoon, so I want to pick her up."

"Whatever you say, Jake. I'll see you when you get here then."

Jake poured over the files of all of the victims of this serial killer. The files were strewn all over his desk. He even called the Portland police department to ask if they had learned anything new on Sara's death. They hadn't gotten anywhere with that. Nothing had changed on Sara's case, which frustrated Jake immensely. He could relate to the slow going on some murder cases, so he let it go for now. He also called Sam, to check up on him and Ann. They were doing okay. There weren't any attempts on Ann's life, so that was good news.

Jake was frustrated, like he always was when he worked on this case. He didn't know if he had the patience to wait for the DNA results. He looked up when he heard Jenny's voice. "Oh man, I got caught up with work, and didn't look at the clock! I'm sorry, Jen. How did you get here? You didn't walk, did you?"

"Of course she didn't walk." Dr. Hall stepped in the door behind Jenny. "Hello, Jake. Good to see you again."

Jake stood. "Dr. Hall, good to see you too. I'm sorry you had to come all the way down here."

"Don't worry about it. It's not that far out of my way. Besides, it gives me a chance to talk to Jenny some more. Off the record, of course. She's a great girl, Jake."

"Thanks, but I can't take the credit for that. Sara did that all on her own."

"Yes, I'm so sorry for your loss, Jake. From what Jenny says, Sara was a special person."

"She was special. That's what makes this so hard." Dr. Hall stared so hard at Jake he felt like she was reading his mind. "Don't get into my head, Dr. Hall. You won't like what you see."

Nancy Hall smiled at that. "I'll be the judge of that, Jake. Well, I better get home. Bye, Jenny, I'll see you next week. Bye, Jake."

He nodded to the doctor, and frowned when Jenny gave her a hug. After the doctor left, he turned to Jenny. "You seem to be getting pretty close to Dr. Hall. Do you think that's a good idea?"

"I do like her, and yes, I do think it's good for me. Don't you?"

"Yes, I guess I do. You need a female figure nearby, and I like her. Now, let's go get that pizza."

It was such a fun night. Jenny didn't want it to end. She was getting to know her dad, and she could honestly say that she loved him very much. She missed her mom so much, but she was very glad her dad was here. She only wished he would at least try and understand what her gift was all about. Thank God for Dr. Hall. Jenny was so happy to have her in her life. Jenny was learning so much about her gift, and how to use it. She kept a journal of everything she saw and heard. It all was starting to make sense to her. She talked to her mom almost every night, and she thought her grandpa was there too. Jenny didn't know some of the people, but that was okay, she wanted to help them anyway. She just needed a little more time, and she felt that her mom would be more clear on what she was trying to get across to Jenny.

As they ate pizza that night, Jenny decided to bring it up one more time, to try and explain to her dad what she was seeing. "Um, Dad? Can I talk to you about something?"

Jake looked uncomfortable. "Sure, but if this is about some female thing, maybe you should talk to Nancy—I mean, Dr. Hall—or Ann about it. I'm afraid I won't be much help."

Jenny laughed that laugh that reminded him so much of Sara. "No, Dad, it's not that. It's about my gift. I know you don't believe in it, but I need to tell you something. It's important, okay?"

"Jen, I know you think you see and hear dead people, but that's just not possible, okay? I think you're dreaming, just like your mom did. It's okay to talk to Dr. Hall about that, I just don't buy it. I'm sorry."

"But, Dad, you just don't understand. I *can* talk to mom. I see her a lot, and grandpa. Some other people too. You have to believe me! They're asking me for help, and I need you to believe in me in order to help them. Does that make sense?"

"Not really. What would I have to do with it? Listen, Jen, if you need to talk to me, you can. I will always try to help you in any way I can, you know that. I'll try to be more open-minded, but you need to be patient with me, okay?"

Jenny jumped up and gave him a big hug. It brought tears to his eyes. "That's all I can ask for except...well, there is one more thing. Can we get a Christmas tree? Please? I'll decorate it. One thing Mom and I always did together was go out and pick out a tree. Even if we couldn't afford it sometimes, Mom made sure we had one. Then we would decorate it together, stringing popcorn and anything else we could find to put on it. Please, can we, Dad?"

Jake was a little choked up at her description of what their life was like in Portland. If only he could have been part of it. He had to clear his throat to answer. "Of course we can get a tree. The house could use a little Christmas cheer. Let's go find a tree right now. You've got me excited for Christmas for the first time in a long time."

"I wish you could have been in my life sooner, Dad, but you're here now, and I, for one, love it!"

"I do too, Jenny. Very much so. Nothing is ever going to come between us. I meant it when I said I would try to listen to you if you need to talk about your dreams."

Jenny shook her head. He just wasn't willing to admit that they were more than just dreams. Oh well, she had a feeling he would find out soon enough. Her mom said so.

They had so much fun picking out the perfect tree, that Jake almost forgot about the chaos going on in his life. Almost. He kept getting the feeling of being watched the whole time they were getting their tree. When he would look around, there was no one there. *Must be getting paranoid.* He thought to himself as he hauled the tree to his car. "We got a good one, Jen. I can't wait to buy decorations for it now."

"Me too, dad. Let's go get some now, can we?"

Jake couldn't resist the look on her face. She was like a six-year-old, instead of fifteen. He would give her the moon if he could. "Let's go get decorations then, you spoiled kid!" He loved to hear her laugh. "Did you know you laugh just like Sara? You remind me so much of her."

"Why, yes, she does," Billy said, as he watched from the shadows. He had made a decision. He couldn't wait to talk to his mother about it tomorrow.

When Billy arrived at the hospital the next day, he could tell something was wrong.

Dr. Bell met him at the door. "Billy, come into my office please. There's something I need to tell you."

"What is it? Did something happen to my mother? Is she okay?"

"Please sit down, Billy. I'm afraid everything is not okay. You're mother…she took her own life this morning, Billy. Somehow she got ahold of a lot of medication. We think she hoarded them without us knowing. Anyway, I'm afraid she overdosed, Billy. I'm so sorry."

Billy stood up fast, knocking the chair over. "You're lying! She wouldn't do that to me! We had big plans. I want to see her right now!"

"Of course you can see her, but you need to calm down. I'll take you to her now if you want. Come with me."

Billy followed along, numb with pain and shock. This can't be true. She wouldn't leave him all alone. She just wouldn't, he was sure of that. When he walked into the morgue, the doctor pulled the sheet down far enough so Billy could see his mother's face, white as the sheet covering her. Her eyes were closed. He still couldn't believe it.

Billy looked at Dr. Bell. "How could you let this happen? I blame you for this! You were supposed to be taking care of her! If you would have let her come home with me, this never would've happened! You did this and you will pay!" Billy turned and stormed out of the room.

When the DNA results came in a few weeks later, Jake was a little disappointed, though he was not giving up. There was nothing in the database that matched the DNA from the rope. He still felt like it would pay off eventually, but for now, he needed to move on from that. Christmas was this weekend, and he was taking Jenny to get her car. She was going to be very excited about it. He couldn't wait. For now though, he needed to concentrate on solving these murders. He was going to catch a break soon, he just knew it.

When he got home that night, Jenny had supper ready. He actually got to sit down and eat with his daughter, which was rare. "What did you do today, since you're on Christmas break?"

"I cleaned the apartment, talked to Ann and Sam, and wrapped some gifts. How was your day?"

"Same as usual, but I don't want to talk about it. Speaking of Christmas, I have a surprise gift for you. I was gonna wait a little longer, but I want to give it to you now. Come on, we need to drive somewhere to get it." Jake called the lot, and they were open late, so he took Jen to get her car.

"What is it, Dad? This sounds interesting."

When they pulled up to the car lot, Jenny squealed. "You got me a car, didn't you? I can't believe it! Let's go see it." Her door was opening almost before they got stopped.

"*Whoa!* Hang on, let me get stopped first."

Jenny loved her car, like Jake knew she would. She followed him home. They had a nice time, talking, laughing, playing cards, and just being together. Jenny stretched and yawned. "I'm tired, Dad. Must be the excitement of getting my own car. Did I say thank you? I love it! Thanks, Dad."

"You're welcome. Now go to bed before you fall over."

After Jenny went to bed, Jake brought out all of the files from his safe and started looking them over again. Nothing had changed, still not a clue about who this killer is. He decided to try and get some sleep, maybe something would change tomorrow. After putting the files back in the safe, he peeked in on Jenny when he heard her voice. Jake figured she was on the phone with Ann. When he looked in, she was sitting on her bed, holding her book and talking to thin air. "Jenny, who are you talking to? I thought you were sleeping."

Jenny was startled when she saw her dad. "Dad, you scared me! You probably don't want to hear this, but it was Mom. She was just here, Dad, I swear! Dad, can I ask you something?"

Jake sighed, shaking his head, exasperated. "Sure. You can ask me anything, you know that."

"Dad, who is Molly Jones?"

17

"What did you just say?" Jake was shocked. "Where did you hear that name? Did you hear it on the news? That was a long time ago, Jen. You weren't even born yet. There's no way you would've heard her name anywhere."

"Dad, I know you're not going to believe me, but Mom told me about her. Just now. She said something about Molly being the first one. Then you came in and interrupted us. What did she mean by that, Dad? This Molly Jones must be dead if she is communicating with Mom. Tell me more about her please."

"Jenny, I don't know how you learned that name, but I can't tell you much. She was killed years ago. I never could solve the case. It was the start of the downfall of our marriage. I became obsessed with solving the case, and it drove your mom and me apart. Now tell me where you really heard her name. Did you look at my files?"

"No, Dad, I didn't see any files. Mom was here, and she was talking to me. She kept asking about this nursery rhyme book, and mentioned Molly Jones, just before you came in the room. That's the truth, even if you don't want to believe me!" Jenny turned her back to him. She wasn't going to talk anymore.

"I'm sorry, Jen. I'm going to try and understand this better. Maybe there is something to this gift of yours. I don't know where you would've heard that name otherwise. I think it's time I talk to Nancy Hall myself. Until then, I need you to tell me if you hear anything more about Molly Jones, okay?"

Jenny turned back around to face him again. "Thanks, Dad. I guess that's a start anyway. I will tell you if Mom has anything more to say."

Jake left her room more confused than ever. He went to the

kitchen, and opened up his laptop, typing in "paranormal visions" to do some research. He wasn't quite willing to admit it yet, but maybe there was something to this. He was going to call Dr. Hall tomorrow and get more info, but in the meantime, he was going to learn all he could via the Internet.

Jake called Nancy Hall the next morning, hoping she could see him. She had an opening, and he went to her office that morning.

"Well, it's good to see you, Jake. Does this visit mean you are willing to admit that there's a chance your daughter has a gift? You do know I can't talk about her case. It's privileged information, unless she comes in with you, and is willing to discuss it together."

"I know you can't talk about her, but you can tell me what this *gift* consists of, can't you? Just tell me a little of what you think she's going through with all of this. I did some research last night, and have a vague understanding of it, but I'm sure it's different with everyone. Just explain to me how this happens to some people and not others."

"Well, usually this gift is brought down from person to person in a family. It can go back to ancestors from hundreds of years ago. Sometimes, the visions get stronger the more they're passed down through the ages. I happen to think Jenny's gift is very strong. That's about all I'm willing to say, until you come in with her. My next appointment with her is tomorrow. If it's okay with Jenny, why don't you join us?"

"I just might do that. Thanks, Dr. Hall."

Jake's phone rang the minute he stepped out of the doctor's office. "Long here. Okay, what's the address? Oakdale Hospital? A murder in a hospital? Okay, I'm on my way."

Jake headed for the scene, sirens blaring. He thought about Jenny's abilities, or dreams, or whatever they were. After talking with Nancy, and what transpired last night, he was starting to believe more and more in her gift. He didn't know how she could have heard of Molly Jones, unless it was on the news lately. But Jake didn't think it was—not that he knew of anyway. He was going to check up on it just to make sure, though he didn't think Jenny would lie to him.

He pulled up to the hospital, surveying the scene. The murder looked to have happened in the parking lot. The yellow crime scene tape was strung around a Lexus parked in the lot. Jake noticed that he actually beat Doc there this time. That was a first. He looked around for the responding officer. Seeing him standing by the Lexus, Jake headed that way. "What've we got here?"

"Looks like a shooting, multiple shots to the head and chest. Have to wait for Doc to be sure who it is, but the car is registered to a Dr. Aaron Bell. He works at the hospital here. Oakdale is a psychiatric hospital, so the perp could be a patient, hard to tell. Here comes Doc Miller now."

Jake turned when he heard Doc pull in. "Good. First thing we need to do, is find out who this is for sure, then we'll take it from there."

Doc Miller shuffled up to the car and peeked in. "Well, looks like a shooting. Any idea who it is?"

"That's what we were waiting for you to tell us. We didn't want to touch the body until you got here, but the car is registered to a doctor from this hospital."

"Okay, can you help me lift him a little bit? I'll look in his back pocket for a billfold." While Jake lifted the body, Doc rummaged around and found a wallet. "Okay, ID says Dr. Aaron Bell, and yes, he works here at Oakdale Psychiatric Hospital."

"Well, that answers that question. I'll go in and ask some questions, see what I can find out." Jake turned to the responding officer. "Who found the body?"

"One of the nurses called it in. Says he came out after his shift, and saw Dr. Bell's car sitting here. He thought he'd better check it out. That's when he saw him dead inside."

Jake saw the burly nurse standing by the door to the hospital. "Wow! They must get some messed-up patients in here to need that big of a nurse. I'll talk to him on my way in. Thanks."

The big man looked up when Jake stepped in front of him. "Hello, I'm Detective Long, homicide. Could I ask you a few questions?"

"Sure. I can't tell you much though, never saw anything, really. No other cars in the lot but his and mine. The next shift parks in the employee lot. I park here, because this door is the only one I have a key for."

"I see. What time did you get off work, Mister..."

"Boyd, Chester Boyd. I was done at six in the morning. Dr. Bell always leaves at ten every night, like clockwork. That's why I thought it was weird when his car was still here at six a.m."

Jake wrote some notes in his book as he talked. "Okay, will you stick around, Mr. Boyd? I may have more questions later."

"I need to get home. My wife will wonder where I'm at."

"Please give the officer here your address then. Don't go on any extended vacations. Thank you."

Jake looked around the door when he got done talking to Mr. Boyd. There were surveillance cameras at the entrance, which will definitely help. If they covered the whole parking lot, and not just the entrance. Jake pressed the buzzer to gain entrance into the building, and waited for a response.

The speaker crackled to life in just a few minutes. "Yes, can I help you?"

"Yes, this is Detective Jake Long of homicide. I need to talk to the rest of the employees please."

"One moment, detective."

There was a click, and the heavy doors opened on their own. Jake felt like he was entering a prison when he walked through the doorway. Another huge man greeted him as he walked in. Jake introduced himself.

"Detective Long, I'm Byron, the day nurse. How can we help you?"

"First, I need to see the footage from the cameras covering the parking lot. Then, I need to talk with the director of this facility."

"Of course. I'll call Director Sims right away. We're all devastated by Dr. Bell's death. We'll do anything we can to help. While you're talking to the director, I'll get security to get you the tapes you wanted."

While Byron made the phone call to the director, Jake looked around the sterile environment. It was a sad-looking place, devoid of anything on the walls or floors. Everything was white. Just white. He held back a shiver as Byron finished his call and came toward him. "The director will see you now. Follow me, I'll show you to his office."

Byron opened another door with a key card he kept around his neck. When they walked through the doors, it was like walking into another world. Soft beige-colored walls were covered with artwork, surrounded by two large offices. The carpet was a dark brown, and there was a large desk in each office. Byron led him to the office on the right, where a balding, bespectacled man stood when they entered.

"Detective Long, I'm Director Corbin Sims. I just want you to know we are all deeply saddened by the loss of Dr. Bell. He was a great asset to this hospital. Please, sit down, detective. Can I get you anything? Coffee? Water maybe?"

"No, thank you, Mr. Sims. I just have a few questions for you, then I'll leave you to your work. Exactly what kind of patients did Dr. Bell see?"

"I'm afraid his patients were the worst of the worst, mostly people who were never going to get out of here. They were usually sent here instead of prison. Those were the ones Dr. Bell wanted. He called them a *challenge*."

"I see. Could one of them have done this to the doctor? Have any been released lately? How about a relative of a patient who may have held a grudge against him?"

"There is no one who has been released that comes to mind right now, so I would have to say no on that one. There aren't too many relatives who visit, so probably not that either."

Jake knew this was a long shot but he thought he'd try anyway. "Could I get a list of Dr. Bell's patients?"

The director was shaking his head before Jake even got the question out. "I'm afraid you would need a warrant for that, detective. We can't give you names of patients. They have a right to their privacy."

"I understand, director. I'll be getting that warrant. Well, I guess that's all for now then. Could I talk to the staff now? I would like to find out if anyone saw anything odd this morning. Also, Byron was going to get me the footage on the camera outside the door to the parking lot."

"Certainly. I'll call down and have the staff come in to answer your questions. I believe the footage is in the lobby right now, but it probably won't help you. It only shows the door and part way into the lot."

"That's fine. I want to look at it myself anyway. Thanks for your cooperation, director.”

“Anything we can do, just ask, detective. We’re all very upset by this turn of events.”

Byron showed up at the door almost as if he never left. “I’ll show you back out, detective.”

“One more thing, director. How many people have these key cards to the building? Do they open all of the doors?”

“Only employees have keys, and no, not all of them open all doors. Only a certain few of us have a master key.”

“Can I get a list of employees, and which keys they have please?”

Certainly. I’ll have it waiting for you in the lobby.”

Jake turned, and followed Byron out the door. He couldn’t wait to get out of this place. It was just too sterile and cold for him.

There were about ten people waiting in the lobby when Jake got there. He questioned them all, but no one was here when Dr. Bell left last night. He learned that they kept a skeleton crew on hand while the patients slept, which made sense to him. Jake would need to come back to talk to them. Byron handed him the surveillance video from the night before, and Jake left the hospital, hoping there was some evidence on the flash drive. Everyone was gone from the crime scene by the time he got back out there, so he headed back to the office, flash drive in hand.

Jake didn’t waste any time getting to his computer. He popped in the flash drive, impatiently waiting for it to open. When it did, Jake could see the door to the hospital, but he couldn’t see Dr. Bell’s car in the lot. “Damn! No video of the crime scene.” He kept watching. When it got to 9:50 p.m., he saw Bell leaving through the door. The doctor stepped out, and was startled by something, or someone. “Now this could get interesting.” Doctor Bell was talking to someone standing off camera. It was almost like the person knew how far the camera’s lens reached. It looked like there was an argument going on, as Dr. Bell put his hands up, and started walking toward his car. Then, nothing. Jake couldn’t see anything that happened after that. “Well, that didn’t do me any good. I need to get that warrant for the patient list.” He dialed the district attorney and requested a warrant, only to be told it could take a while. Doctor-patient confidentiality was a big deal. “Well, do what you can, okay? I need that list!"

Jake was totally drained when he finally got caught up enough to go home. Jenny wasn't there when he got home, so he called her cell phone. "Where are you, young lady?"

"I'm just having ice cream with some friends from school. I tried calling you earlier, but you didn't answer. I'll take off right now, and be home in fifteen minutes, okay? Sorry, Dad, but I did try to call."

"Okay, but we need to set up some ground rules about you taking off like that without letting me know. I'll talk to you when you get home. Drive carefully."

Jake didn't like the fact that Jen took off like that. Anything could happen to her. There is a serial killer out there. He didn't see a missed call either, so she lied about calling him.

When Jenny got home, he was waiting for her at the kitchen table. "Come and sit down for a minute please. Listen, I got you a car so you could be more independent, but you need to let me know if you go off on your own. This is a dangerous city, with dangerous people. I don't know what I'd do if something happened to you too."

"I know, and I'm really sorry, Dad, but I just get so lonely sitting here alone all day. Tomorrow is Christmas Eve, will you be working?"

Jake ran his hand through his hair. "It's Christmas Eve already? I have to work. We had a murder today, but I'll try and be home Christmas Day, deal?"

"Deal. Can I go get some groceries tomorrow? So we at least can have a meal on Christmas Day?"

"That would be fine. Just call me when you leave, and when you get home. I'll go get you some money. Why don't you order some food from our favorite restaurant."

Jen rolled her eyes. "I will."

By the time Jake got to work the next day, he was getting a call from Doc Miller. "Jake, I expedited the autopsy on our Dr. Bell since it's Christmas tomorrow. Come on down when you get here. I have something interesting to show you."

"Will do, Doc. I'm just pulling up now, be there in a few." It didn't take Jake very long to get to the morgue. He was ready for some good news.

"You weren't kidding when you said you'd be here in a few, Jake. Well, I won't waste any time either then. Come over here."

"What am I looking at, Doc?"

"Look closely at his neck, Jake. Tell me what you see." Jake leaned in a little closer. "All I see are bullet holes. You're going to have to point this out to me if it's something other than that."

Doc grinned. "I almost missed it myself, so don't feel bad, Jake. It took a magnifier to see it, but there are burn marks on his neck."

Jake looked at where Doc was holding the magnifier and light. "Well, I'll be damned! He may have been killed by our serial. What the hell! He's not in law enforcement, is he?"

"I don't know. That's your job to find out, not mine. But I have to say, I really doubt a doctor would be in law enforcement...Unless he's related to somebody, like some of the others were. You know, just because a stun gun was used, doesn't make it our serial killer. I mean, how hard is it to get a stun gun?"

"Well, it depends on what kind of stun gun it is. Some do require a permit. We already looked into that angle, nothing there. Wow! I mean, *wow*. I must admit, I didn't see this one coming. We need that list of patients, now more than ever. Excuse me, Doc, I need to make a phone call."

Jake rushed upstairs and dialed the number for the district attorney. "Listen, I need that warrant. This guy was killed by our serial. I really do need that warrant...like, yesterday."

"Jake, are you forgetting it's the holidays? No judge is going to sign off on this until after the New Year probably. I'm sorry, I'll do my best, but it's more than likely not going to happen anytime soon."

Jake was so frustrated when he hung up the phone. He really wanted to throw something. Tony could see Jake's anger brewing from his office. He thought he'd better intervene before something bad happened.

"I could see the smoke coming out of your head all the way from my office. What's going on, Jake? You okay?"

"No, I'm not okay, Tony. Now, the time of year is working against me with this serial case. I finally could get somewhere, and even the judges are taking a holiday. I don't get it, Tony. Murder doesn't take a holiday, so neither should we!"

"Listen, sometimes things just don't go the exact way we want them to. It doesn't mean that it isn't going to happen. It's just going to take a little more time. We're going to get this guy, I can feel it. He can only get by with this for so long before he screws up. Now go home, and take tomorrow off to be with your daughter. This case will still be here when you get back. Merry Christmas, Jake."

"I know, but maybe I should go back to the hospital, try to sweet-talk the director into giving me that list of patients. Maybe I could use the Christmas thing to persuade him."

"No way! You stay away from there, you hear! It'll probably make it worse if you go over there now. Come on, I'll help you organize these files. Maybe between the two of us, we'll see something we missed before."

Jake sighed, "Okay, fine. I'm not happy about it, but I do have to agree with you."

They worked later than Jake meant to. He started gathering up the files, when his phone rang. He answered without even looking at the caller ID. "Yeah, Long here."

"Dad, where are you?"

"Jenny, are you all right? What's wrong?"

"Nothing's wrong, Dad. I really need to talk to you right now. Are you coming home soon?"

"I'm on my way, hang tight." Jake rushed to his car, and sped home, not caring if he got stopped. His little girl needed him. He slammed his car door, running to his door, slamming it against the wall when he opened it.

"Jen! Jenny, where are you?"

"I'm back here, Dad. In my room."

Jake was relieved to see her sitting on her bed, but she looked as though she had been crying. "What is it, Jenny? Why are you crying?"

She looked at him with tears streaming down her face. "Dad,

Mom was just here! Grandpa too. They gave me another message. Mom said that if you needed some persuasion whether or not this is true, she wanted me to tell you, she loved every moment of your honeymoon even if it was only in room three-twenty-one. I don't even want to know what that means, but she said you would understand."

Jake was flabbergasted. No one would know that room number except for him and Sara. It was kind of a private joke between the two of them. Three-two-one was code for, *I want you, now!* He stared at Jenny. *It was true! She was talking with Sara!* Jake didn't know where to go from here, but he had to solve these murders. If Sara and Joe wanted to help, then so be it.

He plopped down on the bed next to Jenny. "Okay, I give up. You've convinced me. Tell me what Sara and Joe said to you."

18

Jenny breathed a huge sigh of relief. "Finally, you believe me! Mom said you would come around." She got more excited as she talked, the tears gone now. Jenny opened her journal, and started reading. "Well, I didn't quite understand what Mom and Grandpa were saying, but maybe you will. Two other people are communicating with them, and these two people have a vague description of who they say killed them. Dad, it's got to be this serial killer, right?"

"Okay, settle down. Tell me what they said, word for word."

"Well, they said this guy is pretty big—maybe six foot one, or six two—in good shape, and has sandy-brown hair and brown eyes. That's all they could see before he stunned them. Does that mean he used a stun gun, Dad, or were they surprised? I didn't get it. What does a stun gun do?"

"Well, I'll be!" The police had purposely kept that from the public eye. No one knew about the stun gun. That information just solidified his belief in Jenny's abilities. "Well, a stun gun is used to completely destroy the ability to move. Basically, you are paralyzed. It's a very good weapon for someone wanting to incapacitate their victim, rendering them helpless. So, that's all they said about how he looked? No tattoos or any other features that would make him stand out?"

"Mom didn't say, but I think she wanted to tell me more before you came in the room. I'm sure she'll have more to say, and so will Grandpa. I mean, it's not like I can call them. I have to wait for them to contact me. Sometimes I go a few days before I even see them again. I'm sorry, Dad. I really didn't help much, did I?"

Jake sat down and reached over to hug his daughter. "You did great, Jen! I just want to say that I'm sorry I didn't believe you before now. From here on out, we are going to work as a team, to gain as much information as we can from these visions of yours. Together, got it?"

"Together. Thanks for believing in me, Dad."

Christmas Day went off without a hitch. It was just the two of them. Sam and Ann called; so did Tom. Jake didn't hear from his brother Tom very often. He figured Tom was just as busy as he was. Jake really wanted him to meet Jenny though. One of these days, he and Jenny were going on a vacation.

Jake helped as best he could with the meal, but a cook he was not. Jenny did a great job, and their dinner was wonderful. After some Christmas movies, and opening a few gifts, they were both tired. Jake looked over just as Jenny yawned.

She grinned when he yawned too. "They're catchy, aren't they?"

"Yes, yawns are always that way. What a great day. I'm so glad I got to spend it with you rather than at the office. I really just wish your mom could've been here."

"Me too, Dad. I'm really missing my mom, but she is here, in a way. I'm really glad I've got you." She leaned down and gave Jake a hug. "Well, I'm going to bed. Are you going in to work tomorrow?"

"Yes, I want to run those descriptions you gave me through the database and see if anything pops up. They're pretty vague so I kind of doubt anything will, but it's worth a try anyway."

"Maybe more will come to me tonight, if we're lucky. You know, I kind of like this detective stuff. It's kind of fun."

"Well, fun isn't exactly how I would look at it, but there certainly is some satisfaction to it. Now go to bed, sleepyhead. Wake me up if you see your mom tonight, okay?"

"I will. I'll write everything in my journal too."

No one came to Jenny that night, so she slept soundly. Only waking up when she smelled bacon cooking the next morning. She got up and trudged out to the kitchen, rubbing her eyes. "Morning, Dad. Well, nobody visited me last night. It's funny. Now that I would like them to come to me, they don't. I wish I understood this a little better. Not even the doctors can figure it out."

Jake looked up from the breakfast he was cooking. "Good morning! Listen, I don't want you worrying about your abilities. If it comes, it comes. If it doesn't, it doesn't. Either way, I will catch this guy. I know that it's just a matter of time. We got his DNA. We just need someone to compare it to."

Jenny yawned. "Gosh, why am I so sleepy. I slept really good last night, never woke up once. I think I'll just hang out here today, maybe take the tree down."

"Sounds good. I would rather you stay close to home anyway. If this guy is hurting people because of me, I don't want you taking off on your own unless you have to."

"What do you mean? Why would he be hurting people because of you? Wait a minute! Do you think he killed mom? Oh my gosh! Did he, Dad?"

"Hold on a minute. I don't know if he did or not. It just seems like too much of a coincidence for her to die in a fire. I honestly don't know what to think. There are still no leads on your mom's death. It bothers me, that's all. I don't believe in coincidences."

Jenny sat down on the nearest chair when Jake set a plate in front of her. "Wow! I guess I never thought it could be a serial killer. Mom didn't have any enemies, but I guess you do. So is that why you think Ann and I are in danger too?"

"Yes, you need to always be aware of your surroundings. Call me if you even think someone is following you, or watching you. Promise me you won't take any unnecessary chances."

"I will, Dad. I'll be super careful, I promise."

"Good. I don't mean to scare you, but until this guy is caught, I don't know who could be next." Jake looked at his watch. "I'd better get to work. I'll see you later tonight. Call me if you need anything, okay?"

"I will, Dad. You be careful too, okay?"

When Jake got in to work, Dr. Hall was waiting for him at his desk. She stood when she saw him walking toward her. "Good morning, Jake."

"Good morning, Nancy. What brings you here this morning?"

"Well, the last appointment Jenny and I had, she gave me her consent to talk to you. So, I thought I'd stop in and tell you that in person."

Jake was happy Jenny trusted him enough to give her consent. "Well, I'm glad she did that. I think some of the things she has talked to you about could help me understand this thing better. Maybe even help solve this case."

"I agree, Jake. I want you to know that I will do whatever I can to help. Where do we start?"

"We start at the beginning. How long has Jen been having these dreams, or visions?"

"As far as I can tell, she was around ten when they started. She hid it from her mom until she was twelve. That's when her mom heard her in the middle of the night. It was then, that Sara shared her abilities with Jenny too. She also told her about how her parents died, and about her and Ann's life after that. Jake, I need to ask you something. You don't have to tell me, but it may help Jenny in the long run. Exactly what happened between you and Sara? Did you break up because of Sara's abilities?"

"No, not at all. I didn't even know about Sara's abilities. She never told me about them, not that I would've understood, or believed her, anyway." Jake thought for a minute before he decided to tell Dr. Hall the truth. "Sara left me because of my job. She never wanted me to be a homicide detective. Her father was a detective, and she knew what the job entailed. I was so stubborn, and a little cocky, I guess. I thought she could handle it. Being in homicide was all I ever wanted. I guess I was being selfish. But, looking back now, she had her mind made up from the beginning, I think. Not that she didn't try, she did. It just wasn't meant to be, I guess. I think her getting pregnant with Jenny was the final straw. She always said that she wasn't going to raise a child the same way she and Ann were raised. Her dad was never home, and her mom was always alone, crying all night. I don't blame her for leaving, really. It was probably for the best."

Nancy was listening intently, and waited until Jake was done before she commented. "Well, it's never good to go into a marriage with doubts. But, it sounds like you genuinely loved each other—probably never stopped loving each other. Sometimes, people who care that much about each other, just can't live together. For whatever reason. Not everyone is capable of sharing a home, and the feelings of doubt creep up when you least expect it. I think Sara wanted to tell you about your daughter. She just didn't get the chance, with her life being cut short before she could."

"Yes, according to Ann, that's true. Doesn't really make it any easier though. I should have been there for Jenny's first steps, her first Christmas, her birthdays. But I wasn't there, was I?" Jake shook his head. "The Sara I knew, wouldn't have kept my daughter from me, unless she had a very good reason. I'll never know for sure what that reason was now."

"To tell you the truth, I would have to say that Sara felt that your job was a good enough reason to keep Jenny away. From what Jenny says, her mom was sad through most of the years they spent in Portland. She did miss you, Jake."

"Yeah, well, I missed her too, but she still should have told me about Jenny. I'm having a tough time forgiving her for that."

"Well, for your daughter's sake, you need to do just that. In your own time, you will." Nancy stood up to leave. "I have another appointment, but you can call me anytime you need to, okay?"

Jake stood up with her, reaching out his hand. "I will, and Nancy, thank you for your help with Jen and me. I want you to know I appreciate it."

Tony stepped out of his office when he noticed Nancy leaving. "Jake, could you come in here a moment?"

Jake waved to Nancy and headed his way. "What's up, Captain?"

Tony shut the door behind Jake. He looked like he had something serious to talk about.

"I just got a call from the commissioner. The FBI called, and offered their help in the serial case. They're sending a profiler in to do a profile on this guy so, hopefully, it will help somehow. I don't know if I believe in that stuff, but the commissioner evidently does. I want you to play nice with this guy, give him what he needs from the files, and let him do his job. Who knows, maybe it will help."

Jake sat up straighter in his chair. "You know, Tony, just a month ago, I would have told you to tell the profiler to go home, and don't even bother coming here. But, things have changed since then. I can't share with you right now what is going on, but let's just say my mind has opened up a lot where this stuff is concerned. Besides, we need all the help we can get with this case. Let me know when the profiler gets here, I'll be more than willing to listen to what he has to say."

Tony was a bit shocked by Jake's answer. "Okay, well, that was easy. I expected to have a fight on my hands. I had my speech all written up. You never cease to amaze me, Jake. I'll let you know when he gets here." Just then, Tony pointed toward the door, where a tall, well-dressed man walked in, tucking his sunglasses into his front pocket. "Looks like he just got here. Definitely looks like a federal agent. You can spot them a mile away, I swear."

Jake laughed. "Yeah, you can. Well, here goes nothing."

"Now remember what I said, play nice."

"I will. I'm ready for this case to get solved, and willing to try anything to do it."

Tony made a face at him. "Wow, that daughter of yours has softened you up a bit. I must say, I like it. Good luck with the fed."

Jake had to agree with Tony on that one. His daughter had changed him, in a good way. He headed over to introduce himself to the agent, and put him to work on the profile. He shook hands with the man. "I'm Detective Jake Long, in charge of this investigation. Welcome to Los Angeles."

"Thank you, detective. I'm Agent Beau Torrey, profiler and all-around good guy."

Jake laughed. "Well, that's good to know, Agent Torrey. I haven't been accused of that lately, but I'm glad you are. It'll help us get along better. Have a seat right here. I'll get you the files you need."

The agent's eyebrows rose. "Well, right down to business, huh? Okay, detective, no fooling around. I get it."

Jake plopped the large stacks of files on his desk. "This is what we've got on the murders. There could be more victims of this guy out there for all we know. Maybe some of these aren't his, but from the evidence we've gathered, we think he's killed seven people. Most of them are related to law enforcement in some way. All killed differently, but a stun gun was used in each one. Anyway, I'll let you read the files and form your own opinion. Let me know if you have any questions."

"Thanks, detective. You know, a lot of people are skeptical about profiling, but it's been proven over and over again. It really does help in solving tough cases. I'll do my very best to get in this guy's head. I'll let you know when I've finished the profile."

Jake nodded, sitting down at his desk to make some phone calls. The first person he called was the district attorney. "Jim, have you made any headway on that warrant? I need it right now. I know it will help this case."

"I haven't gotten to a judge yet with the request, Jake. This takes time. I'll let you know when I get it."

"Dammit! I need that warrant! Can't you speed it up somehow? This is a serial killer, Jim. It's just a matter of time before he kills again. Now get me that warrant!" Jake slammed the phone down on the receiver and stalked out of the station. He had to get out of there.

"Damn paper pushers! I can't just sit around waiting for a piece of paper telling me what I can and can't do." He revved up his car and headed to Oakdale. The same nurse let him in the door. "Byron, right?"

"Yes, Detective Long. How can I help you today?"

Listen, I need some information. I know you can't give me patient names. But you can at least tell me if anything out of the ordinary happened around here at the time of Dr. Bell's murder."

Byron threw his head back and laughed. "Something out of the ordinary? You do know where you're at, right?"

Jake didn't find anything amusing about his question. "Yeah, I do know. I'm somewhere people are supposed to get help, somewhere people should feel safe—even the doctors—not killed in their own cars. Now answer my question."

Byron sobered up at Jake's chastising. "I'm sorry. I'll help if I can. I just don't know how much I can say, but I will tell you this. There was a suicide not long before Dr. Bell's murder. That isn't so unusual, but the reaction of a relative was. He threatened the doctor, and blamed him for his mother's death. I can't give you any names, but I really thought you should know."

Jake was even more determined after hearing this news. "Thank you for telling me, Byron. It does help. If you have anything else, you be sure to call me. I'll be back with that warrant, and you *will* let me know who threatened Dr. Bell." Jake gave him another one of his cards and left the hospital. He had more information than he went there with, and it did help.

While driving back to the police station, he called Jenny to check up on her. Everything was good there. Jen was just, "chilling out with a book," which were her words, not his. He couldn't wait to get back and see if that profiler had gotten anywhere. He really wasn't going to hold his breath that it would do any good. After what he's gone through with Jenny's gift so far, he was going to keep his mind open. Jake was surprised that when he got back, Agent Torrey was done with the profile already. Jake picked up the file. "Wow, that didn't take you long! Can you summarize this for me?"

"It's a little hard to summarize it. I would rather you read the report."

"I don't have time right now to read the whole report. Just tell me what it says please."

"Okay, but you need to read it too. Deal?" Jake agreed. Agent Torrey gave him the rundown on this crazy person's personality. "First, this guy is probably thirty to forty years old, white male. Probably a big man, to have been able to subdue trained police officers. He is probably a mama's boy, an only child. With no father in the picture, more than likely. He feels bitter about that, I'm sure. He lives alone, or with his mother, no other woman in his life. I don't think this guy can hold a relationship with anyone but his mother. He obviously has some vendetta against the police. Maybe his father was arrested, or has spent time in prison. That's why the father isn't in his life, would be my guess. This guy is very intelligent, having outsmarted the police all these years. He started killing when he was pretty young, probably small animals. He gets great satisfaction from every kill, maybe even sexual satisfaction. If you're going to catch this guy, you need to look at single men, living in a home with a parent in prison. Maybe he could even be a cop himself, or the dad could be a cop. That's as close as I could get with the profile. I hope it helps, detective."

"I hope so too, Agent Torrey. I'll hand this over to Tony. We'll work on it together. You have given us some good ideas to follow up on, thank you."

"You're welcome. If you need the agency's help on this, let us know. We would be glad to give you a hand."

Jake stood, shaking Agent Torrey's hand. "We will keep it in mind, but I think we've got this. It was nice working with you."

After the agent left, Jake took the file into Tony's office. "This is what he came up with for a profile. He has a few good clues in there. You look it over and tell me what you think."

"Will do, Jake. Don't worry, we're going to figure this out, come hell or high water."

"I know, Tony. I know that I'm starting to sound like a broken record, but we need to figure this out before anyone else dies. Let's hope that happens, and soon. In the meantime, I'm going to go home and hug my daughter."

Minutes later, Jake walked into a spotless apartment. It hadn't been that clean in a long time. Jenny was sitting in the recliner, book in hand. "Well, you look comfortable. Good book?"

"Yeah, it's pretty good. Just something I have to read for school. What do you want for supper?"

"Let's go out. The apartment is too clean, I don't want to dirty it up."

"Cool. I'm ready, let's go."

They left the apartment arm in arm, going out to enjoy their time together. Trying to forget about some madman stalking Los Angeles.

19

Billy just couldn't muster up the energy to leave the house. After burying his mother, he just kept spiraling downward, into an abyss. Not even the thought of planning his next kill could cheer him up. How was he going to do this without his mother? Without her, he was nothing—a nobody. Just some guy who never really quite grew up. He just wasn't sure he even wanted to go on.

The days went by, with still no word from the district attorney on the warrant they needed to get the list of Dr. Bell's patients. Jenny hadn't had any more contact with Sara, or Joe either. It just seemed like everything about this case was at a standstill again, Jake was getting very impatient. All they could do was go over and over what they already had, which was next to nothing. There were so many strange things about these murders. The first one, Molly Jones, had pins and needles in her body. What was up with that? Another was missing a foot. This guy had to have taken it as a trophy. Jake was beginning to doubt himself. Had they all been killed by a serial killer? Molly was the wife of a cop, Harvey Anderson was a former cop, Martin Parker was a cop's son, and in the police academy. Ryan Sands was a cop, Mary Sax was a wife of a drug enforcement agent, and Jack and Sue Martin were two rookie cops. They were all incapacitated with a stun gun. The two cases that really confused Jake was Sara, (no stun gun, but she was his wife) and Dr. Bell, (had stun gun marks, but wasn't involved in police work). Jake wasn't sure if these two murders were connected with the serial killer, but he had a feeling they were.

Jake stood in front of the murder board, staring at the faces of the people this nutcase took away from their loved ones. He shook his head when Tony came up beside him. "I don't know, Tony. I just feel like we're missing something here. Do you think we are ever going to solve this?"

Tony let out a long sigh. "Yes, I do think we will. We're nothing if not persistent. We'll get him."

"Well, I hope it's soon, I don't know how much more of this I can take." Jake sighed, turning back to walk to his desk. "I made a list of some of the weird things about these murders, like the pins and needles, missing foot, fireplace chimney, and posing on a wall. Those things tell me, that this guy had to have planned for a while, before committing these murders. That's probably why he waited so long between kills sometimes. You know, maybe he had help. If there are two murderers, all he had to do was the actual killing. Maybe whoever is helping him, is along for the kill, and helped him carry them out. I don't know. I think it's a possibility."

"Maybe, but I get the feeling he doesn't want to share the spotlight with anyone. He's too egotistical for that."

"I guess so. Anyway, I guess we'll keep plugging along the way we are, until something breaks in the case. It's getting late, I think I'll head home. Good night, Tony."

"Good night, Jake. Try forgetting about this case for a while. Take it easy."

Jake walked through the door of his apartment, tired, and a bit cranky. Jenny bounced over and gave him a big hug. "Hey, Dad! How was your day?"

Jake hugged her back. It made him feel better having someone to come home to. "It wasn't too good, Jen, but it's better now. Getting a hug from you definitely helps. What did you do in school today? Everything good?"

"Oh yeah. You know, same old, same old. Did you eat supper? I ate with some friends already, but I can fix you something."

"I'm fine, I ate earlier. Let's just veg out in front of the television for a while. I'll make us some popcorn."

"Sounds good. I get to pick the movie." Jenny bounded off, grabbing the remote. Jake made popcorn. The rest of the night was spent zoning out to a good movie.

When the movie was over, Jenny yawned and stretched. "I'm tired. I think I'll go to bed. Good night."

"Good night, Jen. Sleep tight."

It was late, but Jake couldn't sleep…again. He walked over to the liquor cabinet, staring into it. He rubbed his hands down his face. Oh, how he wanted a drink. Jake slowly opened up the cabinet and drew out a bottle of whiskey. Setting it down on the table, he grabbed a glass from the cabinet. His hands shook, as he poured the whiskey into the glass. Just before Jake could raise the glass to his lips, he heard Jenny cry out. Jake rushed into her room, not knowing what he was going to find.

Jenny was sitting up in her bed. "Dad, Grandpa was just here! He was talking to me, clear as day! I knew if we were patient, they would come back."

Jake tried to hold back his excitement. "Okay, that's great, Jen. Tell me what Joe said, word for word."

"He said something about his past being related to these murders. You need to look at his past cases, or something. He said to look for some notebook. I don't know what that means, do you?"

"A notebook? I'm not sure what that is, but I can look at his past cases. That's a while back, but I'll see what I can do there. I don't know if they keep case files for that long. This is good, Jen. Real good. It could be the break we've been waiting for. Was that all he said?"

"Yes, that's it. Do you really think it might help? I sure hope so."

"I think it will. Now try and get some sleep. I'm going to go to work early tomorrow, so I probably won't see you in the morning. Be careful going to school, okay?"

Jenny hugged her dad. "I will, Dad. I'll be careful."

Jake went back out to the living room and spotted the glass, still full of whiskey, sitting on the table. He went over to it, picked it up, and dumped it down the sink. He was actually feeling hopeful for the first time in a long time.

Jake didn't get any sleep. He was at the police station bright and early the next day. He rushed into Tony's office. "Tony, I need all of the case files, and anything that was left in the desk, of Joe Olsen. Don't ask me any questions, it's just a feeling I have. Can you get them for me?"

"Ah…I can try. That was a long time ago, Jake. You're talking thirty-five years. Didn't Sara get her dad's belongings after he died?"

"I don't think so. All she said she had left was that nursery rhymes book. I don't think she got his things from the police. I just have a feeling that these serial murders may be connected to Joe Olsen somehow. It came to me last night." Jake wasn't going to share how he really got the idea about Joe's past.

Tony picked up his phone. "I'll get right on it. I know the captain from Joe's old precinct. I'll give him a call right now, and see what he can do."

"Great, I'll wait, if you don't mind." Jake sat down before Tony could even answer. He listened intently as Tony hung up, dialing another number. Jake's patience was wearing thin, but after the third phone call, Tony grinned and gave Jake a thumbs up.

"I can't believe it, we actually found it! There's a box of Joe Olsen's things in the cold case room at his precinct. How lucky is that? I guess they just couldn't throw it away, probably were waiting for a family member to pick them up. I guess that's you, Jake. I told them you would be right over."

Jake flew out of his chair before Tony even stopped talking. He looked over his shoulder as he left the room. "Thanks, Tony!"

Jake drove as fast as he could, and rushed into the ninth precinct where Joe used to work. He took the stairs two at a time, slowing down only when he reached the captain's office. He knocked, and let himself in when the captain answered. "Captain, I'm Jake Long. My captain called earlier about Joe Olsen's belongings?"

"Yes, come in, Jake. It's nice to meet you. I understand you were married to Joe's daughter?"

"Yes, Sara was my wife."

"I heard she passed away, I'm sorry. May I ask why you want her father's things?"

"It may be connected to a murder case I'm investigating. I won't know for sure until I go through his things. Any past case files in there?"

The captain shook his head. "I don't believe so. All of his cases were solved either by him, or the cold case unit. We don't keep them for forty years, I'm afraid. Sorry about that. I think this box is mostly personal belongings that never got picked up. I hope it helps."

Jake grabbed the box and turned to leave. "I hope so too, captain. I hope so too. Thank you very much for going to the trouble of tracking this stuff down."

"No problem. I'm glad it finally got into the hands of someone who needs it."

Jake hurried back to the station and plopped the box on his desk. Tony spotted him, and came out of his office. "Well, that didn't take you long. Need any help?"

"Sure, I won't turn down help." He slid the cover off the box, and set it down on the floor. The two men looked inside. There really wasn't much in there. An old coffee cup that said "World's Greatest Dad" on it, a pair of glasses, and some pens and pencils. Jake pulled out Joe's badge, which had fallen to the bottom of the box. "Jenny or Ann deserves to have this. I think they'll treasure it. I wish we would've thought of this when Sara was alive. Why wouldn't they have contacted her?"

"They probably did, but she was so young then. She didn't want it. Sara probably forgot about it after that."

"I suppose. She certainly never mentioned to me that there was anything of her parents left from the fire. It's kind of sad, holding this in my hand, knowing it belonged to Sara's dad. Well, it doesn't look like this is going to pan out. I guess my feeling was wrong."

"You never know. There are a few other things in there. You should take it home, and go through it with Jenny. She could learn more about her grandfather, about his life as a cop. It might interest her, and maybe you'll learn something too."

"Good idea. It's sad to think our lives can be summed up in one lone box. Makes you wonder if it's worth it really."

"Don't doubt for a moment that what we do is worth it, Jake. If it weren't for us, killers would be getting away with their crimes. We put them away where they belong."

"I know, I know, and I do feel like we make a difference. It's just frustrating sometimes. Well, I'm gonna take these home and go through them there. If I find anything, I'll let you know."

When Jake got home, Jenny called, asking permission to stay overnight at a friend's house. He thought she deserved a break from it all, so he gave his consent. He set the box down on the table, wondering if he should go through it without Jenny. Jake ultimately decided that if he could find something that pertained to his case, he wasn't going to waste another minute, so he dug in.

Most of what he found were odds and ends, nothing interesting really. He pulled out a dusty picture. When he wiped the dust off, he saw a striking couple. The woman was dark-skinned, with long, black hair; the man was blonde, with striking blue eyes. Sara resembled them both. He knew it was Joe and Ali Olsen. All of these years, Sara thought there were no pictures left of them, and here it was. *Ann will be thrilled to have this.* It felt a little thick to him, so Jake turned the frame over, loosening the back. Sure enough, a notebook fell out. *Oh my God! Jenny said that Joe told her about some notebook. Could this be it? It had to be.* Jake sat down on the couch, and carefully opened the book. It was personal notes, written by Joe. Jake almost felt guilty reading it. *Okay, here goes.*

"Monday, June fifteenth-Ali and I took the baby to the park together. It isn't very often that we get to spend time together, all three of us. I really miss my family when I'm working all the time. Ali didn't want to be a single mother, but she says that's how she feels. Ali is staying strong, but I know she is frustrated." *Sounds familiar. I can relate, Joe. Let's see what else you have to say.*

He turned the page. "August tenth, 1975-Today, my captain called me in. Evidently, I'll be getting a new partner. I hope he's better than my last one. We never got along at all. I get to go home early again, Ali will be pleased. Sara loves it when I get home in time to read to her. That nursery rhymes book is almost as important to her as I am. I love my girls more than life itself, and Ali too. I only hope they know that."

Jake turned another page. " October first, 1975-I did get a new partner. It's a woman, for God's sake! What on earth would possess a woman to join the homicide division? I don't know why the captain stuck me with her, but I don't think it will last long. Oh well, it's their decision. I guess I'll just have to accept it...for now."

"March, 1976-I guess having a woman partner isn't all that bad. Liz and I are getting along great, and she's really good at her job. I think we'll be okay. We work together quite well. It's like she knows what I'm going to do before I do it."

There wasn't anything written for a few years after that, so Joe started up again in 1978. "Liz and I are growing closer now, maybe too close. I'm trying to keep my distance, but we are partners, and it makes it very hard to do that. We spend so much time together, she really knows me. Ali and I are growing apart, and Liz has been there for me all the way. I feel like we understand each other."

"April, 1978- Liz and I are definitely in love with each other. Our significant others are growing suspicious now. I feel so guilty, but just can't help myself. The two of us meet whenever we can get away to be together. I don't know what to do about it.

June, 1978-Ali has given me an ultimatum, Liz or her. I chose her. Liz is not happy, she says she is pregnant.

December, 1978, Liz has given birth to a son. She claims it's Kurt's, but I'm just not sure. There is a way of finding out for sure, it's called a paternity test. Liz wouldn't agree to do it. If the boy is mine, I don't know what I'll do. I believe it's more than likely Kurt's.

"1979, Well, I found out the boy is mine. I'm very upset, but excited too. I have a son! I'm not going to turn my back on them. Liz's husband, Kurt Rommel, is crazy. They have named the boy Billy. I spend time with him when I can, but Kurt believes it's his son, so that makes it hard. Maybe it's for the best for Kurt and Billy to think they're father and son."

That was the last entry in the notebook. *"Whoa!* This is some interesting stuff. Sounds like old Joe was in it up to his neck. It's probably a good thing Sara didn't see this. I wonder if she knew about her father's affair. So, if Joe had a son, I wonder where he is now. He would only be about Thirty-nine years old. For that matter, where is Liz?"

Jake knew that Kurt Rommel killed Joe and Ali, and then took his own life. Jake opened up his computer and typed in Liz Rommel. When her name popped up on the screen, all it said was that she had been in the police force, and was married to Kurt Rommel. A son was listed as Billy Rommel. No information after that. Jake had a feeling that he needed to use the computer at the station to see if Liz or Billy had a police record. Was this the clue that Joe meant by looking into his past? Jake thought it was. He couldn't wait to share this information with Tony.

Jake beat Tony into the station the next day. He had already looked up Liz and Billy on the police computer. Neither one had a record, but their information stopped abruptly, and he wanted to know why. He showed Tony what he had found, and asked if he knew what Liz and Billy were up to now. Tony had no information on either of them. Jake went back to his desk, hoping to find something out from Joe's old boss. When he called the old police captain, Stan, he couldn't answer any of Jake's questions either. He only remembered that Liz was pretty messed up by her husband Kurt committing suicide. She basically went off the deep end. Stan had to fire her, so she took her young son and left. Stan thought that maybe they moved to Portland for a while, but wasn't sure.

Jake was very interested in that statement. "Portland? Are you sure? Now that's interesting. Thanks for your time, captain." When Jake hung up, he thought about the murder in Portland that they had originally thought was connected to these serial killings. Jake dug through his files, until he found the one he was looking for. Could be just a coincidence that Liz and Billy were living in Portland for a while. He wasn't going to jump to conclusions. Jake's phone rang just as he finished up reading the case file from Portland. "Long here."

It was the district attorney, Jake finally got his warrant. He headed straight to Oakdale Hospital the minute he had the warrant in his hands, hoping that this was the break they'd been waiting for. If Dr. Bell was killed by the serial killer, like Jake thought he was, this could be it.

When Jake buzzed the doorbell, it didn't take long for Byron to let him in. Jake shoved the warrant in his face and demanded to see Dr. Bell's patient list. Byron checked with Mr. Sims, and the list was handed over to Jake. He couldn't wait to look at it. He set it out on the counter at the hospital, and started reading down the list. He was surprised at how many patients Bell had. One name suddenly popped out at him, Liz Rommel. Jake looked up at Byron. "Liz Rommel, did you know her?"

"Of course I did. She was especially difficult. Some days you couldn't even tell she belonged here. Other days, she was nuttier than a fruitcake. Sorry, not very professional of me, but she really wanted out of here. Dr. Bell was wise to her, and refused to release her. The son was about as bad as she was."

"Wait a minute, her son was here too? How often did he come to see her?"

"Every day. As a matter of fact, when she killed herself, he blamed Dr. Bell, and threatened to get back at him."

"Do you know where he lives? Did he leave an address where he could be reached? Or a phone number? I need the camera footage so I can identify this guy. Can you tell me what he looked like?"

"No, I don't know where he lives. Like I said, he was here every day anyway. He refused to give us any information about himself. He's a big guy, younger—around thirty-five, or forty, maybe—and with sandy-brown hair. A nice-looking kid."

Jake was beyond excited about this turn of events. He hurried back to the station and showed Tony what he'd found out. "Tony, this guy is our killer, I know it! If we can find this Billy Rommel, we'll have our serial killer!"

"Are you sure Dr. Bell was killed by our serial killer? I agree that Billy probably killed him, but I'm just not sure that makes him a serial killer."

Jake knew it was him. He needed to get this camera footage up on his computer. Jake noticed as soon as he saw the footage, that this Billy was deliberately avoiding the cameras. He knew exactly where each one was at, and covered his face with a ball cap whenever he came into view. All Jake could get was his build, and hair color. The very same as described by the people communicating with Jenny through Sara. This was him, he was sure of it.

20

Jake was so close to catching this guy he could taste it. He had a name; he just needed to find him, and then go about proving he's a serial killer. But, he needed to catch him first. There wasn't an address anywhere for Billy Rommel. He didn't even have a social security number. Jake went to Tony for advice. "I mean, who doesn't have a social security number? This guy's a ghost."

He cringed a little at that comment, knowing that's just what was helping him solve this case. They put out a "Be on the lookout," or BOLO, as it was nicknamed, for Billy Rommel, with his description and general build. It wasn't much to go on, but it was better than nothing. The footage from the hospital wasn't helpful either. Billy hid his face with a ball cap pulled low over his eyes.

"Damn, who is this guy? He has to be around here somewhere. He visited the hospital every day. I think I need to start there. Maybe someone overheard something, or found something in Liz's belongings." Jake sighed, "Back to Oakdale I go."

When he arrived, Byron was waiting for him. "You know, detective, I've been thinking since you left the other day. Liz spent an awful lot of time on the computer, when we would let her. Some of the patients are allowed computer time for just a short time once a week. It seemed like Liz would get very excited after she got done, and very angry if we cut her short. She would scream and yell, or throw a temper tantrum, basically. We would have to subdue her sometimes, and ban her from the computer for two weeks—maybe longer, depending on her doctor."

Jake was very interested in this information. "Do you know what she was looking at on this computer?"

"Yes, we monitored it quite closely. She was looking up names of people who lived in Los Angeles. I wrote the names down if you want them.”

“Oh yes, I want them. Why didn’t you show me this before? You could be in trouble for obstructing justice. I could’ve used this information earlier. It may have saved lives.”

Byron held up his hands. “*Whoa*, wait a minute! I was just doing my job. I couldn’t very well show you this without giving Liz’s name now, could I? As soon as I remembered it, *and* you had the subpoena, I told you.” He reached into his pocket, and handed Jake a list of names.

Sure enough, listed in order were: Molly Jones, Harvey Andersen, Martin Parker, Ryan Sands, Mary Sax, Jack and Susan Martin. Jake almost dropped the piece of paper. He couldn’t believe what he was reading. It was a murder list. “Is there any way possible that Liz Rommel could have gotten out of this hospital, even for a short time?”

“No, no way. You’ve seen how hard it is to get into this place. It’s harder getting out. There are alarms on every door and window. If anyone even tried to open either one without a key, the alarm would blare very loudly.”

“How about if someone let her out? Think very hard about your answer, Byron. We’re talking about murder here, and a serial killer. Could Liz be capable of that?”

“Of course she could be capable, anyone here could be, but our staff is very well-vetted. We don’t have a huge staff in the first place. This isn’t a very big hospital but, believe me, no one would let a patient out, for any reason!”

“I hope you’re right Byron, for your sake as well as the hospital.” Jake picked up the letter, folding it, and slipping it into his pocket. “Thank you for this, Byron. It helps me out a lot. I just wish we could find the son. Maybe he helped her out. We won’t know until we talk to him. Any ideas where he might be?”

“No, I’m sorry. I don’t even know if he drove here, or walked. I don’t remember seeing a car, but that doesn’t mean he didn’t have one.”

“Okay, if you think of anything else, don’t hesitate to call me... anytime. Don’t wait this time, call me right away.”

Byron walked with Jake to open the door. “Will do. I’m sorry I couldn’t get that list to you sooner. I only just thought of it yesterday, and

I knew I had to wait for the warrant before I could give it to you.."

Jake nodded, breathing deeply of the fresh air, while he walked to his car. He called Tony when he got in. "Tony, I obtained a murder list that Liz Rommel made from a computer search. I think she may have helped commit these murders. I don't know how she did it, but all of the names of our victims are on that list, with the exception of Sara and Dr. Bell. Those two may not have been planned, but I still think they were murdered by our serial killer. We need to find the son, Billy, and question him. I think she gave him the names, and he killed them for her."

"Good work, Jake. That's definitely good news. Bring the list back here, and we'll try and figure out where this guy is. He could be homeless. That would make it very difficult to find him. We have every police officer in the city on the lookout for this guy. We'll find him."

Jake took the steps two at a time, and went straight to Tony's office. Tony grabbed a sheet from the printer. "Jake, we got lucky! I found a Billy Rommel in the police academy files. He was trying to be a police officer, can you believe that? I got a picture, and fingerprints. They're right here."

Jake yanked the printout out of his hands so fast, he gave Tony a paper cut. Looking at the photo, he frowned. "This guy looks familiar to me, Tony. I just can't place it right now. It'll come to me. I can't imagine where I would've met him though. Anyway, this is great. Now we know what he looks like. Any other information on him? An address maybe?"

"The address he gave is an empty lot, and get this, he failed the psych exam. That's why he didn't make it in the academy."

"Go figure! This is more than we knew a couple of hours ago. I think it's just a matter of time now. He is definitely our serial killer, and his days are numbered. I just don't know why either one of them would kill these people. I guess Liz maybe held a grudge from being fired, but why the son? Was he just carrying out her wishes? I'm going to read over the files again, with fresh eyes, and see if that will explain something."

Before Jake knew it, the clock chimed ten, and his eyes were burning from all of the reading he had been doing. He quickly called Jenny to let her know he was on his way home. He could tell she was half asleep when he called, so he grabbed a sandwich on his way home. She even had him eating healthier these days. Jake quietly opened the door, creeping slowly into the apartment. He was too excited to eat or sleep. They actually were getting closer to catching this guy. This is why he loved this job. This is what he lived for, cracking the case.

All of a sudden, Jenny squealed and started yelling his name. When he rushed in, he found her standing over the nursery rhymes book. "Jenny, are you okay? What is it?"

Jen looked up, her eyes shiny with tears. "Dad, Mom just won't stop with this book. It flew at me, almost hitting me in the head! It landed down on the floor. You need to read it. I think there's some clue in there. I don't know, she's insisting you read it."

Jake bent down to retrieve the book. It had fallen open to a specific rhyme.

"Eeper, weeper, chimney sweeper,

Had a wife but couldn't keep her.

Had another, didn't love her,

Up the chimney he did shove her."

"Wait a minute here, what's this? Are you sure this is how it landed? On this exact page?"

"Yes, I didn't touch it. What does it mean, Dad?"

Jake wasn't about to tell his fifteen-year-old daughter the gory details of a murder. "Nothing. Try to go to sleep, okay? You have school tomorrow."

Jake wanted to tuck her in, but he resisted the urge. He had missed out on so much of her younger years. He shut the light off, carrying the book to his recliner, and just started reading. It took him most of the night, and a lot of reading. Jake compared all of the murders to the nursery rhymes. By the time he was done, he had compiled quite a list.

Mary Sax, "Eeper Weeper, chimney sweeper." Killed because her husband, in the Drug Enforcement Agency, was gone all the time.

Molly Jones, "Needles and Pins, needles and pins, when a man marries, his troubles begin." Probably killed her because her husband left her.

Harvey Andersen, "Goosey, Goosey gander, whither shall I wander,

Upstairs, downstairs And in my ladies chamber.

There I met an old man

Who wouldn't say his prayers, I took him by the left leg,

and threw him down the stairs."

Jake figured Harvey was thrown down the stairs, and killed, because of his affair.

Ryan Sands, "Humpty Dumpty sat on a wall, Humpty Dumpty had a great fall,

All the king's horses and all the king's men, couldn't put Humpty together again."

Jake wasn't too sure on this rhyme, but it was the only one he found that was about a wall, and falling.

Martin Parker, "Diddle, diddle dumpling, my son John,

went to bed with his breeches on,

One stocking off and one stocking on,

Diddle diddle dumpling, my son John."

Even though his name wasn't John, he did have one sock missing, along with his foot.

Jack and Susan Martin, "Jack and Jill went up the hill, to fetch a pail of water,

Jack fell down and broke his crown, and Jill came tumbling after." These two were killed in just this   way.

This made sense on a lot of levels, except why them? Jake had to show this list to Tony and see what he thought. In his mind, these killings followed this damn book. Why? He didn't know, but he was sure he was right on this one.

Jake scratched his head and yawned. It was four in the morning. He needed to get some sleep, if that was possible. His mind was whirring, he doubted sleep was in the cards for him. If Tony agreed with him on this, Jake didn't even know what to do with it. So the guy liked nursery rhymes, and decided to kill people using them. Big deal. He still didn't know where he was. He still didn't know why he did it in the first place. What drove him to kill? That's the question that needed answering. Jake was right, sleep was elusive. He was up and pouring milk into his cereal bowl when Jenny came out of her room. "Do you want some cereal? It's all we've got. We really need to pick up some groceries soon."

"Sure, sounds good. Did you figure out what the nursery rhymes were all about? I could hardly sleep. I kept waiting for Mom to come back and tell me more, but she never did."

"Actually, I think I did find a connection to the murders. I'm not going into details with you, but I do think the rhymes were used in the murders. I just don't know why."

"Well, Mom will be happy to hear that. What about Grandpa's clue about the notebook?"

"Yes, that helped too. We just need to piece everything together. We have certain pieces of this puzzle, just need to put it together. You've been great, Jen. Thank you."

"You need to thank Mom and Grandpa really, they did all the work. You know, Dad, I miss Mom a lot. I miss seeing her, hugging her. The day we had her service, everyone was so kind. The things they said and their condolences, even that creepy guy, was kind of nice."

Jake suddenly remembered. "Jen, what was that guy's name? Do you remember it? It was Billy, wasn't it?"

"Yeah, I remember thinking that Mom never mentioned knowing anyone by that name. I guess I wouldn't know all of her coworkers. I'm gonna be late for school, I'd better go." Jen kissed Jake on the cheek and took off for school.

Jake couldn't help but worry, as he watched her walk out the door. He shook it off and left for work himself.

When he showed Tony the list of rhymes, and told him he was pretty sure this Billy was the very same guy at Sara's service, Jake was surprised at how open he was to his ideas. "Okay, say I agree with you on this, let's put it all together as a hypothesis. Say Billy is just following his mother's instructions. They got ahold of a book like this, read through it, and decided to kill people in the same fashion as some of these songs.

Then, they made sure to pose them in the exact same way as some of the rhymes. The murders may or may not have something to do with Joe Olsen, probably because Liz hated him for leaving her. I still can't figure out what drove them to this. Why now?"

"I think they just both went off the deep end, and just enjoyed killing. Liz was a cop, married to a cop, and Billy wanted to be a cop. That's the connection there. They just hated the police because they couldn't be one themselves. That's all I've got so far. It still doesn't get us any closer to finding Billy. Any clues there yet?"

"Not one clue. But we will find him, I know it."

Jake shrugged. "I believe it, Tony. The question is, when? Before, or after, he kills again? I need to call Sam and Ann, let them know what's going on, and see if they remember this guy." He dialed Sam's number as he walked back to his desk.

"Jake, we haven't heard from you in a while! What's up? Is Jen okay?"

"She's fine. Great, as a matter of fact. That's a long story. I just called to tell you that we got a lead on this killer, and I need your help. Remember that creepy guy—as Jen called him—at Sara's service? I need you and Ann to look at a photo. I think he's our killer. Like I said, it's a long story."

"You know, I remember him clearly. He was strange. Listen, Ann and I have been talking, and we want to come to Los Angeles for a while. When you told Ann about the things belonging to her father that you found, she wanted to come and see them for herself. She's been worrying about Jenny, and I also miss you both. What do you say? We could get together and figure this whole thing out. We would leave soon. Maybe in the next couple days, and be there by the weekend."

Jake was ecstatic with that news. "Of course, you're welcome here any time. You'll stay with us, we'll figure something out for sleeping arrangements. Ann can bunk with Jen, and you can have the couch. It's pretty comfortable, I can attest to that. Jen will be so excited when I tell her. Call when you leave so we can keep track of you. I'll see you this weekend then."

"We'll be there late Friday night. See you then, bro."

Jake let out a *whoop* that had everyone looking at him. He shrugged, and grinned at their incredulous looks.

Jake was right, Jen was beside herself when he told her about their visitors for the weekend. She started cleaning on Thursday night, preparing for their arrival on Friday. By the time Ann and Sam got there, Jen was crawling out of her skin. She kept looking out the window. Finally, when they drove up, Jen shrieked, running out the door to greet them. "Ann, Sam! I'm so glad you're finally here. I didn't think tonight would ever get here!"

Ann hugged Jenny back. "Oh, Jen, I've missed you so much! I'm so happy we made the decision to come here. It was past time."

Jake hugged his brother, and grabbed their luggage. "Come on in. Welcome to our humble abode."

The group stayed up late, talking and laughing. Mixed with some tears, when Jake showed Ann the picture that he found of her parents. When he explained how it came about, that Joe himself was telling Jenny to look at his past, Ann cried more. Jake left out the part of the notebook, with the story of Liz. They just didn't need to know that sordid detail just yet. Jake was taking the weekend off. Sam and Ann were going to stay at least a week, which thrilled Jen immensely.

Jen could hardly sit through school, with Ann being there. The days flew by, she knew it was coming time for them to go back to Portland. She begged them to stay longer. Jen had to admit, she missed them more than she thought.

Billy had enough of this moping around, it was time to finish his job. It was the least he could do for his mother. He missed her. This one was going to get done especially for her. First, some surveillance, then some action.

21

This was just too much of a coincidence. Billy couldn't believe his luck that Ann was here in Los Angeles with that little brat. His mother must still be helping him from beyond the grave. He probably would have to act fast on this one. Who knows how long they'll all be there. It was time for planning this final act, then he would be done. "I'll see you soon, Mother. Maybe not in the same way we planned, but together, nonetheless." This kill definitely had to be special. It's what Billy and Liz had talked about forever. It made him sad that she wouldn't be here to see it come to fruition. "Ah well, I'll make sure it's enjoyable anyway."

He waited patiently for just the right time. When it came, he felt the familiar buzz in his head. It was so loud this time, it almost paralyzed him. This was it, the moment he'd been waiting for. It almost fell right into his lap. He laid down on the seat, barely able to stay still so he wasn't detected.

Ann and Jenny were laughing and giggling all day. It felt as if the past, and all of the bad things that had happened to them, were melting away. Just a distant memory. Although Sara was never far from their thoughts and conversations.

"Your mom would be so proud of the young lady you've become, Jen. I want you to know that I'm proud of how you have accepted Jake into your life. I know it wasn't easy, forgiving him for everything that happened, but I'm glad you did."

"Yeah, I'm glad too. I think my dad and I have grown close. I really love him a lot, Ann."

Ann put her arm around Jenny as they walked to the car. "That's great to hear. You have to remember, you had fifteen years with your mom that Jake didn't have. He loved her, and I'm sure he was confused about her leaving like that. Now let's call up our men and figure out a place to go for supper, I'm starving!"

Jenny pushed unlock on her key, and opened the trunk to throw in all of their purchases. "I think we bought out the stores. You shouldn't have spent money on me, Aunt Ann, but I'm glad you did."

The two laughed at that comment, and jumped in the car. Ann had her cell phone in her hand, and was just dialing Sam's number when she was startled by a noise in the back seat. By the time she could turn around, she felt the cold steel of a blade against her throat, and a voice in her ear.

"I don't think you want to call him right now, Annie dear. Put your phone down, or I'll slit your throat right here in front of your lovely niece." Ann gasped, and Jenny screamed, ready to grab her cell phone and call for help. "Why don't you just give me that phone, Jenny darling. Or would you like the blood of your aunt all over your car?" Jenny quickly handed over her phone. "That's a good girl. Now drive!"

Jake loved having his brother around. He could really get used to it. He was explaining to Sam about Sara's help with this case. Showing him the nursery rhymes that he thought the murderer used in his kills. The photo of Billy was being circulated around every police station in Los Angeles, and Portland. It was just a matter of time now.

While the girls went shopping, Jake and Sam were busy at the police station, searching every social media sight there was. They were hoping Billy would have a profile, but no luck there. They also searched every police database, looking for any ideas on where this guy could be living. Still nothing, Billy was very careful not to show his cards. Jake was hopeful, but still frustrated, about things moving along so slowly. By the time they got their heads out of the computers, it was dark outside.

Jake looked at his watch. "Sam, weren't the girls going to call when they were done shopping? They should be done by now."

Sam glanced up from the computer screen and looked at his watch too. "Yeah, they should have called by now. We were supposed to meet for supper somewhere. I'll call Ann. They probably just got caught up in their shopping and girl stuff." Sam dialed Ann's number only to get the answering machine right away. "Her phone is always running out of battery. Try Jen, will you?"

"Yeah, she makes sure that her cell phone is always charged up and ready to go. She'll answer. It never leaves her side." Jake held the phone out and frowned. "I just got the answering machine too. Do you think they went somewhere out of service? Kind of hard to do around here. We'll give them a little while, and try again."

Billy threw Ann's cell phone out the window after he pulled out the battery. "You girls won't need these where we're going, but I think I'll leave yours for a bit, Jenny. Your dad will be so worried when he can't reach you. I'd better reassure him that you're okay. Now give me your phone." After shutting Jenny's cell phone off, he put it in his pocket. "There, I can talk to Jake later. We wouldn't want him wondering what you're up to." Billy laughed at his own comment.

Jen was shaking so badly she could barely drive. "W-w-who are you? What do you want?"

"*Tsk, Tsk*. Don't tell me you don't know who I am? That would be such a shame. Oh well, everyone will know who I am soon enough. I am quite famous actually."

Ann tried to turn her head to look at him, but she could only move her eyes. "You're Billy, aren't you? I remember you from Sara's service. What do you want with us? Just let us go, we won't tell anyone anything, I promise."

Billy swiped the blade against her cheek. Ann bit back a sob. "Oh, sweet Ann! I am definitely not letting you go. I've waited too long for this moment. I plan to cherish each moment of our time spent together. So, don't think those idiot cops are going to help you two. I've outsmarted them all. Taking you two was almost too easy, but it was exciting. Now take a right up ahead. There's a dirt road there, follow it!"

Jenny glanced over and looked at Ann, silently pleading with her to tell her what she should do. Ann shook her head a little bit, so Jenny kept on driving, doing what she was told. She couldn't take the chance of anything happening to Ann. It seemed like they drove for hours, when they finally saw a huge old house looming in the distance.

"There, that's it! Park out front." Billy put the knife closer to Ann's neck when Jenny shut off the car. "Now you just stay put, little girl, or I will kill her, you understand?"

Jenny nodded, silently praying her dad would call when her phone got turned back on. For now, she would continue playing the game, until she could get both of them out of there. She knew her dad and Sam would find them; she only hoped it was soon. While Billy walked in front of the car and opened the door, Jenny watched him closely. He was much too big for her to fight him. She needed to use her head. What would her dad do? She had no idea, but somehow she and Ann would come up with something. It was just a matter of time. She got out of the car.

Holding on to Ann's hand tightly, the three of them walked to the huge old house. They were in the middle of nowhere, not a neighbor around for miles. The old house was a two-story, but it looked like someone had been trying to keep it up. The windows were all intact and the doors had all of their hinges. Jenny's dad told her to always study her surroundings, so she looked around the house when they walked in. Whatever work had been done to the outside of the house, they had let the inside go. There was mouse feces all over, and the smell of rotting food threatened to overwhelm them. She held back a gag, as Billy grabbed a gun out of a cupboard drawer. Now, with Billy armed with both a knife and a gun, Jenny and Ann felt their chances of getting away dwindling. They headed up the stairs, entering a room that held nothing but an old bed. The window was barred from the outside. He had definitely planned ahead for this. Jenny prayed that her dad would figure out soon that they were missing, and find them. She didn't know if they had much longer before this guy lost it completely.

Jake stared at the clock as he dialed Jenny's phone one more time. This time, he heard someone answering. "Hello? Jen, where are you two? We've been worried sick! Jen?"

There was a long pause on the other end, before a strange voice came over the line. "Well, hello there, Jake. It's been a long time. I'm sure you know who I am by now. Well, you don't need to answer that. I know you do. Everyone does. Everyone is scared of me, the papers say. Well, they should be. *You* should be. You're never going to see your daughter or sister-in-law again. Say goodbye, Jake."

"Wait, don't hang up! What do you want, you crazy bastard! Wait!"

Sam was watching Jake's face turn from concern to panic. "What? What's wrong, Jake?"

Jake's face was white as a sheet. "He's got them, Sam! He's got the girls."

Billy laughed, and hung up the phone, yanking out the battery and crushing it on the floor. "We wouldn't want the detective spoiling our fun now, would we? We're just beginning." Billy backed toward the door. "You can try to escape, it won't do you any good. If I were you, I'd save my strength." Jenny could hear the key locking the door when Billy left them alone, singing as he walked down the hall. "Oh, where have you been, Billy boy, Billy boy."

Jenny turned to Ann as soon as she heard his footsteps walking away. "Are you all right? Did he hurt you?" Jen looked closely at the small cut on Ann's cheek where he swiped the knife blade.

"I'm okay, Jenny. We have to get out of here! He's going to kill us!"

They ran to the window and tried everything to get it open. It had been nailed shut from the outside, and there were bars. Next, they tried the door. It was locked up tight. There were no other windows or doors anywhere, just a rickety old bed. They were totally helpless and in the control of a madman. Ann and Jen crumpled in the middle of the floor and held each other, sobbing uncontrollably.

Sam jumped up from the chair, knocking it over. "Oh my God, Jake! How did this happen? The girls were in a public place. We thought they would be safe! What did he say? You were talking to Billy, right?"

Jake nodded, stunned. "He's got them, Sam. He's got my little girl. I can't lose her too!"

Sam grabbed Jake by the shoulders and shook him a little. "Jake, you need to snap out of it! We need to figure out where he took them! It's up to us to find them!"

Tony saw the commotion and stepped out to see what was up. "Jake, are you okay? What's happened?"

Jake snapped out of his trance when Sam shook him. "Tony, Billy kidnapped Ann and Jen. I just called Jenny's phone and he answered it. He hung up before I could hear much."

Tony took charge after that. "You need to go home in case he calls there, or one of the girls get ahold of a phone. We will start a trace on their phones, and put out a BOLO on Jenny's car. That's what they were driving, right?"

"Yes, we need to get video of the mall too, and question the store employees, to figure out where they were shopping last. Maybe we'll get lucky with a surveillance camera. I'm not going home to sit on my thumbs waiting for a phone call that'll never come. You know that, and I know that." Jake was all business now. "Let's roll!"

Jake and Sam headed for the mall, hoping to get some information from the employees. They went from store to store with pictures of the two girls. Finally, they struck pay dirt. An employee at the ice cream store remembered seeing them. Jake took over the questioning. "Was anyone following them? Were they acting strange, or scared?"

"No, sir. They were laughing and talking normally. Nothing was wrong when they were here. I saw them walking toward the mall main entrance. I think they were leaving. They were alone, I swear!"

"Okay, you've been a lot of help. Do you know where I could find the head of security? I need to see the video from today."

"He's in the main offices upstairs. His name is Kevin Cross."

"Thank you." Jake and Sam took the escalator to the second floor, and quickly found the head of security's office. Jake knocked once, opening the door before Cross even invited them in.

"Mr. Cross, I'm Detective Jake Long from homicide. I need you to bring up the security camera views of the main parking area outside of the main entrance. There may have been a kidnapping that took place there."

"Of course, right away, sir." Mr. Cross turned to his computer.

After clicking a few keys, the image of the parking area came into view.

Jake sat down next to the security guard; Sam stood behind. Both of them were staring intently at the screen. The camera panned the whole parking lot slowly. "There! That's Jenny's car! What time is this, Mr. Cross."

"Five o'clock. Do you want me to keep going?"

"Would you rewind a little? I want to see the car pull into the lot." Kevin kept rewinding until they reached the time Jake wanted. "Okay, now keep the view on the car if you can. I need to see if anyone gets in the vehicle." After about two hours, a man slowly approached the vehicle. He had some kind of device in his hands, which he expertly used to break into Jenny's car. "That's him, dammit! That's Billy! He didn't even care if he was seen this time. Keep going please."

Soon, Jenny and Ann could be seen walking out to their car, laughing, and carrying some packages they were putting in the trunk. Nothing was wrong yet, until they got in the car. They could vaguely see a figure jump up from the back seat, then Jenny drove off, heading east. "Well, now we have an idea which way they went anyway. A lot of good that'll do us. Thank you, Kevin. Can you make me a copy of that tape?"

After the mall, Jake wasn't sure what to do, so he called Jenny's cell again. Of course, nothing. Jake threw his phone down. "Figured he'd take out the battery so we couldn't trace him that way. What are we going to do, Sam? We have no idea where he took them, not a damn clue! He's going to kill them, Sam!"

"Jake, Ann and Jenny are a couple of strong women. They're going to keep fighting to escape, and we're going to fight to save them." Jake nodded, and they headed back to the station.

Days passed with Ann and Jenny biding their time until Jake found them. They didn't dare eat, for fear of poison, so they were growing weaker. Billy brought them bottled water so they drank that and nibbled on some food.

"Ann, what is he waiting for? Why not kill us already?"

"I don't know, Jen. He's growing more unstable every day. It's like he's preparing for something, or waiting for a certain time. I'm really scared. Do you think we could take him down? He's pretty big, and we're growing weaker. We have to do something!"

"We have to try. Maybe we could do it, I don't know. I thought Mom or Grandpa would be there when I needed them, but they haven't come either. Ann, I'm scared!"

"I know, so am I." They heard the key turning in the lock so they sat quietly.

Billy walked in. "Hello, girls."

"W-w-what are you going to do to us?"

"Oh, I have a grand plan. That's all you need to know. Now let's get down to business, shall we?"

Tony called in the FBI, and Beau Torrey met Jake at his desk. "Jake, you look like hell! The FBI will take it from here. You need to go home, get some rest. You're not doing anyone any good by not sleeping or eating for a week. Now go home!"

"I am not leaving until we find this guy, and where he took my daughter. So forget it!"

Tony stepped in, glaring at Jake. "You are going home for a little while, Jake, and that's an order! You can come back, but you two need to get some rest."

Jake and Sam stood abruptly. "Fine, we're leaving, but if anything—and I mean *anything*—happens, you call me, you hear?"

"We will. Now get out of here."

Jake almost lost it when he walked into the empty house. Sam was very quiet, trailing behind him. They were both exhausted. "Sam, why don't you go lie down in my bed. I know I won't sleep anyway."

"Are you sure? I can stay out here with you. You haven't slept much either."

"I'm sure. Go to bed."

Sam reluctantly went to try and sleep for a couple of hours. Jake walked to the liquor cabinet, craving a drink. He shook it off, and walked into Jenny's room instead. "Oh, Jen! I hope I haven't let you down like I let your mom down." He sat at the edge of the bed and put his head in his hands, breaking down. "Sara, I know that I don't have any kind of a gift, but I really need your help right now. Our daughter needs your help. If there was a time for you to show up, now would be it."

Nothing happened. Jake laid down on the bed. In an instant, he was asleep. He was startled awake by a loud noise right next to the shelf. The nursery rhymes book fell off the shelf. Jake jumped up, rubbing his eyes and looking down at the book. *Could this be a sign from Sara?* He hoped so. Jake carefully picked up the book. The rhyme it fell open to was called "The Hunter of Reigate."

It read: "A man went a hunting at Reigate, and wished to leap over a high gate. Says the owner, 'Go round, with your gun and your hound, for you never shall leap over my gate'." Jake scratched his head. *It's worth a try.* He went to his computer and typed in "Reigate." Sure enough, an image popped up of an old, two-story white house on some land east of the city.

"Well, I'll be damned!" Jake printed out the directions and ran in the bedroom. "Sam, wake up! We have to go. I think I know where he took the girls!"

Sam was groggy, but woke up fast at Jake's words. "What? How did you figure that out?"

Jake was already out the door. "I'll fill you in on the way. Come on!"

They jumped in the car and peeled out of the driveway. Sam looked over at Jake. "Are you going to call the FBI?"

"No, not yet. Anyway, this could be nothing. If we find anything, we'll call them." Jake threw the sheet of paper at Sam. "Tell me which way to go, Sam. These are the directions." He looked sideways at his brother. "Okay, I'll tell you. I fell asleep in Jenny's room. Just before I went to sleep, I asked Sara for help. I know, but I was desperate. Anyway, I woke up to a noise. That damn book was lying on the floor, open to a page with a nursery rhyme called 'The Hunter of Reigate.' So I looked it up, and sure enough, there is a place called Reigate. So here we are, on our way there."

"Jake, you know this is a long shot, right? It's probably nothing. Don't get your hopes up."

"I know, I know, but it's worth a try." They drove on in silence; the only words spoken were Sam's directions. Before too long, they were going down a dirt road and saw a house up ahead. "Sam, take this gun and stay behind me. I don't know what we'll find here." Jake parked well away from the house, and the two men got out, slowly making their way closer to the old house. Jake held up his hand to stop their progress, and waved Sam to his side. He pointed at the house, staying silent. He mouthed the words. "Jenny's car."

There it was, Sam couldn't believe it. He picked up his phone and looked at Jake, who nodded in agreement. Sam stepped away and called the police station, informing them of their situation. He turned back and rejoined Jake. "What now, Jake?" he whispered.

"We go in, you get the girls, and get out. Billy is mine. I only see one entry point in the front. Let's go around back and see if there's a door."

They creeped to the back of the house, and sure enough, there was a door. "We'll go in here. If things go right, we'll make it to girls undetected. We just can't take the time to do any more surveillance. We're gonna have to wing it. You up for that?"

Sam nodded. They crept silently toward the house. Jake slowly opened the door (it creaked loudly) and he cringed, holding his breath. There was no response, so they entered the house. There were some noises coming from the basement, so the two men headed that way, staying silent. Sure enough, they heard voices. Jake breathed a sigh of relief. The girls were still alive. He glanced back at Sam, a little less worried now. Taking the steps slowly, Jake spotted Billy standing over a table. He had to hold back a gasp. Jenny was tied to one table, and Ann to another. Billy had a hammer in his hand and a box of nails next to him. Jake glanced back at Sam who had a shocked look on his face. He knew how he felt. They had never seen anything like this before. That crazy bastard was going to nail them to the table! "Not on my watch."

Jake yelled out. "POLICE! FREEZE!"

Billy slowly turned, grinning; his eyes looking crazed. "Well, well, we have company, ladies. How did you find me? Never mind. It doesn't matter anyway. You're too late! You're not going to stop me."

Jake stood frozen to the spot. Billy was holding a gun, and it was pointed straight at Jenny's head. "Okay, settle down, Billy. We can talk this over. Let's not do anything rash here." Jake glanced at Jenny's face. She was petrified and sobbing silently. Ann was too quiet. Jake was worried about her.

Billy made a crazy sound that sounded like a laugh. "It's a little late for that!" He screamed, spittle spraying out of his mouth. "Now back off, or I'll kill her right now...and you! Put your gun down, detective. You too, Sam. I mean it!"

Jake thought about his options. If he put his gun down, and couldn't get to his other gun in time, they were defenseless. If he didn't, they may be dead. He had to buy them some time for the FBI to get here. Jake made the only decision he could, he put down his gun, nodding for Sam to do the same. "Let's talk about this, Billy. You don't need to do this. These girls haven't done anything to you, just let them go. Keep me instead."

Billy was going off the deep end now, drooling and shaking. "You don't know what you're talking about! They need to die, just like the others, and Sara—especially Sara."

"So, you did kill Sara. Why Billy? Was it because of your mom? Did she hate them that much?"

"You don't speak of my mother! She was perfect! She didn't deserve to be treated like he treated her!"

"Who, Billy? Who treated her badly? Your dad, Kurt? That wasn't Sara's fault, Billy...or Ann and Jen. I'm trying to understand here."

Billy moved away from Jen, screaming louder now. "WHAT? Kurt Rommel wasn't my dad, you idiot! Joe Olsen was. Not that anyone knew that. He was ashamed of me! The only time I ever saw him, was when he could drag himself away from Sara and Ann. I hated them for that. So did my mother. We vowed we would get revenge, and we have." Billy looked over at Ann who was lying very still. "Almost."

"But what about the others, Billy? Why kill them?"

"That was my mother's idea. She wanted to get back at the police for firing her. They deserved it anyway. Harvey Andersen was one of the people who fired her. Sands just needed to be killed, no one should have an affair with their partner. Those two last ones, she decided it wasn't right for them to be married and be partners...and so on and so forth.

What does it matter? They all deserved to die!" Billy paused, picking something up from the table next to Jen. "Can you believe it! This book is all I ever got from my father, a stupid book of nursery rhymes. He even wrote in it. Do you want to hear what he said? Well, do you?"

Jake crept slowly closer to Billy, not wanting to alarm him, since he was waving the gun around now. "Sure, Billy. Tell me what it says."

"Don't come any closer, detective! I'll kill her!" He opened the book to the first page. "To my son. That's the only time he ever called me that. 'To my son, I know I haven't been there for you and your mother, but please keep this book close, and think of me when you read it.' Oh, I did, *Dad*. I thought of you with every kill!"

Billy was losing it completely now, Jake had to do something. He grabbed his gun, hidden in his holster. As he drew it, Billy pointed his gun at Jen, getting ready to pull the trigger. Jake shot first, right between the eyes. Billy fell backwards, dead. Jake ran to Jenny's side; Sam to Ann's.

Jake untied his daughter and hugged her close. "*Shh*, it's over now, Jen. You're safe, I've got you. It's over." He just held her, as she clung to him, sobbing into his shoulder.

"Daddy, is Ann okay? I think he poisoned us! We tried not to eat, but we were so hungry."

He lifted Jen off the table. "Can you walk?" They could hear sirens now. "It's about time they show up! Sam, carry Ann. Let's get them out of here."

When the FBI and ambulance pulled up, Jake and Sam were carrying the girls out of the house. The ambulance crew got out two stretchers and laid the girls down.

Tony ran to Jake just as he got Jenny on the stretcher. "Jake, are they okay?"

Jake addressed the EMTs and Tony at the same time. "They may have been poisoned. Let the hospital know when you get there." He turned to Tony. "Here's my gun, Tony. I shot Billy. He's in the basement, he's dead. I'm going to the hospital with my daughter. I'll leave you to take care of this. Billy confessed to everything. I'll explain it to you later. It's over, Tony. I got him! It's over."

Epilogue

Jake and Tony were gathering all of the evidence from the murder board. There was a lot. These murders were over a span of twenty years. Each face staring back at Jake told a story. Billy and Liz held a grudge for a lot of years. Jake found out that almost all of the people killed were killed for a specific reason.

Molly Jones was murdered just because she was a single mom, trying to raise a son alone, and her husband was an ex-cop. Harvey Andersen, who Liz knew from her police days, actually fired her. Ryan Sands was having an affair with his partner. Martin Parker was the son of Liz's ex-captain. Mary Sax was the wife of a DEA agent. They couldn't figure out her connection to Liz. Jack and Sue Martin were killed just because they were married partners. Billy killed Sara for the obvious reasons. Lastly, Dr. Bell died because he supposedly let Liz kill herself. Billy certainly did a lot of surveillance on these people to get to them so easily. Most of them were in the police force and well-trained individuals. Billy probably would have made a good cop, if he wasn't crazy.

Jake was so tired. Twenty years of his life was spent chasing one madman after another. He knew he was a good detective, but he had made up his mind. He just needed to let his captain know.

Jake shook his head, as they put the last of the evidence in the box, and shut it up. "I just don't understand how people can keep killing each other. I mean, this guy was born into a crazy family. Liz forced Billy into that life. He really didn't have a choice. Do you think it would've been different if Joe would have acknowledged him, maybe treated him like he did his girls?"

"I don't know, Jake. It's hard to say what might have been, but there are a lot more out there just like Billy. Young boys, confused about their lives, trying to find a place in the world. It never ends."

"Tony, I don't think I can do this anymore. This job was my life, but look at what it's cost me. I lost Sara, and came close to losing Jenny. I can't lose my daughter because of this job. I think I finally realize that there's more to life than police work. Do you know what I mean?"

"I do know what you mean. I was actually thinking the same thing. But, are you absolutely sure about this? We never would've gotten this serial killer if it weren't for you. I still don't know how you came up with all of that new information."

Jake snickered a little. "Let's just say, a little birdie told me. Let's leave it at that."

"Well, we'll miss you around here, but I do understand. What will you do now?"

"Sam offered me a job at the ranch, and I accepted. I'm going to be there every day for my daughter. We'll live on the ranch, and breathe the fresh Oregon air. Who knows what will happen next in our lives but, I plan to be there every step of the way."

Jake Long handed his badge and gun over to his captain. They shook hands, and he walked out the door, taking a deep breath. He was just Jake Long now, not Detective Jake Long. A new chapter in his life was beginning.